Praise for the Works of Maggie Brown

Reinventing Lindsey

I'm a total sucker for matchmakers falling in love, so I leapt at the chance to review this one. Despite being into the premise, I was still pleasantly surprised by how much I enjoyed it, and I couldn't put it down! I was totally engrossed by Lindsey and Daisy and the slow burn that crackles between them. Everything about the writing style worked for me.

-The Lesbian Review

Playing the Spy

The characters in this book were great. It wasn't just the two mains, but the supporting cast was well done too. Everyone was fleshed out and I remembered all of their names even if they didn't play a huge role. Brown definitely writes characters well. This is a book that is easy to recommend to romance fans. I really enjoyed this and expect others will too.

-Lex's Reviews – *Goodreads*

Mackenzie's Beat

A fast-paced, well-done detective story. It is exciting and interesting—a classic page-turner that could easily keep you up all night. The plot uses established crime-drama ploys to keep the story moving along, from the gradual piecing together of clues to the detective herself being threatened—and it accomplishes this very well. The main characters are well-drawn, powerful, independent women and they have a wide-ranging, and at times, amusing supporting cast...

-Curve Magazine

In the Company of Crocodiles

This book was great from start to finish. Hard to put down, there was always something happening or about to happen, and I genuinely wanted to reach the end and never let it end in equal measure. Maggie Brown did a superb job of keeping everything so twisted and suspenseful that the revelation at the end was exactly what you want in a good thriller—surprising yet believable.

-The Lesbian Review

PURSUING PANDORA

About the Author

Maggie has now eight published works, which include two GCLS finalists.

She lives in Brisbane, Australia, where the weather is warm, the people are laid-back and the lifestyle relaxed. As well as liking a good joke, her favorite way to relax is to chill out with a glass of wine with friends. Most of the time she sits too long at the computer, drinks too much coffee when typing, and becomes a hot mess when struck down with writer's block.

Check out her website. Maggiebrown-books.com

Other Bella Books by Maggie Brown

I Can't Dance Alone
Mackenzie's Beat
Piping Her Tune
The Flesh Trade
In the Company of Crocodiles
Playing the Spy
Reinventing Lindsey

Pursuing Pandora

Maggie Brown

2020

Copyright © 2020 by Maggie Brown

Bella Books, Inc.
P.O. Box 10543
Tallahassee, FL 32302

All rights reserved. No part of this book may be reproduced or transmitted in any form or by any means, electronic or mechanical, including photocopying, without permission in writing from the publisher.

This is a work of fiction. Names, characters, businesses, places, events and incidents are either the products of the author's imagination or used in a fictitious manner. Any resemblance to actual persons, living or dead, or actual events is purely coincidental. The publisher does not have any control over and does not assume any responsibility for author or third-party websites or their content.

Printed in the United States of America on acid-free paper.

First Bella Books Edition 2020

Editor: Cath Walker
Cover Designer: Judith Fellows

ISBN: 978-1-64247-123-6

PUBLISHER'S NOTE

The scanning, uploading, and distribution of this book via the Internet or via any other means without the permission of the publisher is illegal and punishable by law. Please purchase only authorized electronic editions, and do not participate in or encourage electronic piracy of copyrighted materials. Your support of the author's rights is appreciated.

Acknowledgment

Thanks again to Cath Walker for her patience and advice. Take a bow—you're an awesome editor.

My appreciation to Bella Books for their continuing support in publishing my books.

And lastly, my heartfelt appreciation to Belinda, who battled with me to design my website. After many frustrating hours, we finally managed to produce something that (we think) is eye-catching.

Dedication

To Anna.

CHAPTER ONE

Winter stopped briefly at the door of the office to savour the feeling. After nearly two years, the bitter wrangling was finally over.

She was free.

When she entered the room, Lionel Miles QC, her legal representative and one of the finest divorce lawyers in the city, ushered her to a chair. "Welcome, Ms. Carlyle. The documents are ready for you to sign."

She smiled at the formal title, even though he knew her well. Politeness in a business that brought out the worst in people. When he took the seat next to hers, the leather groaned under the weight of his expanding body. No doubt a side effect, she thought as she eyed the sagging chair, of the expensive dinners paid for by his exorbitant fees. But he had been worth it. Though the settlement had cost her, most of her investments remained intact.

Without another word, he placed the papers on the desk and handed her a pen. After a quick perusal, she scrawled her signature on the dotted lines at the bottom of the three pages. With a satisfied nod, he gave her arm a pat before he slid the documents across the polished top. A long slender manicured hand reached over to take them. For the first time since her arrival, Winter looked directly at the woman opposite who was co-signing the agreement.

At the sight of Christine, she was surprised how quickly old resentments came rolling back. Even though Winter had moved on with her life, she couldn't forget what happened. Not that she had cared for her by then—it had been a minor miracle they had lasted five years. But the shock to her self-esteem and pride had hurt like the devil. All she wondered was how the hell their relationship had deteriorated to such trash.

It had been easy to be charmed by Christine Dumont. As soon as Winter met her, she had been captivated. The TV presenter was perfectly groomed, with a mature attractive face and slender body that turned heads. But it wasn't only her looks that had claimed her attention—it was the way she could converse with wit and intelligence. It wasn't surprising she was so articulate, for over the years she had interviewed everyone imaginable: prime ministers to royalty, murderers to millionaires.

Their dating had been mostly social events and dinner parties to fit in with Christine's lifestyle. After a year, she had given up her inner-city apartment to move in with Winter.

Maintaining their relationship was another thing entirely. The woman she admired and respected soon proved a figment of Winter's imagination. Christine was the master of pretence and an expert in emotional manipulation. Whether it had been love Winter had felt for the TV star was immaterial, for all feelings were systematically destroyed by the games Christine was adept at playing. But ultimately, it was infidelity that finished their relationship.

Winter could never—ever—forgive that day when everything blew up. Two thirty in the afternoon to be precise.

Funny how she remembered the trivial details. They seemed just as indelibly etched into her mind as the scene in the bedroom.

* * *

Two years ago, the first of March hadn't been a pleasant day. The city sweltered in the summer's muggy heat, and dark grey storm clouds were already forming on the horizon when Winter exited her office building. She rubbed her temple to lessen the headache that still throbbed behind her eyes even after two painkillers. The morning's meeting had been a bitch. The merger negotiations hadn't gone well, and it had taken all her diplomatic tact to calm frayed tempers. By the time the meeting was over, she was mentally exhausted. Though it was rare for her to take time off, she figured the logical, sensible thing was to go home to lie down.

She ignored the surprise on her personal assistant's face as she said briefly on her way out the door, "I'm off home, Nancy. Only ring if there's an emergency. See you tomorrow."

When she rolled her dark Lexus sedan beside the red Lamborghini in the garage, she glanced over at the other car in surprise. Christine always left for the studio by noon. *Damn!* So much for peace. She wouldn't have come home if she had known she was still in the house. For a moment she simply sat to enjoy the quiet, knowing she was going to get a frosty reception after their row last night.

An argument that wasn't new.

She'd learned through bitter experience that Christine hated to be told she didn't have free rein with Winter's money. Nor did she seem to understand that Winter's sizable savings were the result of hard work and astute investments and weren't Christine's to squander. Christine liked the good life—the very good life—and expected to be provided with the expensive things she couldn't afford even on her own lucrative salary.

As quietly as she could, Winter crept through to the kitchen. Relieved to find it empty, she made herself a sandwich before she slipped out the back to the area beside the pool. With a contented groan, she pulled her hair out of the French twist with quick flicks of her wrist and stretched out on a deck chair. She closed her eyes to let her head settle. After the throb finally subsided, she turned to her lunch.

The sandwich was half-eaten when her gaze latched on to a discarded bikini top on the pavers. Winter's vision wavered in the heat and she blinked to clear it. Another flash of red—the other half of the bikini, she presumed—was further down past the end of the pool in front of the guest bungalow. She continued to doze in the chair until she was woken by the rumbling of thunder. Time to go inside. By the darkening sky, the storm wasn't far off.

She glanced at her watch. Nearly two thirty—Christine should have definitely left by now. On the way, she made a detour to pick up the bikini, but when she scooped up the bottom half, she caught snatches of sound inside the bungalow. Puzzled, she peered at the small building. No one had used the place since Christmas. It had also been the subject of one of their most bitter arguments. As far as she was concerned, it was just another extravagance of Christine's that was unnecessary. Six bedrooms were enough to accommodate any friends and family.

Winter had lost the argument of course.

Curious, she jogged up the three steps and pushed open the door. The kitchen cum living room was deserted, but an empty bottle of wine, two glasses and the remains of a plate of cheese and antipasto sat on the table. From the cries coming from behind the closed door of the bedroom, the action had moved there. It didn't take any imagination to know what was happening. Christine was always vocal during sex. Tightness crept into Winter's muscles and a drop of perspiration trickled down her back. Her brain went into overdrive as she tried to come to terms with what was happening. She was being cuckolded and she didn't have a clue who was in bed with the woman who shared her life.

She knew their relationship was in big trouble, but that Christine was unfaithful had never entered her head. Mentally she tried to tick off the possible women who could be the other party but gave up in the end when she realized with a dejected feeling that they hadn't socialized much together the last couple of years. While in the beginning they made time for each other, now they didn't bother or care. As their lives became busier, they had become strangers living in the same house. She couldn't even remember when they had made love tenderly or held each other through the night. Sex had become as impersonal as it was infrequent.

In two minds about what to do, Winter looked at the door. By the shouted words of pleasure from within, Christine was reaching her climax. She could wait in the kitchen until they came out, but that would save *them* humiliation, not her. Aware that if she caught them in the act it would be irrevocable, she hesitated. But then she had wanted out of the relationship for some time now. As much as the cheating clawed a hole in her insides, a feeling of release was also there. She could be free.

For some reason in the midst of her turmoil, her mother's words floated into her mind as if she had prophesied this very scenario. "When a woman acts without constraint, it always ends in tears." There was no way this wouldn't end in tears. Any good memories would be lost in the recriminations to follow.

Moisture filled her eyes. She brushed it away irritably, squaring her shoulders, reclaiming her anger. She knew she had better make sure she had watertight proof. Christine knew how to shift blame and was malicious if crossed. Winter reached into her pocket for her phone and set it ready to take photos.

Time to sever the ties forever.

Not giving herself a chance to second guess, she opened the door with a determined twist of the knob. As her eyes focused on the two people in the bed, she had to steady herself on the doorframe to keep upright. Christine had her back to her, her head thrown back, her hips pumping with abandon as she straddled someone on the bed.

Winter snapped off two photos before her gaze settled on the legs under her. She gave an involuntary cry, "What the hell!"

Christine's head whipped around at the sound and her eyes widened in alarm. She scrambled off, then tried to jerk up the sheet. It was too tangled to cover them. Winter took another photo before she realized who the other person was. She stared in disbelief. It was their yard and pool handyman. Furious, she bared her teeth. The woman was having an affair with a young man in his early twenties.

God damn the bitch!

Winter pulled herself together with an effort. "Get out of here," she barked at him, "and don't ever set foot on my property again."

Christine finally reacted, her eyes darting in panic. "You'd better go, Jason. I'll call you later."

He didn't hesitate. After hastily dragging on his underpants, he bolted out the room with the rest of his clothes bundled in his arms. When the door clicked behind him, they glared at each other. Winter's hands formed into fists. She couldn't remember when she had been so angry. Given her place in the corporate world, her temper was something she could control, particularly if it accomplished nothing. But the emotions she was experiencing here were another matter. Anger seeped across her skin, into her mind, through her bones, until it took all her willpower not to slap the woman.

With a deep breath, she shifted forward until they were face-to-face. "I expect you to be gone in half an hour, Chris," she said coldly. "Take what clothes you need for the night and I'll have the rest packed and sent to you. Email your forwarding address and leave your keys to the house on the dining room table on your way out."

Christine paled. "Damn you, Winter. I won't be tossed out like this. I have my rights. This is my home too."

"Not anymore. You forfeited that right. It's my house and you're not welcome here."

"And if I don't?"

Winter smiled, though it didn't reach her eyes. "There's no use arguing and you know it. I've photos to prove it. If you have any brains, leave with some dignity left."

"Screw you."

"No, Chris. That's what this is all about. You screwed someone else. A man. A young one and an employee. How could you?"

"Because I like variety. Because you're married to your fucking work. You never—"

"Enough. Don't make this about me," interrupted Winter, feeling bone weary. "Now for shit sake get into the bathroom and clean yourself up. You stink of him."

Unable to control the tremors, she turned her back on the bed. The room was so claustrophobic with the smells of perfume and sex that Winter barely made it out the front door. When she hit the fresh air, her stomach began to heave. A few seconds later, she succumbed to the turmoil and vomited into the bed of azaleas. Thunder rumbled in sympathy as raindrops began to mingle with the tears on her face.

* * *

Winter brought her mind back to the present as, with precise strokes, Christine signed her name. After her lawyer added her signature as a witness, she pushed the papers back across the table. "There. We're finished with each other now. I hoped you'd show more compassion, more gratitude. But you always were a self-serving businesswoman."

Winter's mouth thinned and her eyes hardened. Christine knew how to hit her buttons. "Get over it, Chris. You've done very well out of me."

"Whatever." She glanced at her solicitor. "If that's all, I'll be off. I have an appointment at twelve."

Her legal representative, a brash fiery redhead with the tenacity of a bulldog, gave a nod. "That wraps up everything." She glanced across at Lionel Miles. "My office will be in touch to finalise payment."

Christine rose to follow her out the door, but on the threshold turned to look back. "We can all point fingers, Winter, but you do have to take some responsibility in all this. You were never invested in our relationship. There were always three of us in it: you, me and your work. And quite frankly, I was very tired of coming in a distant third. You have no idea what passion means. The only thing you're really good at is making money, because you certainly were a disappointment in bed."

Feeling as though she'd been kicked in the stomach, Winter gulped. This could easily be her most humiliating moment. After Lionel finished shuffling the documents into his briefcase, she avoided his eye when he looked up. Instead, she concentrated on a small brown stain on the desk, trying to think of something to say. Nothing came. The settlement had been negotiated through their lawyers. This meeting to sign the papers was the first time she and Chris had been face-to-face in two years. All very civilized, but that façade had flown out the door.

She cleared her throat and raised her eyes. When she saw he was looking at her with compassion, involuntary tears welled up. She blinked them away hastily.

"Don't take her words to heart, Winter. Breakups are never pleasant. She's just venting her anger," he said with a shake of his head.

She fought for restraint and calm. Above all, she admonished herself, keep away from self-pity. But, how could she? Her personal life was a train wreck. Even though she hated to admit it, she knew Christine was partly right. From the beginning, she had never felt that fierce longing depicted in love stories. She had liked her, been charmed by her, but the first sexual pull hadn't blossomed into something deeper. She should have realized after dating for a year that they should never have moved in together. But Winter had become comfortable with the status quo—it was very pleasant having an attractive, bright woman share her life.

She pushed aside the embarrassment and held out her hand. "Thanks, Lionel, for all you've done. It's time to get on with my life."

As she spoke, she wondered if it were indeed completely over.

No one broke free from Christine without some scars.

CHAPTER TWO

Seven months later

A shade of uneasiness fluttered through Winter as she rang the doorbell of her aunt's house. The lunch invitation had sounded more like an SOS than a social visit. When her eighteen-year-old cousin, Tracey, answered the door and announced, "She's in a fluster. Go on through…she's waiting in the lounge," she knew something was definitely wrong. Except for advice on financial matters, Augustina Hamilton was usually unflappable and handled her own problems.

Winter bent over to give her a kiss on the cheek before she took a seat opposite. "Hi, Aunt. You wanted to see me?"

"I did, Winter. I've just brought the tray out so the coffee's hot. You'll have a cup?"

Winter nodded and watched as she added milk and sugar. Gussie, as she was known to friends, looked the epitome of everyone's favourite aunt: pleasantly plump, with a soft pretty face and a jolly disposition. Her blond curls were stylishly cut, the grey kept at bay by regular touch-ups at her hairdresser's.

Underneath her cheery exterior though, like all her four sisters she had a stubborn streak.

The youngest of the sisters, Gussie had been widowed at forty-seven when her husband died in a motorbike accident. Left with two children, the eldest just turned twelve, with a determined attitude she took whatever life threw at her. The sale of their large cattle property left her a wealthy woman, and she moved to Brisbane to raise her children.

Today she looked out of sorts. Her usual bright smile was missing and dark shadows smudged the pale skin beneath her eyes. Winter sipped her coffee, content to wait rather than ask what was wrong. Gussie never liked to be rushed. Once she had inquired briefly after Winter's mother, her eldest sister, Gussie came to the point. "I asked you over because I want you to do something for me."

Winter studied her. By the way her aunt was nervously fiddling with her cup on the saucer, it must be something serious—or delicate. Intrigued, she replied with a lift of her eyebrows, "Oh?"

"It's about Michael."

Now Winter was surprised. Tracey was the wild child of the family. Michael was a nerdish boy, and the apple of his mother's eye. "Is he in trouble?" she asked, then added with a wave of concern. "Not sick, is he?"

Gussie's soft chin quivered as a look of unease crossed her face. "No, it's nothing like that. But...well...I'm very worried about him."

"What's he up to? Knowing him it wouldn't be too much."

"He's taken up with a most unsuitable girlfriend. Let me rephrase that—not a girl but a woman well into her thirties."

"So?" Winter drawled. "He's twenty-one. Guys that age are obsessed with girls...or women. And we both know Michael's no different. He was dating Nanette when he was nineteen."

"I'm well aware of that, but he's so fragile emotionally," groaned Gussie. "You know how *dreadfully* depressed he got after breaking up with her, and this is *far* more serious. He's obsessed with this woman and claims he's in love with her."

Winter nearly rolled her eyes. In her opinion, Michael wasn't fragile just spoilt rotten. "Let him alone. Even if she's a lot older, there's nothing you or I can do about it. I wouldn't fuss. At his age, it won't last. Besides," she added with a shrug, "he might learn a thing or two from an older woman."

"I'm going to ignore that last remark," said Gussie solemnly. "It is not funny. This has been going on for months. He's talking about marrying her and he's still got two years left at uni. He'll be lucky to pass."

Winter was suddenly struck with a feeling of déjà vu. Was the woman another Christine, wanting a toy boy? "I'm hardly an expert on the subject," she said with a bitter edge.

"Of course you are. Christine had an affair with a young man. That's why I'm asking you to help."

Winter grimaced at the words. She had only discussed her breakup with her mother and in private, but given Christine's high profile in the media, their failed relationship had become public gossip. Somehow, her extended family had found out there was a young man involved. Her broken life had been painful enough without having to face that humiliation as well. She pushed aside the feeling of hurt and said in a disapproving voice, "You're not seriously asking me to interfere in your son's love life?"

"Well…not *interfere* exactly. Just get him to see it will never do."

"And how do I go about doing that? He'll probably tell me to get lost and I wouldn't blame him," Winter sharply replied. What did her aunt think she was…a sex counsellor?

"Nonsense! He thinks the world of you, Winter."

"Huh! So…what does this *cougar* do?"

Gussie flinched at the word. "She's a singer at a nightclub."

"What's the problem? She probably has more talent in her little finger than that giggly airhead, Nanette."

"Her occupation is not the biggest problem—it's the club where she works. I have on good authority that it's something to do with the Russian mafia. And apparently, Michael haunts the place."

"How do you know where he hangs out?" Winter asked, narrowing her eyes.

"I have my sources."

Winter stared at her aunt. It was about time she cut the apron strings. Gussie was such an indulgent and clinging mother. Tracey was already rebelling and if she continued with this, Michael would do the same. "What's the name of the nightclub?"

"The Silver Fox. Have you heard of it?"

"I was taken there once by clients, but that was a few years ago. It seemed respectable, very nice actually…certainly not a dive. It wasn't one of those gaudy loud nightclubs but catered for a classier set. The drinks were expensive enough. Who told you it had something to do with Russian gangsters?"

"I play bridge with a friend whose husband is a judge. Apparently, the place is known to be pedalling drugs and laundering money," answered Gussie.

Winter shook her head in disbelief. All this drama came from the damn Bridge Club gossip vine. "What do you expect me to do? Drugs are everywhere and I know nothing about organized crime."

"I want you to go there and have a look at what kind of woman my son is mixed up with," said her aunt.

"You want me to *go* to the club?" Winter asked incredulously. But then gave a resigned sigh, knowing she didn't have a choice. She loved her aunt dearly and hated refusing her anything.

"Well, I can't very well go. Please, Winter. For me. Michael will listen to you."

"Whoa there. I'll go there for a night out with a couple of my friends and have a look but that's all. I'm not interfering in Michael's love life."

Gussie relaxed back in her chair with a smile. "Thank you, dear. Now come and I'll show you the sculpture I bought at that auction last Saturday."

Winter followed her out the door, aware she had been adroitly manoeuvred into agreeing. And it was just as obvious that the Russian mafia was fabricated rubbish. Her aunt had no intention of letting her son marry a penniless lounge singer from a bar. It all sounded ridiculous. Besides the fact he was far too young.

* * *

As soon as Winter opened her front door, a black furry body twined around her ankles. When she reached down and tickled the cat under the ear, she was rewarded with a satisfied purr. "Miss me, Jinx sweetie, did you? Come on and I'll get you something to eat."

She chuckled as he immediately padded off to the kitchen—she swore he knew what she was saying. A friend had given her a kitten after her breakup and she had accepted him gratefully. Mainly because, although she loved cats, it was the first step in claiming back her life. Christine hated cats. Winter could never understand why she disliked them so much, she thought them ideal pets: cute and cuddly with a mind of their own, loyal but not cloying and could look after themselves. Jinx proved a godsend. It had been difficult to remain too depressed when listening to the soothing purr of a contented kitten curled up in her lap.

Winter filled his bowl with Meow Mix, then kicked off her shoes and rummaged in the fridge for the open bottle of sauvignon blanc. After pouring herself a glass, she headed for her study to her laptop. When she typed *The Silver Fox* into the search bar, up appeared a number of sites. She settled herself more comfortably in the chair, logged on to their main web page and began to scroll through the images.

The club appeared as she remembered: a long silver bar curved in a semicircle, surrounded by a troop of silver stools with thick black leather cushions, a shiny ceiling covered with myriads of small LED lights, solid rectangular tables on pedestals that rose up from a stone-grey floor and a row of booths nestled against the back wall. All the furnishings were black and silver, with touches of rusty red trimmings to set off the fox colour scheme.

It looked smart and edgy, a very classy lounge bar for higher-end clients with more disposable income than the average sports-bar patrons.

The blurb contained the usual enticing tropes. It also boasted of its unique range of cocktails for "serious drink connoisseurs." Winter smiled at that. In layman's language, it meant that a night out on the town was going to cost. She clicked on the entertainment section and a small stage with a piano appeared, along with the name of the main artist: Pandora. Excited now that she had reached her goal, she shifted the cursor down to the name.

The image caused her to take in a sharp breath. The woman sitting on the stool next to the baby grand was above stunning. A modern version of a vintage 1940s femme fatale: sexy, mysterious and darkly dangerous. She wore a body-hugging low-cut gown, gloves, and high stilettos. Her shoulder-length hair was glossy black, her lips ruby-red and her eyes long-lashed and hooded. As she sang into the microphone, a flash of fine black mesh fishnet stockings peeped out from the long split in the side of the dress.

Confronted with such unbridled sensuality, Winter's nether regions tightened into a sudden throb. She swallowed, unsettled by her body's reaction. Her libido was never this receptive. As she squirmed in her seat to dispel the ache, she put the acute response down to need. Two and a half years was far too long without a special someone. She had to forget Christine's last scathing words and shrug off the feeling of failure. It was time to get back to the dating scene—her body was wound up like a tightly coiled spring.

With a snap she clicked off the computer. Little wonder that Michael was so enamoured. And she had to agree with her aunt who had obviously done her homework. Pandora wasn't a suitable girlfriend for her son. She could understand Michael's crush, but why would a woman who looked like that even give him a second glance? He was so far out of her league it was laughable. Maybe it was all in the boy's mind. But then Winter was struck with a perturbing thought. Perhaps she did have some ulterior motive for leading him on. He was, after all, very well set up financially by his mother.

Determined now, she reached for the phone. At the second ring, it was answered.

"Dr. Drummond speaking."

"Hi, Jessie," she replied, smiling as she heard the familiar deep drawl.

"Hey, Winter. Sorry for answering so abruptly. I'm on call so I thought it was the hospital. What's up, babe?"

"Well…I was wondering if you'd like a night out."

A laugh resounded in her ear. "You're kidding, right? Winter Carlyle never goes out. She works all the time."

"Very funny. I'm serious. I figured it's about time I got back into the social scene. Would you be interested in going to the Silver Fox on Saturday night?"

"Shit yes. I've been meaning to give it a visit. I heard they've a really hot singer there. Dana will be itching to go as well. She's not with anyone at the moment. Would you mind if Linda came along too?"

Winter bit back the groan. She had met Linda at the party Jessie had put on after her split from Christine was finalised. The following week, she'd asked Winter on a date which proved a disaster. Though the woman was nice enough, they hadn't clicked at all. She was more interested in trying to get her into bed than getting to know her. "If you want to ask her then go ahead. I think I eventually got across I wasn't interested."

"She can be annoying but she grows on you."

"Yes, like mould. I had to scrape her off at the door."

"Don't worry. She got the message," said Jessie with a chuckle. "You can be intimidating sometimes when you're cranky."

"Yeah…yeah. What time Saturday?"

"Let's say we have something at that new Thai restaurant up the road from my place, then go on from there."

"It's a date. See you at seven."

With a satisfied hum Winter tapped off the phone. Even though she had an ulterior motive for the night out, she felt a flush of excitement. Cruising a bar with Jessie would be like old times and she had missed their close friendship. Christine hadn't liked her, which made socialising together too awkward. Not that Jessie had objected—they were too staid for her. She remained the perennial player, never forming any lasting relationship as she drifted from one woman to another.

They'd been friends for years, beginning as roommates in the on-campus women's college of the university. That first day, Winter was unpacking when she looked up to see a lanky, wildly handsome girl studying her from the doorway. She wore a clingy shirt, tight faded jeans with a big buckled belt, and black chunky boots. Her short hair was tipped blue to match her eyes, and a row of silver studs ran down the side of one ear. Two more studs winked above her eyebrow and the side of her nose.

The smile she turned on Winter was friendly enough, but there was a measuring gleam in her eye. Then seemingly satisfied, she announced she was a lesbian and if she had a problem with that then she'd better ask for another room. Taken aback, Winter, who still half-hovered in the closet, blurted out she was one too.

Jessie had simply remarked, "Thought so," and dragged her battered suitcase through the door. From then on, they became fast friends. By the time Winter began work as a corporate lawyer and Jessie as a medical intern, they had formed an enduring friendship.

To this day, Winter never knew how Jessie picked her sexuality so quickly. She was just an ordinary looking fresh-faced girl with freckles, who dressed a little conservatively. Prior to meeting Jessie, she had been too shy to ask anyone out.

CHAPTER THREE

Pandora attended to her makeup carefully in front of the long dressing room mirror. Though she had arrived a little late, it wasn't something she could hurry. Not if she wanted to look the perfect part. And now thirty-four, she seemed to have gained a few fine lines that needed to be covered up. She worked methodically, first smearing on a dark foundation to sharpen the angle of her jaw and the cheekbones, then applying a lighter foundation, followed by powder and blush. Her last touch was a rich creamy lipstick, the expensive type that slipped on like satin and set like velvet. It was a bold vibrant scarlet that held a hint of promise, a touch of wantonness. Not a colour many women wore. She would never consider it herself in real life.

After she studied her face critically for a moment, she pulled off the shower cap confining her hair and fanned out the thick strands with her fingers. The hair spilled to her shoulders, the longest she had ever worn it. She preferred it much shorter, more manageable, less flamboyant, but this woman she had created was all about illusions and fantasies and seduction.

A rap on the door was followed by a man's voice. "Ten minutes and you're on, Pandora."

"I'll be there," she called back and picked up the pace. She brushed the black waves down the side of her cheeks, then swept the right side as far as the corner of the eye and tucked back the other side against her ear. With another quick glance at her reflection, she rose to put on her dress. She smoothed down the patterned net tights before wriggling into the long black gown. Specially made, it hugged her curves without a crease.

Satisfied all was in order, she reached for the glass on the counter and took a mouthful of the warm Throat Coat Tea mixed with a pinch of salt. She didn't swallow immediately, instead gargled for a full minute, letting the liquid slide over her vocal cords. A pre-performance routine she did unfailingly before going onstage. Too many singers suffered from voice problems. Her throat muscles now exercised and protected, she pulled on the black gloves and eased her feet into the high heels.

Before opening the door, she glanced around the room to see two new bouquets of flowers on the table against the wall. There was no need to look at the attached cards to know who sent them—they had been coming to her dressing room every Saturday for weeks. Tonight, she was tempted to dump the roses in the garbage bin.

Enough was enough. It was beginning to feel like she was being stalked.

As usual, the large bunch of red roses was from Lawrence Partridge, a twice divorced wealthy playboy with an abrasive personality and an inflated ego. No matter how many times she told him *no*, it didn't seem to register. She would like to tell him where to stick his attentions, but then she would have to contend with Yuri. The owner of the club wouldn't take it lightly if she pissed off his best customer. So, she continued to be polite but firm as she fended off his advances.

With more misgivings Pandora reached for the card tucked into the much smaller posy of pansies. She was at a loss to know what to do with this one. Nearly five months ago, she had spent some time having a few drinks with a group of young people celebrating a twenty-first. Usually after her last bracket of songs, it was expected she remained visible in the club for at least half an hour before she left. Yuri insisted it was good for business and she didn't argue. It was always nice to wind down before she went home.

She had stayed much longer than usual that night, finding them a fun crowd. Then ended up spending a deal of time late in the night talking to Michael Hamilton, a shy, awkward engineering student. She indulged in a little light-hearted flirting to bring him out of his shell, which proved a huge mistake. He had taken her attentions to heart and began to turn up regularly every Saturday night at the club. It didn't take her long to twig he had developed a major crush on her. Without being hurtful, she tried to subtly discourage him but to no avail.

The weekly visits increased to twice a week. When his posies began to arrive, she was at her wits' end. Knowing she had to do something, she resolved that if he continued with the infatuation much longer, she would have no choice but to be downright rude. But she hesitated going down that path—she wasn't quite sure how he'd take that sort of rejection. A few things he had said made her suspect he wasn't very stable emotionally. She didn't want him to take things to heart and self-harm.

After a few deep breaths, she exited the dressing room and made her way down the corridor to the back of the stage. As she passed the open door of the main office, Yuri called out from his desk, "Come in for a second, Pandora."

She turned and walked to the door. It was a large room, split into business and pleasure. The front was designed for efficiency, housing his desk, a smaller workstation for his office assistant, filing cabinets, and a wall monitor of the club area. The back was for entertaining, filled with four plush leather chairs, a state-of-the-art TV, and a well-stocked bar. The windows were shielded with blinds.

She smiled at the other man in the room, her friend and mentor, Kurt, the pianist. When she began singing at the club a year ago, he had taken her under his wing immediately. In his early forties, he was a graceful handsome man, with wavy black hair, charming and charismatic, and a favourite of everyone in the club. Though most nights he walked with her the two blocks home to her apartment, he'd never once crossed the friendship line.

Yuri waved a hand at the monitor. "The place is packed tonight, Pandora. I'd like you to socialize longer afterward if you're up to it. Keep 'em happy."

She nodded, though hoped it didn't mean his brother Boris was in the club. While Yuri was likeable enough, Boris was someone to be avoided. He was an arrogant cruel pig of a man. The brothers were in their mid to late thirties, both unmarried. She'd learned that the gender dynamics in this close Russian family were very patriarchal, and women were expected to look and act a certain way. Yuri had always accepted that as a non-Russian, she didn't have to live by their rules, but then so he should. They both knew her popularity was one of the main reasons the club was always so full. He couldn't afford to lose her.

"No problems, boss," she murmured, and smiled as Kurt gave her a wink.

"Right-oh. You two had better get along then."

When Pandora walked onstage, the room died to a hush before applause broke out. She let it wash over her as Kurt took his place at the piano. He began to caress the keys, giving her a cheery nod before he began to play a short solo piece as an introduction. She scanned the audience to take in its demographics as she waited at the microphone for her cue. It was a good mix of age, and she was pleased to see more women than usual. They always upped the tone of the night.

Lawrence Partridge was sitting in a booth with a man and a woman around his age. Michael was at the bar with two friends, gazing at her adoringly.

Pandora ignored them both and began to sing.

As she crooned out her songs, a table of four women took her eye. A pang of longing swept over her. Just for one night she wished she didn't have to cater to the men in the room. This job had been too long, become too stressful. She was getting hyper edgy, needing to feel a woman's arms around her again, and if she wasn't mistaken the women were gay. Two were definitely anyhow. But she wasn't her own boss, wasn't able to mix freely with them. With an inward groan, she went back to her routine, becoming the enchantress, the siren.

As the night wore on, she felt more and more restless. She needed to vary her act, stop being so one-dimensional. An idea hit in the last bracket. A walk-through finale would be a change. She had two songs left in tonight's repertoire: Adele's "Someone Like You" and Selena's "I Could Fall in Love." Ideal for the purpose. Out of the corner of her eye she could see Kurt lift his eyebrows in surprise when she took the microphone out of its stand. Then he gave her a grin and nod as he caught on and held off playing until she had descended the two steps to the main floor.

Silence fell as she began to glide through the tables. With her low husky voice, she was power and charm, the embodiment of the ageless courtesan, the stuff of fantasies. Three guys in suits with ties loosened, looked at her expectantly when she slowed. With a shake of her head and a wink, she moved on. She paused at a table where a young couple held hands and sang a few bars to them. They blushed and wriggled closer together. She stopped to sing to a man who looked well into his sixties, while his wife smiled fondly at his embarrassment.

The song finished—she began the last. She stopped here and there, though only briefly after a line or two. No one touched her, nor did she expect anyone would. The crowd knew it would have destroyed the intimacy of the moment. As the song neared its end, she reached the booth with the four women and looked down at them. With a slow deliberate motion, she leaned over the one in the black dress who had been frowning at her all night, and breathed the last line into her ear, "I could fall in love with you."

Smiling as she heard the sudden hissing intake of breath, Pandora turned away to bow and wave at the crowd. When the applause died down, and she'd returned her mike to the stage, she walked back to the table and decided for once to do what *she* wanted for a change. "Would you ladies mind if I joined you."

"We'd love you to," answered a devilish good-looking woman with short spiky hair, clearly the spokesman of the group. They shifted around to make room.

"It's a relief to get off my feet," said Pandora with a sigh as she eased herself onto the seat. "Too long on these heels. Now…who are you girls?"

"This is Linda, Dana, and Winter. And I'm Jessie," the woman replied, flashing her a practised smile so full of charm and arrogance that Pandora nearly laughed. Jessie clearly had an inflated sense of self-worth and used to getting her own way. She'd probably only rarely had a knock-back from a woman. Pandora knew her type very well. Charismatic but a perpetual player who was afraid of commitment, no different from the aging playboys who frequented the club.

Pandora eased back in the chair, sizing the women up as they were introduced. Linda was a curvaceous pretty blonde who looked like she knew how to enjoy herself. Just like any average person who frequented a bar—uncomplicated in pursuit of a good time. And sex. If she fancied women, Pandora doubted she would be her type. Too feminine. Nor was she sending out any vibes that she was interested.

Dana was a tall redhead with an angular androgynous face framed by cropped short hair. She was looking at her self-consciously, as though a little intimidated. She'd probably be more at home in a bar with a pool table than in an upscale club. Both were in their mid-thirties and appeared pleasant women with no agenda other than a night out on the town.

But it was the woman in the black dress who tweaked her interest. Light-brown glossy hair tied up in a back twist, mature strong features and very foxy. Elegant and aloof Winter. Even the name was interesting. Pandora had no idea why she had been studying her with dislike, but she was intrigued. And all that pent-up hostility was rather sexy. Her libido thought so—it was giving definite twitches.

She held her gaze quizzically for a moment. Yes, there were still sparks of temper in her eyes and simmering resentment. Underneath though, there appeared to be a hint of interest as well, but maybe that was only wishful thinking on her part. Winter might not even be a lesbian.

"What would you like to drink?" asked Jessie.

Pandora turned her attention to her and replied with a smile. "This round is on me." She signalled to Frankie, their most experienced waitress and who also, she knew, preferred women.

When she reached the table, Frankie beamed at them. "What'll you have, ladies?"

"Hallelujah," murmured Dana. Pandora smiled to herself as she caught the whispered words. It seemed the waitress was Dana's type. And Frankie was looking at her with a light in her eye as well.

After the others placed their orders, Frankie cocked her head at Pandora. "Your usual?"

She nodded then added to Jessie, "I'm not a big drinker, but I do enjoy a brandy at the end of the night."

"I'm a beer drinker or maybe an odd vodka, but occasionally I'll have a Coke to surprise my liver," Jessie replied with an engaging grin. "So, what do you do when you're not at the club, Pandora?"

She shrugged. "I jog, watch movies, read…you know…what most people do."

"Oh, you're anything *but* like most people," murmured Jessie, angling her body until their knees were pressed together. Then she casually draped her arm over the back of the chair.

Far too close for Pandora. She considered her for a moment before she deliberately eased away. She left the sharp retort on the tip of her tongue, instead said mildly, "I'm just here to have a quiet drink and a friendly chat, Jessie."

"Sorry. But you can't blame a girl for trying."

"Just so long as you know where I stand," Pandora said with a smile to take the sting out of her words. "Tell me now…what do you all do?"

Jessie slid her arm off the backrest with an embarrassed hum. "I'm a paediatrician. Linda's a nurse in the children's ward, Dana's a construction engineer and Winter…well…she's a corporate lawyer and a workaholic, hey babe?"

Winter sent Jessie a good-natured shrug. "Some of us have to keep the wheels of commerce running to pay for your hospitals, my friend."

"Touché, Jessie," chuckled Dana.

Pandora watched the exchange with a small pang. They were good friends and she envied them. When the drinks arrived, she sipped her brandy, enjoying the light-hearted banter and the low recorded background music. She covertly studied Winter as they talked. Her voice was as polished as her designer dress. She didn't say much, but when she did it was worth listening to. A no-frills type of person.

As they swopped stories, Pandora realized she hadn't enjoyed herself so much for a long time. The women were a breath of fresh air. But when Jessie was in the middle of a complicated joke, she noticed Winter's eyes suddenly widen as they focused on something behind her. Curious, she swivelled her head to look.

Shit!

Michael was heading for their table. He was the last person she wanted to see at the moment. She watched alarmed as he stumbled toward them. Normally only a moderate drinker, something must have set him off tonight. She winced—he looked very tipsy and very aggro. This could be a nasty scene.

When he reached their table, he gripped the edge to steady himself then spat out, "What the hell are you doing here, Winter?"

Taken by surprise, Pandora turned to look at Winter. Judging by her glare, she wasn't too pleased with the greeting. "I imagine the same as you. I'm having a night out," she said coldly.

"Mum sent you, didn't she?" he asked truculently.

"Be careful, Michael. I'm not going to answer that. I don't expect you to talk about your mother in a bar when you're half-drunk."

"What I do has nothing to do with you."

Winter's eyes ran over him like a scanner and she curled her lip. "You're embarrassing yourself. Go back to the bar and I'll talk to you later."

"Fuck you, Winter. Don't order me around."

"Then act like a man."

There was an uncomfortable silence, before Jessie said soothingly, "You're Aunt Gussie's son, aren't you? Winter took me out to your property one Easter when we were at uni."

He glanced at her distractedly. "I remember. We thought you were great fun, Jessie." Then for the first time he directly faced Pandora. His voice rose with emotion. "Sorry about that. I guess I was out of line. Will you have a drink with us? I'm with a couple of mates."

Conscious the women were waiting for her answer, Pandora shook her head. "Some other time perhaps." Then turned to Jessie before he could say anything more. "Now what about giving us the punch line of that joke."

Jessie launched back into the story immediately. At the rebuff, Michael stood for a moment swaying from one foot to the other before he shuffled off. The uneasiness hovering over the group melted away when he vanished back to the bar. Pandora cast a look across at Winter. Her eyes were downcast, locked on her drink. Pandora felt a sharp jab of anger. And hurt. Winter wasn't here for a night out—she had come to check on her cousin. That explained the antagonism.

Obviously, the family thought Pandora was unsuitable for their precious boy.

CHAPTER FOUR

Winter clutched her glass tightly, wishing she could sink under the carpet.

What a clusterfuck.

When she eventually had the courage to raise her head, she found Pandora studying her. Her expression was neutral but her eyes were cold. Winter flinched. It was her own damn fault for letting Gussie talk her into this ridiculous charade. Not that she thought the singer was a suitable partner for Michael. She wasn't. But it wasn't any reflection on Pandora. She was all class. He was far too immature to be with a woman like her, and from what she had seen of the Silver Fox, it wasn't a place he should be frequenting.

On the surface it was sophisticated and upmarket, but to her there was something not quite right about it. She'd seen enough of wealth and power to get the vibes that it had a not-so-nice underbelly. But then again, she thought, maybe she was worrying too much. Perhaps all clubs were the same. Having been out of circulation for years, she had lost touch with this sort of night life. She and Christine had never visited places like this, and with her crazy work schedule, clubbing wasn't on her agenda now. But whether she was being overprotective or not, Michael should be socializing somewhere more suitable, somewhere with a crowd his own age. Too long in a place like this spelt trouble with a capital T.

She snapped out of her thoughts when Jessie called out, "Have another drink, Winter?"

"I should be going home."

"Come on. Don't be such a party pooper. There's nothing to go home to except your cat."

"Oh, all right. I guess it's about time I had a night out. I'll have another scotch and dry, but make it a half."

"You live alone, Winter?" asked Pandora as she scooped up an olive and a piece of cheese from the dish on the table.

"I have for over two and a half years," she answered quickly—too quickly—aware Pandora was looking down at her ring finger. She tucked her hand into her lap.

"Ah. Sorry. That must sound like I was prying." But from the gleam in her eye, she didn't appear too sorry.

"What about you, Pandora? Someone at home?" broke in Jessie. Winter leaned forward to hear the reply.

The singer's eyebrows lifted fractionally. "Not when I looked last."

"Leave the woman alone, Jessie," said Linda, "and stop being nosy. She can have anyone she wants."

Pandora smiled at her. "Why thank you. That was a sweet thing to say."

"True enough though," replied Linda wistfully.

"Trust me," murmured Pandora, waving at herself. "All this is only an illusion. A skin I shed as soon as I go out the door."

"Maybe so, but—"

"Hello, Pandora," interrupted a male voice.

Winter glanced up quickly at the sound, momentarily caught in the pinpoint lights that shimmered on the ceiling. A bulky man around five ten in a dark suit, stood in front of them. He was facing Pandora, half turned away from Winter. When his head swam into focus, she gave a hiss of surprise. Lawrence Partridge. Thankfully, he hadn't looked her way—she had no wish for a public confrontation. He hated her, and the feeling was mutual.

Last year, she had counselled a client against buying a half-billion-dollar company in which Partridge was a major shareholder. After a great deal of research, she found the figures of one of the smaller subsidiary holdings of the company didn't add up and had advised against the purchase. The withdrawal of the offer had led to some very heated words in the negotiation chamber. Partridge had stormed out of the room, though not before he had called her some offensive names. She had been tempted to slap a defamation suit on him, but that would have only meant she'd have to have more dealings with him. She'd had no wish to see him again.

Pandora nodded impersonally at him. "Lawrence."

He skimmed a glance over her chest. "Would you like to come over to my table for a drink?"

She remained unsmiling as she shook her head. "I'm sorry."

"I've waited all night to speak to you," he said, his congenial grin slipping a notch.

"Maybe another time. I'm with friends."

At that statement, he gazed around the table. When his eyes settled on Winter, his beefy face hardened. "You prefer to be with this bitch Winter Carlyle?" he snarled.

Winter's face went red hot as her temper spiked. "Hello to you too, Lawrence," she snapped back, not bothering to hide her dislike. "And call me that again and I'll see you in court. I'm not joking."

"You think you—" he began, then must have realized she was quite serious, for he bit off the sentence with a swallow. "Shit. You're not worth wasting my breath on." He turned back to Pandora and skimmed a hand over her shoulder. "Come on, honey. My friends want to meet you."

Something about the possessive way he was touching Pandora, sent another wave of anger rippling through Winter. This time fiercer. Every inch of her body stiffened. She couldn't explain why she had such a reaction, or why it mattered, but it made her mad as hell. Struggling for calm, she half rose in the chair. "Didn't you hear her. She said *another time*. In my book that means *no*."

"Piss off, Winter. Have you told her you're a bloody lesbian yet?"

"That's enough, Lawrence. You're being rude and insulting," Pandora interrupted. Her voice was still low, but disdain and cold anger radiated in the tone. Far more chilling than if she had shouted the words. "You'd better go. Oh…and don't bother sending any more flowers. I won't be accepting them."

For a long moment he stared at her, the high colour in his face beginning to fade to a pasty grey. He looked undecided for a moment, then abruptly turned and strode off. No one spoke. Winter sat mortified, wondering if she should just get up and go. She'd made a complete fool of herself, never having been involved in so public an altercation before. Could this night get any worse? God knows what Pandora thought of her now. Not knowing what to do, she clasped her hands in her lap and avoided looking at anyone.

Linda patted her arm and a chuckle from Jessie broke the silence. "Who exactly was that fuckwit, Winter? I've never seen you so riled up."

She gave her a sickly smile. "We had a business run-in. I'm bound by confidentiality, but I can say that I cost him a lot of money…and I mean mega dollars." Feeling obliged to say something to Pandora, she turned to her. "I owe you an apology. I shouldn't have interfered."

Anger flared in Pandora's eyes. "You think I'd encourage a man like that?"

"Well…um…I wouldn't presume to know whom you'd like. I personally find the man repugnant, but that doesn't mean you would. I've often been baffled by the laws of attraction. Some people are drawn like magnets to the most unsuitable partners."

Pandora snapped her glass down on the table. It gave a resounding clunk. "This isn't about quantum physics. This is about my integrity. And you're bringing that into question, Winter."

She winced. Could she muddle this up much more? "That wasn't what I meant. I was only trying to help."

"I know perfectly well how to handle men, and women, like him," Pandora said quietly. "Money is power, but it's not the only power."

"Perhaps I'd better stick to the laws of economics. Human relations aren't my forte," muttered Winter ruefully.

Linda leaned forward to snuggle into her side. "Hey, baby, I think you did just great. You're kinda sexy all hot and bothered."

"Yeah, come on," said Dana. "Don't let that dropkick spoil our party. I could do with another drink. Where is that waitress. What was her name again?"

Jessie slapped her arm. "Frankie…as if you didn't know. You're so full of shit, Dana."

To give her feelings a rest, Winter sat back just listening to them happily babble away. Pandora seemed to get over her hissy fit quickly enough to join in the friendly wisecracks, though Winter noticed she didn't look her way again. It was also very annoying that Linda had her hand on her thigh. She wanted to push it off, but that would probably appear petulant on her part. The less attention to herself the better now.

Frankie proved a pleasant distraction, hovering around their table as much as she could and accepting their ribbing in good heart. It wasn't long before she realized that Jessie was acting completely out of character. Gone was the arrogant assured player. She was actually behaving normally around Pandora, rather than turning on her usual bold charm. Winter studied her quietly. If she didn't know better, it looked like Jessie was genuinely interested in the singer and not just as a casual pick-up. At this epiphany, a bad taste filled Winter's mouth. She had no idea why the thought of the two of them together annoyed her so much. She didn't know Pandora and she'd been waiting for years for Jessie to find someone she could care for.

Time flew and it was past two when Pandora announced, "I'm off home. It's been a long day."

"I think we're all ready to head out too. It's been a great night and thanks for your company," said Jessie.

"My pleasure. Look…next Saturday is a special night at the club to celebrate a Russian holiday, if you'd like to come. It's themed…everyone usually wears something red."

"Sounds like a plan," said Jessie enthusiastically. "I'll make sure I'm not on call."

Dana and Linda nodded, promising they'd make it as well. Unsure if she was included in the invitation, Winter remained quiet. But as they rose to go, Pandora put her hand on her arm. "You girls go on and order a cab. I want a quick word with Winter."

She glanced at her in surprise, though didn't argue. Trying to ignore the pleasant warmth of the hand on her skin, she tilted her head at Pandora enquiringly after the others had moved out of hearing range.

"Would you have lunch with me sometime during the week?"

Winter stared at her incredulously. "You're asking me out?"

Pandora flushed and said brusquely, "It's not a date. We need to talk. You seem to have formed an opinion of me that's upsetting."

"Why would you worry what I thought of you? You made it quite clear you don't care for my opinion."

"You're taking everything too personally. I'm not a fool…I know you came here to check up on Michael and I'd like to put things straight. But not here. Somewhere where we can talk quietly and rationally. When we're not so tired." Pandora lightly squeezed her arm as she spoke.

The squeeze was friendly, feminine, and Winter melted into the touch. "Okay," she muttered, not hesitating anymore. Lunch with her sounded nice—super nice actually. "Would Wednesday suit? Say twelve thirty at the White Lace in the city. It has a decent menu and there are tables out the back where we won't be disturbed."

"Perfect."

"Will you be safe going home by yourself? It's very late. We can drop you off."

"I have an apartment only a few blocks away and Kurt always walks me home. I have to change into street clothes before leaving the club so I'll still be a little while," replied Pandora with a smile.

"Kurt?"

"He's our pianist and a good friend."

"Yes, of course. I forgot. You have a man to protect you… that's good. I'll say goodnight then."

Winter made her way to the door, resisting the urge to run. The woman had her in a dither. She'd never felt this attracted to Christine, even in their first months together. Theirs had been a quiet orderly romance with very little spontaneity or overwhelming passion.

She shook away her thoughts as she spied only two of her friends on the footpath. "Where's Dana?"

"Gone home with Frankie." Jessie looked at her curiously. "Care to share?"

"Not really. It was between the two of us."

She was saved from any more questions when a yellow taxi pulled up at the edge of the pavement. They dropped Linda off first then continued on to Jessie's house. As they sped through the nearly deserted streets, she turned to look at Jessie. Her friend's face was only visible by the glow of the streetlights streaming by, but to Winter she seemed pensive. "I hope you haven't got your eye on Pandora, Jess. Straight women will break your heart."

Jessie's teeth flashed white in the night as a laugh exploded from her. "Geez, Winter, you really are clueless. Pandora is a big ol' lesbian, just like us."

CHAPTER FIVE

Pandora stripped off her dress, whimpering a little as she pried off her shoes. Five-inch heels were far too high to be comfortable. She needed to visit a shoe shop before she wrecked her feet or broke a leg. Besides, it would hardly matter if she went down to three inches. She doubted anyone would even notice. Most would be focused on her face and body. After easing off her fishnet stockings, she slipped into her jeans and T-shirt. But as she pulled on her old comfortable Jimmy Choo boots, she began to wonder why on earth she was going home. Her lonely apartment was the last place she wanted to be tonight. Winter Carlyle had her so wired it was pointless trying to sleep. She needed to unwind, go somewhere where she was anonymous, where Pandora didn't exist.

And she knew the very place.

Revisiting the wardrobe, she took her light blue dress shirt off the hanger and discarded the T-shirt. Determinedly, she scrubbed off the layers of makeup, for tonight she needed to purge the club from her skin. When satisfied her face was perfectly clean, she ran her fingers through her hair to feel the texture as she always did before she tied it up. The black tresses were thick and silky, a legacy from her dear old Irish grandma. After quickly braiding the ponytail, she glanced at her reflection in the mirror. She was herself again and not some show pony on a stage.

After sending Kurt a text to tell him she was going out rather than heading home, she ordered a taxi.

Light rain had begun to fall as the cab reached a plain wooden door in the narrow side street. The entrance to the small private "ladies only" club was situated far enough away from the main social strip to remain discreetly hidden from passers-by. After scrutinizing her ID, the doorman waved her inside. As soon as she stepped into the room, every sense in her body sparked to life. The dancing was in full swing. She stood mesmerized by the flashing coloured lights and the pulsing beat of the music: vivid, frenetic, mind blowing. Just what she needed.

She made her way to the bar, though didn't plan to drink. She wanted to dance, to let off steam, to forget everything for a few hours.

"Ginger ale," she ordered, raising her voice above the din.

When it arrived, she swivelled on the barstool and idly sipped as she gazed around. A friend had brought her here over a year ago when she first came to the city, and the place hadn't changed. It still had the nineties look with its preppy pastel walls covered with psychedelic posters of women, and the air held that slight smell of countless spilled beers. But it felt warm and inviting, an intrinsic feeling that the Silver Fox lacked for all its cultivated interior design.

She didn't have long to wait. A dark-eyed woman in her late twenties with an olive complexion, wearing a tube top and spandex black pants that showed every inch of her athletic body, sidled up beside her. Her short hair suited her square face and when she smiled, two dimples peeped out. After giving Pandora the onceover, she asked, "Wanna dance?"

"You bet," she replied and followed her to the floor.

And then she was lost in the rhythm, the beat, the mindless mass of gyrating bodies. It was wild. It was fast. It was perfect. Her partners came and went but she danced on, until finally just before five, the DJ announced, “Last song, girls.”

When a slow love song started to play, the dancers began to couple up.

The spandex girl was moving towards her, when a tall well-built woman in red leather veered in between them and pulled Pandora into her arms. She felt the hot heat from the strong body, the warm breath on her cheek. Fingers cruised up her back as a whisper echoed in her ear. “Would you like to come home with me?” Her voice was deep and husky, her cologne sharp and spicy.

Pandora considered the offer as they swayed together to the music. Anonymous sex. No strings, no unwanted ties, no recriminations. It’d been months since she’d been with a woman, and this Amazon looked like she knew how to satisfy her, how to have her screaming out her name.

For a moment she was tempted, but sex with a stranger wasn’t really her thing. And she had already met the one who caught her interest. Anyone else just wouldn’t feel right. But it was just her luck it was an uptight high-flying corporate lawyer who had made it quite clear she disapproved of her. Who thought she was straight, willing to seduce a boy and encourage a sleazy fifty-year-old playboy. Not to mention that Winter already had a pretty blond nurse fawning over her.

With a touch of regret, Pandora slowly drew out of the embrace. “Sorry, babe. I only came to dance tonight.”

The Amazon rocked back on her heels with a rueful smile. “My loss then. You certainly are a fine-looking woman. Maybe you’ll visit the place again one night when you’re more in the mood. Now come on and I’ll escort you out the door so no one will bother you. There are a few girls on the make who’ve been drinking too much. I’ll wait with you until your taxi comes.”

Pandora took her hand with gratitude. Though she knew how to look after herself, it was nice to be the object of such chivalry. The big woman was a real treasure.

* * *

When Pandora reached the White Lace a few minutes before twelve thirty, Winter was already waiting outside. Dressed in a dove-grey pin-striped suit, a cornflower-blue shirt opened to the top of her cleavage and a pair of natty designer sunglasses, she looked the epitome of a successful woman. Even in the bustling crowds of the city, she stood out. Pandora was pleased now she had chosen to wear the silk knee-length dress, her favourite in her wardrobe. She smoothed down the front self-consciously, aware she had dressed for a date rather than a casual luncheon with an acquaintance.

When she realized she'd never see Winter again once they left the club, the invitation had been a spur-of-the-moment thing. While the others enthusiastically agreed to come the following Saturday night, she doubted Winter would bother to return. Clubbing didn't seem her scene. So, Pandora made up a pretence of wanting to talk about Michael, knowing full well it was just an excuse. She was actually surprised Winter agreed to meet her so readily, considering she had studiously avoided looking at her most of the night.

She adjusted her bag on her shoulder, then stepped forward to greet her. "Hey, Winter. Thank you for meeting with me."

"Hi. Really, it's nice to have lunch with someone other than my office colleagues. We tend to talk shop too much. Shall we go in?" said Winter, looking serene as she waved her inside the restaurant.

After they placed their orders at the counter, Pandora followed her out to a small courtyard filled with tables covered with checked tablecloths. This secluded section was quiet, the sound of the traffic so muted it was almost musical. "This is really quaint," she exclaimed.

"It's one of my favourite places," said Winter. "A little secret I don't share with the office. A hideaway when I want to get away by myself if I'm too stressed."

"I know what you mean. When I perform, I can't avoid public scrutiny which becomes wearing. Alone time becomes precious."

Winter's eyes were shrewd and probing. "I can believe there would be complications with an act like yours. I imagine some customers wouldn't have the wit to separate the woman on the stage from the real one underneath. You must have lots of unwanted advances."

"You get used to it. It comes with the territory. I've learned to make it plain from the beginning that I never mix my work at the club with my personal life."

"Then tell me why you haven't told Michael that?"

Pandora grimaced. Winter hadn't taken long to ask that question. "And you think I haven't?"

"I don't know what to think. He told his mother he intends to marry you."

Pandora blinked at her, speechless. She snatched up the glass of water and gulped, then managed to get out, "You're kidding me."

Winter's eyes turned dark. "Do I look like I'm joking?"

"No, I guess you don't," she answered reluctantly. "But I suggest I give my side of the story before you continue to judge me. Are you interested in hearing it?"

"Of course I am. Look," Winter replied, her voice lower, softer, "we started off on the wrong foot. I admit I went to the club with the preconceived idea you were playing around with Michael. Don't get me wrong. I couldn't care less who he's seeing. He's an adult and can do what he likes. If it's someone more…ah…mature, then that's his choice. But my aunt is panicking. This marriage declaration has her in a flap. She asked me to—"

Her voice trailed off when a female voice interrupted. "Your meals, ladies."

They both looked up with a start, then hurriedly leaned back to allow the waitress to place the plates on the table.

After smiling her thanks, Winter waited until the woman disappeared before she continued. "She asked me to…well…assess the situation."

"Why did you agree? You just said yourself it was none of your business."

"It's very hard to say no to Gussie," Winter said with an embarrassed shrug.

Pandora let out an exasperated huff. "You know, all this could have been avoided if I hadn't been so stupid."

"What do you mean?"

"I made the mistake months ago of paying a bit too much attention to him one night. He was with a crowd celebrating a twenty-first. They were so much fun I stayed to closing time partying with them. Because he was the shy one in the group, I decided to make him feel special with some light-hearted flirting."

Winter poked her fork in the air. "Bad move. Knowing Michael, he would have taken you seriously. His mother mollycoddles him."

"I know that now," Pandora said impatiently. "Ever since that darn night, he's haunted the club like a lovesick puppy. I've tried everything to discourage him, except being downright nasty and I don't want to do that. Quite frankly, I'm at a loss how to handle it." She looked at the composed Winter thoughtfully as an idea formed. "Perhaps your appearance at the club may be a good thing. You should be able to get through to Michael that I'm not interested because I certainly can't. It's like talking to a brick wall."

Winter nearly choked on the piece of chicken. "Certainly not. He won't listen to me. He's twenty-one for Christ sake…he thinks I'm a stick-in-the-mud. I only promised Gussie I'd have a look. Nothing more. That's it."

"Rubbish. You can't get out of it that easily. You poked your nose into my business so you have to help me."

Winter scowled at her. "How do you suggest I do that? He'll hate me for life and he *is* my cousin."

"Maybe we should get together and make a plan. I'm fresh out of ideas."

"Humm…I suppose I could help. I have to go back to work soon. Do you have any nights off?"

"Sundays, Mondays and Thursdays. Singing four nights a week is enough. Any more and you start getting voice fatigue. They have recorded music Sunday and Monday, and every Thursday the club features a different artist."

"Right," said Winter, suddenly all business. "How about coming over to my place tomorrow night for dinner then. I enjoy cooking. Say about six? You might like to have a dip in the pool before eating. We'll work something out."

Pandora was tempted to hug her. It seemed Winter was a woman of action once she made up her mind. She could see why she would be good at her job. And it was nice to be looked after for a change. She already owed her a debt when she'd given her a way out to get rid of Lawrence Partridge. Not only had she put him in his place, Winter had come like a shining knight to Pandora's defence.

"Dinner sounds delightful," she murmured.

CHAPTER SIX

Winter conceded that if it had been anyone but Pandora, she'd never have agreed to be part of this. She always shied away from getting involved with other's personal affairs. Give her a flow chart or a commercial contract and she was quite at home. Catch phrases like "better solutions," "broader perspectives," and "accountable risks" were her bread-and-butter buzzwords. Not words like emotions, love, or soulmate. She'd been wracking her brains to come up with a solution to Michael's infatuation, but every idea would be sure to hurt him. She didn't want to be responsible for his winding up in the same state after Nanette broke up with him. He had been close to being hospitalised. Then in the end, she decided it was probably better if she and Pandora bounced ideas off each other—two heads would be better than one.

She prepared the Dijon salmon and roasted vegetables ready for the oven later and went upstairs to shower and dress. She dithered over her outfit. Though it wasn't actually a date per se, just a get-together to discuss things. All the same she did want to look her best. Pandora knew how to wear clothes—her dress yesterday was stunning. Eventually she decided on mid-way—not too dressy nor too casual. But that didn't prove easy. By the time she'd tried on half her wardrobe, it was nearly six.

With a "For heaven's sake, this is absolutely bloody ridiculous," she pulled on the charcoal jeans and the embroidered beige shirt that she'd tried on first. Then she rushed to the mirror, applied a touch of makeup and put her hair up in its usual French twist. This time she slipped in her tortoise-shell comb as well. With two minutes to spare, she made it downstairs before the doorbell tingled. Pandora stood on the landing with a small bag and a bottle of wine.

"Hi," said Winter, keeping her expression calm. "Come on in."

Pandora flashed her a wide smile. "Your house is great."

"I'll take you on a tour afterward. You'll have a dip in the pool first?"

"I've brought my swimmers," Pandora announced, holding up the bag. She handed over a bottle of wine saying, "I hope you like this."

"Excellent. Come around the back and you can change there."

"You're not coming in?"

"I'm not much of a swimmer. I put the pool in for my…um…ex. It'll be nice to see someone use it again."

"Then I'm happy to oblige," said Pandora cheerfully.

Once her guest disappeared into the change room, Winter took the bottle to the kitchen. She glanced approvingly at the label before popping it into the bar fridge. Then she poured herself a glass from an opened bottle and went back out. Stretched out on a deckchair beneath the shade of a wisteria, she watched Pandora swim laps. The woman certainly was at home in the pool as she churned through the water with economical seemingly effortless strokes.

When Pandora finally hoisted herself out, Winter found herself fixed on the graceful body. Drops of water gleamed on her skin like golden pearls as the muted rays from the setting sun bathed the yard in warm colours. She looked breathtaking.

Pandora towelled off, drying her hair vigorously for a minute before combing it into order with her fingers. "That was wonderful. I haven't had for a swim for ages," she exclaimed before she dropped onto a deckchair beside Winter.

"You're like a fish."

"I was into competitive swimming at school." She wriggled her toes. "Big feet."

"You make it look so easy. Would you like to sit out here for a while before changing?" Winter asked, staring up into the evening sky. "It's too pretty a time of day to be indoors."

"It certainly is," agreed Pandora with a wistful lilt in her voice.

"Ready for a wine, or a beer perhaps?"

"A beer sounds nice after the exercise. I'll have a wine with the meal."

Winter was back in a few minutes with a frosty beer, a refill for herself and a small plate of nibbles.

Pandora took a long swig, then sank back in the seat. "It's so peaceful."

Winter entwined her fingers behind her head, pillowing it as she looked out over the pool and surrounds. "Yes, it is," she murmured.

An orange tinge reflected in the still water and the gardens were tinted mauve in the evening light. They sat silently content, letting the calm of the evening wash over them. Winter shifted her attention to Pandora, studying her as she gazed out over the yard. With only a trace of makeup and hair tousled, she looked just as appealing as her onstage persona but in a far different way. In fact, it was hard to even see the singer in the woman stretched out on the chair beside her. She seemed not so soft, not so sleek. In a one-piece bathing suit, she looked super fit like a competitive athlete. Though essentially very feminine, the muscles in her upper arms and legs were quite defined.

Pandora turned her head with a quirk of her eyebrows. "What?"

Winter took another a quick swallow from her drink, embarrassed to be caught staring. "Just thinking how fit you look. Do you work out?"

"I do. Standing for hours singing requires a certain degree of stamina so I do some gym work and jog in the mornings."

"You put me to shame. I need to get in better shape," Winter said, patting her stomach.

"Nonsense. You're very nice how you are. Only..." she leaned forward suddenly and reached a hand over to Winter's hair. With quick fingers, she plucked the comb and bobby pins out of her bun and shook the locks free. The hair tumbled to below her shoulders in a mass of thick waves. "There," Pandora murmured. "That's better. It's way too pretty to be kept up when you're not at the office."

Winter blinked at the intimacy of the gesture. Something heady and unexpected shot through her. Tongue-tied, she felt herself blush as the fingers continued to fan out the strands. "You think it's pretty?" was the only thing she could think to say.

"Very much. It's such a beautiful shade, like light chocolate," Pandora murmured. "And you have beautiful eyes...autumn brown and gold. Gorgeous."

"Um..." Winter stared blankly at her, fumbling for a witty retort. Finally, she just muttered, "I guess we'd better go in. We have a lot to discuss. Change and come in when you're ready."

Pandora dropped her hand and smiled. "Sure thing. I'll see you inside."

Her nerves tingling, Winter put the vegetables into the oven. She'd have to pull herself together or she'd make a fool of herself. When Pandora stroked her hair, she'd nearly leaned into her and purred. It was not surprising her hormones had come so alive at the touch. She had been far too long without any loving. And even before the split, the sex had been infrequent and mostly one-sided in favour of Christine.

Thankfully, by the time Pandora appeared back in her black jeans and red top, Winter had herself in check. She placed the salmon in to cook and smiled at Pandora. "Let's sit in the lounge until dinner's ready. I'll get us another drink."

Pandora took a seat opposite her in the soft leather armchair and crossed her legs. Without stage makeup, her face was not quite so symmetrical, her chin stronger and a tiny scar was visible above her left eyebrow. To Winter, the little imperfections enhanced her beauty rather than distracted from it. And with her full lips shimmering with a rosy lip gloss and the damp ends of her hair twined into little curls, she looked bewitching. When she handed her a drink, Pandora immediately raised her glass and said, "Cheers."

Winter lifted her glass in the air to return the salute with a smile. "To you too. Shall we get down to business before we eat, or talk about it later?"

"Let's get it over with," Pandora said, leaning casually back. "Have you come up with anything?"

"There is one thing that baffles me," Winter began, searching her face. "If you've let Michael know you're not interested, then why are you so worried about just telling him he's an irritating shit and to leave you alone. Is there something you're not telling me?"

Her fingernails drummed a staccato on the arm of the chair before Pandora replied. Her expression became strained. "Two reasons. Firstly, I'm expected to encourage paying customers, not drive them away."

"Yes, but there are limits surely."

"True. But unless they become physical or too aggro toward me, I have to ignore them. It's part of the job. It's a nightclub not a church social."

Winter pulled a face. "Lucky you."

Pandora gave a noncommittal shrug in return. "I can handle aggression."

"I'm beginning to believe that. What's the second reason?"

"This one is more complicated. It's a feeling I have. I've studied human nature and I'm not so sure Michael will take rejection well. Not an unpleasant knock back anyhow. He strikes me as the type who could go off the rails and self-destruct."

Winter nodded. "He gets very depressed if he can't cope."

"The depth of his infatuation is alarming. I've honestly ignored him but he still turns up at the club twice a week, plus sends flowers every Saturday. And we can't forget he has developed a fantasy that I'm going to marry him. If he makes a public scene, the bouncers won't hold back with the punches."

"I didn't imagine it was that bad. We certainly must do something," Winter exclaimed, feeling a touch of panic. "Have you any ideas?"

"I'm fresh out of them other than to tell him to get lost," said Pandora.

A loud ringing emanated from the kitchen. "That's the oven timer." Winter rose to her feet. "We can continue the discussion while we eat."

"Do you want a hand?"

"I'm fine with the meal. The wine you brought is in the small fridge behind the bar. If you could fetch it while I bring the dishes to the table that would be great."

Winter scanned the salmon with satisfaction. Cooked to perfection. Pandora was already seated with the two glasses filled when she bustled in with the long serving platter. After another trip for the dinner rolls, she took a seat, pleased how nice everything looked on the Queen Anne rosewood dining table. She'd picked it up at an auction and had it restored, the finest piece of furniture she had acquired since moving into the house.

"This looks fantastic," said Pandora.

"A true-and-tried recipe, so I hope you like it."

"I'm sure I will," Pandora replied, then enthusiastically filled her plate. "You like cooking?"

"I do."

"Not a party animal?"

Winter laughed with a shake of her head. "Workaholic actually. But I've decided to cut down on my workload and get out more. Jessie keeps telling me I should."

"I'm intrigued you're such good friends," said Pandora contemplating her. "You're nothing alike."

"You mean because she's bright and funny and attracts women like bees to a honeypot."

"Some people prefer light and bubbly," said Pandora holding the glass of red up to the light, "but I prefer more robust, more depth."

Winter flushed and dropped her gaze. "Jessie and I have been friends since we were eighteen. She's a good person but needs to find someone to settle her down."

"You were never lovers?"

"God, no. I was too awkward and naïve for her in our university days. She always dragged me along to bars as her wingman."

"I bet she did," murmured Pandora. They lapsed into silence while they ate, content just to enjoy the food. When Pandora finally put down her knife and fork onto an empty plate, she gave a satisfied groan. "That was absolutely delicious."

Winter was flattered. She imagined this woman would have had many gourmet restaurant meals. "Thank you. Would you like a brandy nightcap?"

"No thanks. I drove over."

"Okay. Then I'll make us a coffee. Go into the lounge and I'll tidy up. I won't be long."

"Nonsense. I'll help clean up."

As the coffee trickled into the mugs under the coffee machine, Winter watched Pandora fill the dishwasher. This was what she was missing, someone in her house again to share a meal. Even if it were for only one night, it felt liberating. Life after Christine had become full of culinary contradictions. Winter loved cooking but had lacked interest in preparing anything other than quick and simple. Sometimes, she just opted for takeaways. The occasions she socialised with friends were usually at a bar or a show, and family dinners were always at her parents' house. Her kitchen had become as sterile as her life.

She put the mugs on the tray, feeling a spurt of optimism for the first time in what felt like eons. She wouldn't allow herself any more time hiding away. With an airy wave, she gestured to the door. "Let's go to the lounge."

Pandora pointed to the bundle of black fur curled up asleep in one of the chairs. "Who's that?"

"That's Jinx," Winter said, then picked him off with a "Tsk, tsk," and shooed him out the door. He protested with a loud meow, flipped his tail in the air and padded off to the kitchen. "Sorry…I hope you're not allergic to cats?"

"No, I love them. You could have let him stay."

"Don't worry, he'll creep back shortly. He has the run of the house. I've spoilt him, I'm afraid."

Pandora chuckled. "Cats are always the boss." She gazed around the room before she settled into a chair. "Your house is lovely."

"I've renovated but tried to retain its original style."

"It's a wonderful legacy. They don't build 'em like this nowadays."

Winter slanted a look at her curiously, catching the wistful tone. "Where were you brought up, Pandora?"

"All over. My father was in the army so we moved constantly."

"So, this city is not your home?"

"No," Pandora answered, offering nothing more.

"Pandora…is that your stage name?"

"Yes. Though I prefer to go by it all the time." She ducked her eyes down to her watch. "Wow, is that the time. I guess we better get back to business."

"Oh…yes, of course," said Winter disconcerted at the change of topic. "I've been giving it a lot of thought but can really only come up with two feasible options," she began. "You either convince him you're keen on someone else or tell your boss he's becoming a pest and ask that he not be allowed into the club."

"I thought of those but can't see a way to make them work. You have to understand that Yuri comes from a male domineering family where women are expected to do what they're told. Though Michael's not a big spender, unless he causes trouble Yuri's more likely to tell me to put up with him than refuse him entry to the club. A lot of customers come just to see me."

Winter gave an exasperated sniff. "Then you'll have to make out you have someone else. What about your friend the piano player?"

"No. That would only make things awkward between us. He's never shown that sort of interest in me. I suspect he has a secret lover somewhere."

"Anyone else?"

"Unfortunately," said Pandora, "I have a policy never to pay particular attention to anyone for more than one night in the club. It would just cause more trouble."

"What about somewhere other than the Fox?"

"Somewhere else? But where? I would hardly be anywhere Michael goes."

Winter shot up in her seat as an idea began to form. "I've got it," she said, taking a sip from her mug to organize her thoughts. "What about here. I could throw a party for my birthday. It's coming up. All the family will be invited, as well as my friends. You could bring a date."

Pandora's eyes widened. "That's very generous of you."

"Michael *is* my cousin so I do have a vested interest. Besides, everyone's nagging me to get out of the rut I'm in and be more social. It's a fabulous place for a party and I haven't thrown one here for years."

"If you're prepared to do it, then I'm all in. It should solve the problem. Just as long as the subterfuge is believable."

Winter eyed her shrewdly. "No reason why not. You know how to put on an act."

"True. And it would be even better if I turned up holding hands with a woman. If I came to the party with Jessie, he'd *have* to get the message I wasn't interested. I'm sure she'd be happy to play the part."

"I've no doubt she'd jump at the chance," Winter replied crossly. Forcing herself to act off-handed, she asked the question she'd been dying to ask. "Does that mean you…ah…bat for our team?"

Chuckling, Pandora leaned forward in her chair. "What do you think?"

Winter's pulse danced under the probing glance. "Jessie says you do," was all she could think to say.

"Ah...Jessie. I imagine her gaydar would be well honed."

"It is. I, on the other hand, am a bit of a blockhead with things like that."

This time Pandora laughed full and long. "I can't imagine you're stupid at anything. Maybe not so observant but never a fool." She stood up with a distracting smile. "Now I'd better be off because I've a few things to do tomorrow morning, and I imagine you're always at the office early. Thank you for the lovely evening. The meal was superb."

Winter barely had time to put her coffee cup down before her guest was at the door. On the porch though, Pandora lingered, shuffling from one foot to the other. "Will you come with the girls to the club on Saturday night?"

For a moment Winter couldn't think. "I...I haven't made up my mind."

"Do come. It should be fun. And you could ask me to the party there in hearing range of Michael. That would make sure he comes."

"Okay. I guess I can," said Winter, her cheeks warming when she realized from the coaxing tone that Pandora wasn't just being polite. She actually wanted her there.

"Good. Then I'll see you Saturday." Without warning, she pulled Winter into a quick hug. Before Winter had time to react, Pandora had hurried down the driveway to her car.

Winter stared into the night long after the car disappeared out the gate, her thoughts in a jumble. After spending the evening together, she wasn't any closer to knowing Pandora. The woman was an enigma. Not only had she deftly avoided answering every personal question, she did so with the ease of a seasoned campaigner.

Winter's heart thudded in apprehension. Something in her had shifted with the hug, something long dormant.

Desire.

And she didn't even know Pandora's real name.

CHAPTER SEVEN

The next call from Gussie couldn't have come at a more inopportune time. Saturday lunch definitely didn't suit. Winter had a late contract to review, which she had hoped to have finished before she met the girls at seven for dinner before they moved on to the club. So much for that. She found it hard to ignore Gussie's pleading tone. It was her own fault. She should have reported back in person about her trip to the Silver Fox, instead of a quick phone call on Sunday telling her not to worry. She knew Gussie was anxious and would want to discuss it fully.

All the way over, she tossed around how to handle the conversation. In the end, she decided to be vague but positive. Exactly how she had no idea—she'd have to play it by ear. She climbed the two stairs to the front door of the stately house.

When she jammed a finger on the bell, a police siren went off inside the house. It forced a smile—Tracey had been programming the sound effects again. When footsteps sounded in the hall, she tried to wriggle the tightness out of her shoulders.

Her body was too tense. Like so many other things in the last few years, she had forgotten how to relax.

Tracey answered the door with a "Heyya, Cus."

"Hi, Tracey," answered Winter somewhat distractedly as she took in the outfit. The girl had passed through her grunge stage to a gothic one. Dressed all in black with spiky jelled hair and eyeliner applied so thickly she could have cut it with a knife, she looked like Dracula's daughter. Winter tore her eyes away from the new shiny tongue stud to ask, "Where's your mother?"

"In the sunroom. She's in a real tizz."

"Right. I'll see you later then."

"Kk," came the reply. Winter heard her following quietly as she walked down the hallway—Tracey had clearly no intention of missing the drama.

The sunroom was bright and airy, delicately scented by vases of flowers scattered around the room. Gussie was sitting in a white cane armchair, her face creased in a frown. "Winter. At last."

Out of the corner of her eye, Winter caught a flash of black near the potted palm in the corner. It was not lost on Gussie, who called out, "What I have to say to Winter is private, Tracey. I'll call you out of your bat cave when lunch is served."

This was met with a sulky, "Whatever."

"On second thoughts, you can set the table, please."

The faint "bor—ing" floated on the air as Tracey vanished out the door.

"That girl has her father's love of the outlandish," muttered Gussie with a long sigh.

At this statement, Winter involuntarily glanced up at the framed photograph on the wall. Gussie's husband, Jim, smiled broadly down at them, rugged and devil-may-care handsome in black leather motorbike gear. She looked back at her aunt who was quietly contemplating her with a glint in her eye. She was reminded of the scene in *Jaws* just before the shark burst out of the water. You know any moment it'll happen.

"Sorry I didn't come sooner," Winter began, getting in first, "but I've been extra busy at work this week."

"Really, Winter? You *knew* this was important. I've been off my mind with worry. You told me nothing on the phone."

"Hardly nothing. I went there as you asked. I even met the woman and found her very nice. Certainly not some predator. I told you there was nothing to worry about. She barely paid Michael any attention."

Gussie puffed up until the veins in her temple stood out, a sure sign she was ready to explode. "*Nothing to worry about!*" she exclaimed. "For your information, we had a blazing row Sunday morning and he hasn't been back since. He has it in his head that I sent you there to turn this woman against him."

"Well...you did," Winter reminded her. She didn't like how this was heading. The fault was going to be dumped solely on her head.

"That's not the point," snapped Gussie. "You should have been more discreet."

"*Discreet!* What's that supposed to mean?"

"Apparently, you and your friends drank with her all night. I merely asked you to watch quietly from the sidelines, not party on with her."

"*Her* name is Pandora," said Winter, trying to tamp down her rising anger.

"Yes, I'm aware of that. Not a name I'd forget in a hurry."

"Then I wish you'd use it," she snapped.

Gussie formed her fingers into a steeple and gave her an appraising glance. "You seem rather taken with this...ah... Pandora yourself."

Winter returned the gaze steadily, deciding to ignore that last remark. But if Michael had fallen out with his mother then it was time to be frank. The situation was accelerating. Though not an alarmist by nature, she figured it was time to say how it was. "Pandora is a bright, pleasant woman who sings for a living. She is not some man-eating siren as you seem to think. That's it, end of story. You should accept that and face the real problem. Michael's infatuation has reached the level of stalking. His feelings are not reciprocated and never will be. If he continues to make a nuisance of himself, it will only lead to big trouble."

Gussie blinked rapidly at her. "What sort of trouble?"

"The management won't condone that sort of behaviour for too long. He'll be lucky if he doesn't find himself bashed up in an alley one night. As far as I'm concerned, he should be mixing with his own age group and not obsessing after a woman way out of his league."

From the look of dismay on her aunt's face, Winter knew she hadn't been expecting her to be so blunt. She thought she'd be upset, but it was worse. Gussie began to crumble. Tears leaked down her cheek as she slumped back in her chair with a low sigh of pain and twisted her hands tightly into a ball in her lap. A wave of compassion immediately quelled Winter's anger. It had been a long time since she had seen a real crack in the armour of the usually pragmatic, cheery woman. Seeing her reduced to tears was upsetting—misery was not a quality she associated with her aunt. She always appeared so capable.

"Do you think he's on drugs?" Gussie asked, pulling a tissue from inside her blouse to dab her eyes.

Winter gazed at her sympathetically. Like every mother, her aunt was terrified of drugs. It was an adversary bigger and stronger than her, a fight she knew she would lose. "Noooo. What gave you that idea?"

"It's out of character for Michael. He has always been such a steady boy."

"I'm positive he's not on drugs," Winter said with a confidence she didn't feel. "He's just fixated on an unavailable woman and needs to back away."

This seemed to satisfy Gussie for the minute. "What can we do to get his mind off her?"

Noting the *we*, Winter felt a dull ache begin in the ball of her neck. Whether she liked it or not, she was expected to help. It was just as well she had planned to. "I've given it some thought. The best solution would be if he found out Pandora was already involved with someone else."

"Is she?"

"No. But Pandora and I had a chat about it."

"Really? You've become that friendly with her?"

When she caught the sceptical look, Winter leaned forward in her chair to emphasise what she had to say. "He made a fuss like a spoiled brat when he saw me talking to her. Believe me, she is sick and tired of his attentions. Because he's a customer she can't tell him to get lost, but she wants him off her back."

"Did..." Gussie took a hitching breath, "did the two of you come up with any ideas?"

"I'm giving a party at my house for my birthday and she's coming along with a date. That should get the message across."

"Really? That's very generous of you, Winter."

"I have another motive. It's about time I got back into the social scene. I'll ask family as well as a few friends, so that will include Michael."

"He won't go. You're not his favourite person at the moment," said Gussie morosely.

"He will. We're off to the Silver Fox again tonight and I'll make sure he knows Pandora is invited."

"You're going again? That'll make things worse."

"I'll do what I please," Winter retorted. "Besides, I have to go if the plan's going to work."

Gussie moved restlessly in her chair. "I don't know if I want to meet the woman. Even taking in all you said, I still can't help holding her partly to blame for flaunting herself in front of the boy."

"For shit sake, Aunt, she's a lounge singer. What do you expect? Michael needs to damn well grow up," Winter exclaimed.

"There's no need to get onto your high horse. You're not a mother, so you wouldn't understand. Now let's have lunch. You go in...I want to freshen up before I eat."

Winter watched her go upstairs before turning toward the dining room.

Tracey was shuffling her feet by the table when she entered. "How's Mum holding up?" she asked with a wan smile.

Winter met her gaze, not surprised to find under the teenage defiance there was genuine concern. Gussie always maintained that the girl took after her father, but in truth she had her mother's resilience. Jim had been flamboyant and outspoken, but Gussie had always been the rock of the family. Once Tracey grew out of her rebellious stage, she would be the sibling her mother would lean on. Winter gently squeezed her shoulder. "She's fine. I'll look after things."

Relief flickered across the girl's face. "I'm glad she's got you, Winter." At the sound of her mother's footsteps, she sprang back and draped herself over a chair.

Gussie bustled into the room. "Do sit up straight, Tracey. Pour Winter some juice while I serve."

"Yeah…yeah." She poked out her tongue to let the light flash on the stud.

Winter smiled. *Yep…they are so alike.*

CHAPTER EIGHT

Pandora skimmed her eyes around the room as she acknowledged the applause. A merry festive atmosphere shimmered through the club that sparkled in every shade of red imaginable. All the stools at the bar were occupied, as well as the seats on the floor. Four waitresses worked the room—Yuri had put on an extra one for the expected crowd and she was pleased to see Frankie working. In glittery low-cut red tops and short skirts, they balanced drinks on the trays with practised skill as they glided through the crowd.

Three men tended the bar: one, young and handsome, openly flirted with a trio of women on stools at the end, another filled beer glasses from the taps, while the last, an older dapper man and a good friend of hers, conjured up a complicated cocktail with clever hands.

She stopped searching when her eye caught the four women at a middle table. When they gave discreet waves, her gaze latched on to Winter's shapely legs in full view at the end of the seat. She smiled appreciatively. Very nice. A warmth settled in her stomach. Very nice indeed. She just managed to catch herself before she said the last out loud. She pulled herself together quickly when her cue note sounded and launched into her opening song.

She was well into her second number before she noticed that the concertina partition to Yuri's private alcove at the far end had been folded back. A number of men were drinking inside, Boris prominent in the middle. While he sometimes visited the club, it was only every couple of months that this particular Russian crew came. She guessed some big business was going down, for when they were due in town Yuri was always extra vigilant about locking his office every time he stepped out.

At the halfway interval of her performance, instead of retiring backstage to rest for the twenty-minute break as per her normal routine, she headed for the bar. Winter was already there as arranged, leaning on the curve diagonally across from Michael and his two friends. Wondering whether he had said anything to Winter, Pandora gave him a curt dismissive nod before she slid in next to Winter and turned her back on him. Thankfully, he took the hint and didn't approach them.

"Hi," Winter said with a shy smile. "You look lovely. That red dress is exquisite."

Normally flattery left her cold, but coming from Winter, Pandora felt a rush of pleasure at the compliment. "Thank you. It's my favourite gown…I only wear it on special occasions."

"You should wear red more often, it suits you. Can I get you a drink?"

"I don't drink until I finish." She nodded her thanks to the bartender who had already placed a glass of Perrier sparkling mineral water on the coaster in front of her. "I'm glad you came, Winter."

Winter raised her glass in salute. "Me too. And many thanks for organising our guest passes. There was a huge lineup outside. Most of the people who arrived when we did, had been turned away."

"It's a popular night for the city's Russian community. All Yuri's family and friends are here, so I've promised him I'll circulate later. Which means unfortunately, I won't be able to party on with you ladies," she said with genuine regret.

"We understand." Winter cleared her throat, then said a little loudly as if nervous, "I'm throwing a party at my home on Sunday week and I was wondering if you'd like to come."

"I'd love too. It's one of my nights off. What's the address?"

As Winter rattled it off, she began to idly stroke the top of Pandora's hand on the bar with a fingertip. Then flushed pink when she must have realized what she was doing and pulled her finger quickly away. Though acutely aware of the pleasant tingling sensation on her skin, Pandora gave no sign she had noticed. Instead, she gave a tiny toss of the head towards Michael. Winter replied with an imperceptible nod.

Satisfied they'd gotten the message across, they lapsed into small talk until Pandora reluctantly stood up. "I must go. Lovely to see you again, Winter. I'll try to have a quick word with the girls before you go. Enjoy the rest of the night." As she turned, she called over her shoulder, "I'll see you at the party."

Kurt was already seated at the piano, fixing a sheet of music to his stand when she walked onto the stage. Dressed in grey pants, white shirt, a shiny grey waistcoat and red bowtie, he looked like he'd stepped out of a nineteen forties bar. "Are you doing a walkthrough tonight?" he asked over the top of the baby grand.

She inclined her head, more in resignation than enthusiasm. "Yuri wants me to, after the move was so successful last Saturday."

"I'm guessing from your expression you're not too keen to repeat it."

"It's not that I don't want to. The idea was to put more variety into my act, but—" she paused briefly before she continued, "but I'm not sure about the crowd tonight, or more specifically, the men in Yuri's alcove. From their loud comments during the first act, they sound like they've been drinking heavily."

"Yeah. They're lowering the tone of the place. It's a wonder the boss doesn't tell them to shut the hell up. He's always usually quick to get the bouncers to toss people out. But I suppose being Boris's friends makes it a bit hard." He sent her a sympathetic look. "If he wants you to do it then I guess you haven't an option, so all I can advise is to stick to the main area and don't go near them."

"I should be able to manage that," she said with an easy smile, though it didn't extend to her eyes. Her stomach was beginning to clench. If she got too close, she would be pawed at for sure. "I'll limit it to one song and start up the other end of the room."

He winked. "Good thinking. Now—ready?"

As Pandora sang through her repertoire, she couldn't help regularly glancing over at Winter's table. Probably too often, she admonished herself, but her eyes just kept going back there like a magnet. She hoped it wasn't too obvious. But by the time she was nearing the last song, she had more pressing things to worry about. The gang in the alcove was getting progressively louder and cruder, and she had to steel herself to descend from the stage.

Come on, you're a performer so act the part.

All right—she could do this. With a slow sway, she began the long walk, singing the love song in a low husky voice.

She stuck to her plan, cruising through the top and middle tables, stopping here and there to eat up the minutes. The noise level bumped up several decibels in the alcove, but she ignored them. As she reached the final lines of her song, she scanned the length of the bar and spied a group of six well-dressed men and women clustered around the far end. She glided towards them, timing the last words as she came abreast of the big-shouldered man in their centre. When she gave him a nod, he called out, "Care to join us?"

She stepped toward them with a wide smile to convey her enthusiasm. "I'd love to."

The curvy brunette beside him gave a friendly little wave and moved to the side to fit her in. She looked to be in her late twenties, wearing a very stylish top-label cocktail dress.

With a breezy "Hi" to the group, Pandora entered their circle.

They crowded around, and soon the air was filled with the easy comradeship of people sharing a night out. Nothing heavy, just drinks and laughs.

Thirty minutes later, they were about to order another round when she heard a man's voice behind her. "The boss wants you to entertain Boris and the boys, Pandora."

She turned her head to look at him, though was well aware who had spoken: Eddie, the chief bouncer, a huge man with biceps the size of tennis balls and thighs like tree trunks. No one argued with him. When he jerked his head towards the end of the room, her heart sank.

Damn!

There was no hope of avoiding them now. With a shrug she nodded, but took her time saying goodbye to the partygoers before she walked through the room. As she neared the men, she could see they were very drunk. She helped herself to relax with slow breaths as she had been taught, beginning from the abdominal muscles and moving up. By the time she reached the top of her chest, she was calm enough to take in everything.

Yuri had vanished. Six hard men who looked like they would be perfectly at home in the criminal underworld sat with Boris in a semicircle of comfortable chairs. She quickly scanned the ceiling and walls of the small room, noting the absence of security cameras. If they closed the partition, she was on her own with them. She forced away the prickle of fear. The boss would have insisted they keep it open—she knew he wouldn't be happy if something happened to his prized singer.

But the ripple of unease blossomed into dread when her gaze settled on Boris. For an awful moment, she realized she'd underestimated the situation. Something about him was different tonight. The Russian looked darker, more vicious. She had never liked his looks. No doubt some women would consider him handsome, but she thought him sinister. He was a tall man, wide shouldered, sinewy rather than muscular, with distinctive Slavic features: pale skin, deep-set blue eyes, a prominent forehead and high cheekbones. His dark brown hair was brushed back and stubble lined his square jaw.

"You took your fucking time coming over," he growled.

"Excuse me? I'm mixing with the customers as Yuri expects me to, Boris, and I didn't appreciate being ordered to come. Nor being sworn at. I'll be happy to have a quick drink with you, but I won't be staying long. If you're after female company for the night then I suggest you look elsewhere. I'm sure there are plenty of women in the room who would welcome your attentions," she replied, forcing a note of finality into the words.

He jabbed a finger at his lap. "Sit here."

She sucked in a breath, readying herself for a quick exit. Immediately, her nostrils filled with the ripe stench of sweat and stale beer. She nearly gagged. "I won't be sitting on your lap now or in the future. If that's the only seat I'm to be offered then I'll say goodnight."

The others ceased their drunken chatter abruptly, silent as they watched intently. Her hands involuntarily clenched. Hunched forward in their seats, they stared at her like vultures waiting for the kill.

"I told you to sit," he snarled.

She took a quick instinctive step in retreat. "Goodnight," she said in a rush, anxious to be gone. It had been a long time since she found herself in a situation so completely out of her control. Boris was a far cry from the club's customers who sometimes got overfriendly. A dangerous man.

But before she could move off, he sprang up suddenly and grasped her arm. With a swift tug, she tried to pull away. He shifted his grip so his fingers wrapped around her wrist, then yanked until her body jerked against him.

"Let go of me," she ground out.

His grip tightened until she knew there would be bruises tomorrow. At any other place she would have retaliated with a hard knee to the groin, but they were in full view of the club. One of the men must have noticed some patrons were already looking their way, for he leapt up to close the partition. For the first time she felt a stab of real fear, pungent and sharp. Anything could happen once she was cut off from view—the men were too drunk to reason with.

She had no hope against so many.

Suddenly, out of the corner of her eye she caught a glimpse of a woman in a knee-high dress appear beside her. Too intent on keeping her cool, and balance, she didn't look around, that is until she heard the voice.

"Oh my, you are such a good-looking fella. I was saying to my friends that ya must be the handsomest man I've seen in years."

Pandora stared in disbelief as Winter, waving a bottle of red wine in one hand, playfully swatted Boris's hand that clutched her wrist, with the other. "Excuse me, honey," she tittered, looking at her directly for the first time, "but I'd like to talk to handsome here."

Clearly as surprised as Pandora, his grip loosened. She yanked her hand free. Winter stumbled awkwardly in front of her and a stream of red wine shot out of the bottle onto Pandora's gown. "Oh, shit a brick, I am so sorry," Winter squeaked. "Red wine is the hardest…the very *hardest* thing to get out."

"Fuckity fuck," Winter chanted as she wiped the dress with a tissue. "We've got to wash it immediately. *Immediately*. Here," she said, thrusting the bottle of red at Boris, "hold this while I take her to the powder room."

He took it, though looked like he would have preferred to hit her over the head with it. "I'm sure the dress will survive," he snarled.

"Nonsense," gasped Winter. "This gown would have cost a fortune. A *fortune*. My father's a judge, and he always says that if people valued what they had, then the courts would have only half the people going through them." She shot a look around the room. "You'd have to agree with the judge, wouldn't ya, fellas."

This was met with nervous stares.

"Now," Winter said, firmly pulling Pandora towards the half-closed partition. "It's going to take a while. Sorry I was so darn clumsy, honey. Ya look so nice in it too. I'll have ya cleaned up in no time. *No time* at all."

Bemused, Pandora allowed herself to be led out the room to the hallway that led to the toilets. "Is there a back way out of here?" Winter asked when they reached the ladies' door.

"There's an emergency exit further down the passageway past the dressing rooms."

"Good. Let's go then. I'll text Jessie to bring the cab around the back. She ordered one when I went in."

Pandora didn't argue, content to let Winter take control. She felt completely washed out.

CHAPTER NINE

Winter fought the instinct to launch into full flight, instead led the way down the passageway at a quick walk so not to attract attention. Two women chatting in the passageway, barely gave them a glance. Once past the toilets, she picked up the pace. When the dressing rooms came into view, she groaned in frustration as Pandora dashed into one.

"I'll only be a minute. I want my phone and purse," she called out over her shoulder.

Every nerve in Winter's body was jangling by the time Pandora reappeared. So keyed up, she squealed out a sharp squawk of relief when they rounded the last corner and the bright green exit sign came into view.

It was unbelievable how far her world had tilted on its axis in the last hour. She had become Alice down the rabbit hole: one moment having fun, the next running from thugs. The night had started off so well, with not a hint of the drama to come. As soon as they had entered the club, the festive atmosphere had enveloped them in such an exciting cocoon that they began partying immediately with lots of kidding, lots of fun.

Then Pandora had strode onto the stage, magnificent in a form-fitting sparkling red gown, and received Winter's rapt attention, as well as that of every other person in the club. Starstruck, all Winter could do was blurt out, "Wow," as a warm feeling spread through her body.

"I second that," Jessie had murmured. "Damn, that dress is smokin' hot."

The instant Pandora had begun to sing, Winter was mesmerized. And the way she had kept glancing over at their table sent little shivers down her spine and her heart thumping. She had wondered if maybe her interest wasn't so one-sided, that her attraction might be reciprocated. At the thought, she felt like she could almost believe in fairy tales again.

But that bubble had soon burst when Jessie had whispered in her ear smugly, "She can't keep her eyes off me."

A sharp twinge of jealousy hit—she could have stuck the swizzle stick into Jessie's arm. She muttered back sharply, "She's not like your usual flirts, Jess."

"What's that supposed to mean?"

"Pandora isn't someone you can take to bed then discard like yesterday's news. She's got more substance than that. And deserves to be treated better."

Jessie had narrowed her eyes. "Aren't you the judgemental one. If I didn't know better, I'd think you were interested in her yourself."

"Why wouldn't I be interested? She's nice."

"Come off it. A hot lounge singer at a bar is hardly your type. You always go for the cold princesses who like prestige and money."

Winter had bitten back a retort. This particular debate was an old one—she hated the casual way Jessie treated women, while Jessie hated Winter's choice in partners. Especially Christine. "Shut up and listen to the music," she'd grated out in a low voice.

"Huh!" came the snort in reply. Then after a moment there was a little snicker. "Well, well, Ms. I'm-so-fussy Carlyle. You think she's very foxy, don't you?"

She hadn't answered, aware Jessie had known it was a rhetorical question.

Winter had sat back in her chair, trying to ignore Dana's out of tune humming and Linda's light touches on her thigh. After the next song, she'd glanced at her watch. Five minutes until Pandora's break. If she wanted a place at the bar, she had to move before the interval rush. She'd stood up and said casually, "I'm going to get the next round. I need to stretch my legs."

"I'll come with you," said Linda, half rising.

Winter had pushed her gently but firmly back into the chair. "I'll be fine. I want to have a quiet word with Michael."

"Okay. Just give me a wave if you want help carrying the drinks."

She'd hoped Linda wasn't watching, because she only gave Michael a cursory hello in passing before taking a spot at the bar diagonally opposite. It had been close enough for him to be within hearing distance. He'd glared at her, which she'd studiously ignored. Underneath though, she'd felt an overwhelming urge to grab him by the shirt and give him a good shake. To tell him to get a life, that he was a brainless idiot to be hanging around a place like this, pining after someone who had made it quite clear she wasn't interested. Thankfully, he hadn't said anything insulting and the situation defused when the bartender appeared to take her order.

"What'll you have?" he'd asked impersonally.

After she'd called out the list, she changed her whisky sour order to a bottle of Shiraz. She could drink at her leisure then, rather than keep up with the rounds. "I'll have a half-glass out of the bottle now, please," she'd added.

At the whiff of the familiar perfume, she'd known Pandora had arrived. They had already decided how to play the scene this morning on the phone. And it had worked. It was quite clear Michael was listening to their conversation when she caught him staring intently at the mention of the party. When

Pandora had returned to the stage, Winter turned to scan the area. People were two- and three-deep at the bar, jostling for drinks before the floor show began again. She'd swallowed the last mouthful of wine before she took the tray to the table.

Jessie had looked at her curiously as she settled onto her seat. "What were you talking to Pandora about?"

"I'll tell you later. She's about to start."

"You're always so secretive," Jessie had said testily.

Amused, Winter sat back with a contented feeling. Just being able to talk to Pandora had brightened up her night even more. For the next half hour, she'd barely heard the others' comments, losing the thread of conversation as the songs washed over her. Half-dazzled, she'd sat completely absorbed in the feminine grace of the woman on the stage.

But as the night had worn on, the crude hecklings from the men at the back soured her enjoyment. As they'd became more vocal, her indignation turned to real worry when Pandora descended the stage for a walk-through finale. Winter had watched her intently as she moved through the room, then blown out a relieved breath when she saw her join a crowd at the bar.

The relief was short lived when one of the men who had been on the door, approached Pandora and she'd followed him down the back.

Jessie must have been watching too, because she'd whispered urgently in Winter's ear. "Pandora's going to those bastards down the back. I hope she'll be all right. They're a mean-looking bunch and pretty hammered."

Winter had craned her head to keep a clear sight line. "I know. But she is in full view of the room. Surely nothing can happen."

"Just as long as they don't shut it off."

Winter had grabbed the bottle of wine. "Come on. Let's get closer." When the other two had begun to get to their feet, she shook her head. "Four of us will be too obvious."

Jessie had looked at the bottle in amusement. "What do you intend doing with that? Hit them over the head with it?"

"I have a plan. Come on…let's go."

They had just reached the wall beside the alcove when tempers seemed to explode inside the small room. The man in the chair reared up and grabbed Pandora's wrist. He'd pulled her against him while another began to slide the concertina door closed.

Jessie had clutched Winter's arm to prevent her moving and growled in her ear, "I'll go in."

She'd brushed off the hand impatiently. "No. I'm going. Ring for a cab and tell it to hurry." And with no more hesitation, she'd strode towards the alcove. She had never been more keyed up and petrified all at once. The group of men who had turned to stare at her looked like they belonged on the set of *The Godfather*.

* * *

When they barrelled through the heavy metal door Jessie was waiting as stiffly as a soldier on parade. Still wound up in a tight coil, Winter cast an eye nervously around the alleyway. It was steeped in shadows, the only light a weak glow from an overhead bulb some metres away. The large industrial bin on the other side of the steps smelt like a disused brewery mixed with something putrid. She was anxious to get as far away from the place as quickly as possible.

"The taxi will be here in a sec," Jessie said, handing Winter her bag.

"Good. This alley is giving me the creeps," Winter muttered. She looked back nervously at the door, half expecting the drunken men to burst through. Then quashing back her desire to bolt onto the street, she turned to study Pandora. "How are you feeling?"

Though grimacing as she rubbed her wrist, she simply nodded. "I'm fine. All thanks to you. I—" The words trailed away as she broke into a smile. Winter turned to see a yellow cab pulling up at the entrance to the alley.

"Let's go," Jessie said. They needed no urging, already walking quickly to the street.

Winter looked over at Jessie before climbing in the backseat. "The others aren't coming?"

"Dana texted to say she wanted to keep an eye on Frankie, so Linda stayed with her."

"It's nice to know someone is looking out for Frankie. She's a great girl," said Pandora. She followed Winter into the cab, then moved into the middle to make room for Jessie.

The cabbie threw a glance over his shoulder. "Where to?"

Winter pressed her palm against the top of Pandora's hand. "I'm taking you home with me. Boris might turn up at your flat." When Pandora looked like she was going to argue, she added beseechingly, "Humour me please. Otherwise I'll worry all night."

There was a pause before the answer came. "I guess it would be wise."

"Good. We'll drop Jessie off first," Winter said, with a quick squeeze before she withdrew her hand. After she called out the address, the taxi moved off into the flow of traffic.

Jessie turned to look from one to the other, her gaze assessing. "It might be better if you stayed with me, Pandora. I've an apartment not far from here…a lot quicker for you to go home in the morning? Don't you agree, Winter?"

Winter shifted in her seat, annoyed. For once in her life she defied Jessie. "No, I'd like her to come home with me." Then realizing they were bickering, she cleared her throat in embarrassment. "I'm sorry, Pandora, we must sound childish. It's up to you of course."

"No hard feelings, Jessie, but I'll go home with Winter tonight. An early dip in that delightful pool would be too good to miss."

Jessie stared at her, her eyes less calm, less assured. "You've been there?"

"Yes, I have," Pandora replied with an enigmatic smile.

"When did—"

The cab stopped with a jerk at the footpath. "Your stop," the driver announced.

"Oh…right. Goodnight," Jessie said, giving Winter a quick glare before she climbed out the door.

"Come over for lunch tomorrow," Winter called out. "We've something to discuss with you."

Jessie poked her head back through the window. "What about?"

"I'll tell you when you get there," said Winter with a soft laugh.

CHAPTER TEN

Though the tension from the drama had settled down, Pandora was unusually quiet. When she kept lightly rubbing her wrist, Winter wanted to stroke it, to soothe the bruised skin with her fingertips. But she stopped herself. It wasn't her place to provide that kind of succour, that was for someone closer to do: a mother, a lover. Instead she asked with soft concern, "Is your arm painful?"

Pandora turned to her with eyes hooded. "Not really. It stings a little, that's all. Nothing that ice won't fix. I was just thinking about the night. You could have been hurt. Those men were dangerous."

"Well, I wasn't going to leave you in there with that drunken mob. Not when they were shutting the door."

"You were wonderful. Thank you very much for being my protector," murmured Pandora, fussing with the gold cross that rested on the base of her neck.

"Um…sure." Winter's cheeks went warm at the compliment. "But I'm not usually a woman of action, you know. More a boring desk jockey."

"You're anything but boring, Winter."

"I have been for years. That's why Christine did what she did."

"Christine?"

Winter swallowed hard, shocked that she had blurted that out. "Oh…sorry, I didn't mean to say that. I'm sure you wouldn't be interested in my pathetic life."

Pandora chuckled. "You should know it's human nature to be curious when you're told you wouldn't be interested. But I won't pry…your personal life is your own affair."

"It should be," said Winter wryly, "but mine was splattered all over social media."

"You must—"

"How far down?" called out the cabbie as he turned into the street.

"It's the one on the left at the end," Winter answered, heartily relieved for the interruption. That particular conversation was definitely closed. There was no way she would let Pandora see what a loser she was.

Once out of the cab in front of her gate, Winter took a moment to gaze at her home. She loved the huge old house. The early twentieth century stately "Queenslander" had been built by her father's grandfather when he'd arrived from England. A decorative two-storied gabled building with wrought iron railings on the verandahs, it was surrounded by tailored gardens, palms, and tropical fruit trees. Sitting on an acre block overlooking the Brisbane River and the city skyline, it had one of the best views in the city.

Being the only Carlyle grandchild, Winter had inherited the estate from her grandmother. She had moved in to find a treasure chest filled with gems: antique furniture, Persian carpets, old Royal Doulton china sets, silver candlesticks, and ornate vases. In the cobwebbed attic, she even discovered a small safe containing a remarkably valuable collection of old coins. From their sale she renovated the house, though made sure the classic vintage style was retained.

"Come on in," she said to Pandora and together they walked down the flagstone pathway. She stepped inside to deactivate the alarm. Jinx immediately appeared meowing plaintively. She scooped him up into her arms with a murmured, "Did you miss me, sweetie," then led the way to the living room. "Take a seat and I'll get us a hot chocolate…or a brandy if you prefer…and some ice for the wrist. I'd better feed this cat as well. He gets demanding if he's hungry."

"Hot chocolate sounds fine. I have a call to make so I'll slip out onto the verandah while you're getting the drinks."

Pandora was still outside on the phone when Winter offloaded the full mugs and a bag of frozen gel onto the coffee table, then regarded her through the window curiously. The call must be serious, for Pandora's body language was tense. She jabbed her free hand in the air as if to punctuate points while she talked animatedly into the phone. After she punched the screen to end the call, she glanced up before Winter had time to look away. Their eyes met through the glass. Pandora's grim, stony-faced expression relaxed back to cool and unperturbed as if she had pulled a switch.

Winter eyed her thoughtfully as she stepped back into the living room. There was clearly more to the singer than met the eye. Strangely though, the mystery only added to her appeal. A logical person and a stickler for details, Winter always felt slightly uncomfortable with anyone, or anything, outside her organized world. It was rather odd therefore that she felt so completely at ease in Pandora's company. But then again, she mused, Jessie was anything but predictable and they were the best of friends.

Perhaps Jessie was right all along. The women she dated were the wrong fit: too pretentious, too demanding. Not that there had been many. Before she met Christine, she'd been too busy with her studies and then establishing her career to date much. Maybe now she should be going out with someone more spontaneous, more exciting. Someone to teach her about real passion. Unconsciously, she dropped her gaze to Pandora's chest and lingered on the full breasts spilling over the low-cut bodice of the red gown. Her heart fluttered up a notch. Then realizing what she was doing, jerked her head back up to find Pandora watching her with eyes bright and cheeks flushed.

Winter felt her own face heat too but tried to defuse the situation by handing over the frozen pack with a casual, "Put this on your wrist. After our drinks, we should get out of these clothes. You must be dying to take off that long gown," she shifted her gaze to her feet, "and the heels. You did well to run in them."

"To be honest, my feet are killing me. They're certainly not made for speed."

"No, I imagine your toes would be pinched and feeling ready to drop off." Winter toyed with the handle of the cup, aware she probably was prying with the next question but asked it regardless, "Do you intend to continue singing at the Silver Fox?"

"It will depend on Yuri, my boss. I'll be asking for assurances that I won't be put into that position again."

"Will he agree?"

"He will. He won't want to lose me."

All Winter could do was gape at her. "Why would you even consider going back? You're a wonderful singer. Any club in the city would love to have you."

"It's not as simple as that. I have a few months left on my contract."

The prospect of Pandora going back to the club was so thoroughly unpleasant that Winter snapped in frustration, "For God's sake, Pandora, you're not safe there. Boris won't take any notice of his brother. I deal with arrogant people like him all the time—he's got his eyes set on you and he won't give up. I can help you with the contract. It wouldn't have a hope of standing up in court if you're being sexually harassed."

"Hey…I've got friends to protect me there so don't worry." Pandora downed the last of her drink and stood up abruptly.

"Now, I really do need a shower. Where do you want me to sleep?"

"You're adept at changing the subject," said Winter wryly. She rose, knowing it was pointless to argue further. "Come on. I'll put you in the room next to mine. We're not too different in size so my clothes should fit well enough. I'll give you something to sleep in and to wear tomorrow."

She led the way upstairs to the guest bedroom, leaving Pandora to shower. She searched her cupboard. The sleepwear was easy enough—the silk boxers and tank top were roomy, but the outfit for the next day was more difficult. While they were much the same height, Pandora's breasts were fuller, her hips a little wider. Eventually she found clothes that should fit—track pants and a gaudy tie-dye T-shirt a size too big that a cousin had given her for Christmas. She picked up a pair of backless sandals and slipped inside the guest room. Hearing the shower running, she put the clothes on the bed and disappeared back to her own room.

Twenty minutes later, showered, she tapped on the door.

"Come in," echoed from within.

The sight of Pandora ready for bed sent her pulse hammering and mouth dry. She hadn't realized the sleepwear was so flimsy, so revealing. The woman really was stunning, not that gaunt look of the Parisian magazine models, but curvy, and with the vitality of a sports star. She couldn't help sweeping her eyes over her.

What was it like for beautiful people, she wondered? Did they always feel they had to prove there was more to them than looks? And it must be especially hard for an entertainer. In Winter's profession, getting older usually meant going up the corporate ladder through experience and seniority. But in show biz, where your job continued to depend on your looks, it must be so depressing to watch your beauty slowly fade away with age.

But all the same, Pandora would be a woman who aged gracefully. She had that sort of timeless gypsy beauty.

With a guilty start, she realized she had lingered far too long. After an embarrassed cough, she stuttered, "I'll leave the nightlight on in the hallway in case you want something from the kitchen. We don't have to get up early. Feel free to have a morning dip in the pool if you like. There's a couple of spare bikinis in the pool shower room."

"That sounds like a plan, though since the pool is secluded, I won't bother with the bikini."

Winter nearly groaned. Why the hell did she have to tell her that? She'd now be dreaming all night of her gloriously nude in the water. "Well, goodnight then."

"Wait, Winter," Pandora said, coming closer quickly until they were nearly touching. "I just want to say again how much I appreciate the way you came to my defence. I think you're amazing. Would you mind if I gave you a hug?"

Winter barely registered the question as she felt the warm breath brush across her cheek. All she could do was nod. Then her senses went haywire as the strong arms wound around her and pulled her close. With a deep sigh, she sank into the embrace and by its own volition, her body began to strain for a deeper connection. A barrage of emotions flooded through her at the feel of the pebbled nipples pressed into her skin through the thin material. The unexpected intensity of her physical response made her head reel, her body ache with want.

She tilted her head, her lips pursed. Pandora slid her mouth over hers in a gentle kiss, softly at first as if to communicate her thanks rather than desire. But she didn't pull away as expected. Instead her mouth gradually became more demanding, her tongue and teeth teasing until the contact exploded into something much deeper, much more sensual. Winter moaned, helpless against the hormonal rush that spread into every crevice of her body. She had never experienced a kiss like it. There was no awkwardness, just a sense of how perfectly their lips fitted together like pieces of a jigsaw puzzle.

When she opened her mouth to the probing tongue, another moan sounded, this time from Pandora. Urgently, Winter grasped the back of her neck, pulling her in even closer.

"Oh God," she gasped out when Pandora began to slide her moist mouth down the length of her neck and run her fingers up the curve of her breast.

The words broke the spell.

Pandora stiffened, lifted her head away and dropped her hands. Winter wanted to protest, wanted to scream to keep going but sanity began to sink in. She managed a raw "Wow," then dazed, retreated until there was a respectable space between them. It felt like a yawning chasm.

Panting, Pandora sat down hard onto the edge of the bed and gazed up at Winter with guilt alive in her eyes. "Are you all right?"

"I guess. I have to catch my breath."

"I didn't mean this to happen."

"Nor did I."

Pandora raised her hands in a supplicant gesture. "I'm really sorry."

"Please don't apologise," Winter said, her body still tingling with need. "That only makes me feel you regret what happened."

"I...well...I..."

"Don't, Pandora...I get the message. Just forget it. I'll see you in the morning."

And Winter fled from the room.

CHAPTER ELEVEN

Pandora tossed restlessly on the mattress, replaying what had happened over and over in her head. It was unbelievable how quickly things had lurched out of control. She knew she was skirting danger when she had hugged Winter, especially when they were both clad in skimpy clothes. But she had just wanted to feel what it was like to have her in her arms. What started off innocently enough, had blossomed into one of the most passionate kisses of her life. And Winter's response had been like the flare of a bonfire. Her ex, Christine, must have been an idiot if she thought she was boring. It had taken all Pandora's willpower to stop.

If it had been anyone else, she would have taken them straight to bed without another thought. God knows she ached to do it. But she knew that with Winter it wouldn't be just a night of sex, nor was she the type of woman to be treated casually. As well as deserving better, she had an understanding that Winter would never go to bed with someone lightly. And judging from the depth of her own reaction, Pandora knew she would be left wanting more and it wasn't a commitment she could make at the moment. But even so, she felt a flutter of concern. This wasn't going to be easy to ignore—it had really hurt to walk away.

Somewhere in the night Pandora must have nodded off, because the phone alarm was the next thing she heard. She rolled over groggily to look at the screen: 6.00 am. She felt washed out and it took a concerted effort to switch her brain to alert mode. Reluctantly, she climbed out of the warm bed—a dip in the pool would be the best way to shake out the cobwebs. After a visit to the bathroom, she headed downstairs with a towel to the pool.

Even though dawn had been half an hour ago, the chilly night air still lingered. In the early morning light, the sky was cloudless, the colour of faded blue denim. Not giving herself time to think, she shrugged off her clothes and braced herself before she leapt in. The shock of the cold water literally took her breath away. She sucked in quick gulps of air until her hammering heartbeat settled back to normal. Then with quick strokes she powered down the pool, relishing the adrenaline flowing through her body. Her skin tingled with the exhilaration that came with the freedom of weightlessness. The tension slowly ebbed away as she swam a few laps until with a sigh, she stopped to tread water lazily.

Calm now, she thought back over the events of the previous night and focused on her more immediate problem. Boris had become much bolder in his attentions, more volatile. If it hadn't been for Winter's intervention, she would've been in trouble. It was doubtful Yuri had any influence in controlling his brother, especially since Boris had now aligned himself with a Melbourne Russian crime syndicate. They were an especially nasty crowd. Thankfully, they never stayed more than one night and Boris only appeared at the club without them on special family occasions. If they followed their usual routine, she would have at least two months' grace before they'd turn up again. She'd have to have something in place.

There was no way she'd escape so lightly next time.

Pushing that problem aside for later, she went back to swimming until she couldn't ignore the persistent rumbling of her stomach. She heaved herself over the side of the pool then began a series of Shiatsu exercises, a ten-minute routine she did every day. When she stretched her neck, a flash of something on the upstairs balcony caught her eye. She gazed up to see Winter leaning on the railing, staring down at her. Pandora froze. Shit, she hadn't expected Winter to be up yet. Figuring it was useless covering up now, she gave her a friendly wave before she reached for the towel.

The balcony was empty when she looked up again.

She hurriedly pulled on her clothes and started toward the house. Winter was at a bench as she passed by the kitchen, so she poked her head in with a breezy "See you soon," before walking upstairs to her bedroom.

Winter's clothes fitted well enough, the T-shirt very snug over her chest. She self-consciously flattened down the front with her palm. Her grandmother referred to her as her little Irish colleen, but she was hardly small anymore. More a strapping tavern wench of Irish folklore.

After a last flip of her hair with the brush, she started back downstairs. The top of the rail slipped silky smooth against her palms as she descended the sturdy oak staircase. With a brief stop to admire the polished timber floors and antique furniture, she thought how welcoming the house felt. It wasn't its old-world charm so much as the feeling of being completely protected from the outside world. Safe. So different from her life.

Winter acknowledged her with a welcoming nod and a "Hey there. The outfit looks great on you." Her tone was light and casual but a tinge of pink coloured her cheeks.

"It fits perfectly," she replied and flashed a smile as she peered at the pan on top of the stove. "Whatever your cooking smells divine and I'm starving." However awkward, it was easier to pretend the kiss last night hadn't happened and Winter hadn't seen her naked this morning.

"I'm sure you've worked up an appetite with all that exercise. We're having eggs benedict with sweet potato fritters."

"That sounds heavenly. I rarely have a cooked breakfast... coffee and toast mainly."

"I always make a decent one. My mother drummed into me it should be the main meal of the day. And besides...I like to cook," said Winter.

"You wouldn't have a kitchen setup like this if you didn't. Or herbs growing in a box on the windowsill."

Winter merely smiled and reached for the flipper. "Sit down...the eggs are ready. Tea or coffee?"

"Black coffee, please," Pandora replied, then continued after they settled down to eat. "Tell me about yourself."

"Now you've put me on the spot. There isn't much to tell. I lead a quiet life and work takes up most of my time."

"Come on. Everyone has something they like to do."

"I actually enjoy my job, believe it or not. It's very satisfying." When Pandora merely cocked her head and waited, she continued with a shrug. "Okay. I enjoy reading, watching movies, and painting.

"So, what about you, Pandora?"

"Me? I like movies, music, and jogging in the mornings."

"You're a very talented singer which I envy."

"I've always loved to sing, even as a child. I won a scholarship to the Sydney Conservatorium of Music after high school."

"Really? Did you ever take your singing further?" asked Winter.

Pandora shrugged. "No. Circumstances changed at home. I had to put my music dreams on hold because I didn't have the luxury of waiting for the big break. I needed a regular income, and I was only one of the many hopefuls trying to get noticed. This gig is the first time I've sung in public for years, although I've kept up practising religiously."

"That's a real shame. You've a wonderful voice."

"We all do the best we can. Now there's something I've been meaning to ask you." Pandora gestured in the direction of the front door with her coffee cup. "I've noticed you have quite a sophisticated surveillance system. Even a camera in the hallway. Why is that?"

"It's a necessity in my line of work. I see highly sensitive material. I bring documents home occasionally."

"Tell me about your work."

"Ours is a major international legal firm," replied Winter, looking more relaxed now she was on familiar ground. "I negotiate business transactions in the multimillion-dollar range, so you can appreciate confidentiality is essential."

"I take it then that you're not the junior help."

That brought a smile to Winter's face. "No, I'm a partner."

"Impressive. What do you do if you come across any criminal activity?"

"On two occasions I've had to terminate an agreement." Winter looked at her curiously. "That's not a question people usually ask. Normally as soon as I describe my work their eyes glaze over and they change the subject."

Pandora chuckled. "I bet. Could you trace money laundering?"

"I could, but it would take time. Usually criminal organizations have networks where they can hide the cash by having a lot of other money in circulation. Casinos, shops, and," Winter looked at her with a gleam in her eye, "clubs like the Silver Fox."

"Just so," said Pandora. "Then what would they do with it?"

"Convert the cash to bank drafts and assets which they can resell legitimately. They set up shell companies to buy property, false loans, and so on." Winter tapped a finger on the table. "You think the club is being used to launder money?"

"It would explain those thugs turning up every two months. Either that or drugs."

"All the more reason for you to be careful of Boris."

Pandora gave a hint of a smile. "Don't worry about me. No…it was Michael I was thinking about. If there is criminal activity there, the police probably would have an eye on the place. If he's known to be a frequent visitor, he may be caught up in it. Worst-case scenario, he may be called in as a witness."

"Damn," Winter ground out, going pale. "Then this plan of ours better work. His mother will have a stroke if he's anywhere near that sort of trouble. And the blame will be heaped on me."

"That's hardly fair. You have nothing to do with it."

"Yes, but tell that to Gussie," Winter said with a resigned shrug. "She's asked me to help. I'm the fix-it girl in the family and supposed to pull a rabbit-out-of-the-hat when there's trouble. Usually Gussie only asks for financial help occasionally, but she's like a lioness protecting her cubs when it comes to her kids. This has her unusually rattled."

"How big *is* your family?"

"My mother has four sisters and one brother. I'm an only child but I have twelve cousins. None though on my father's side, hence my inheriting this house. She was my paternal grandmother."

"I take it then you're the only one with financial expertise?"

"Unfortunately, yes. If they want advice, I'm the first port of call. Mind you, when I warn some of them to go easy on the credit cards that's ignored." Winter dabbed her mouth with the serviette. "What say we continue this later? Would you like a tour of the house and garden?"

"I'd love it," Pandora agreed. The more she got to know Winter, the more she liked her. For so successful a woman, she was remarkably humble. It was no wonder her family leaned so heavily on her—she radiated competence and trust. Smart too. She couldn't imagine anyone besting her in business.

Winter turned to her with a smile. "Let's go."

Pandora nodded her approval as she wandered around. In an early century time capsule, the house was a charming picture of old-world sophistication. Where there had been obvious updates—she guessed to replace aging electrical wiring and plumbing—the original materials had been faithfully reproduced. All five bedrooms were roomy and she particularly liked the way a verandah circled around the second floor to give each bedroom a balcony.

When they stood for a moment to gaze down on the swimming pool, Pandora couldn't resist murmuring, "Great view."

Winter said nothing, though fidgeted from one foot to the other. They walked back down the stairs out to wander through the garden. Winter filled her in about her family while the plants soaked up a gentle spray from sprinklers. Pandora had to laugh when she described the idiosyncrasies of her numerous relations.

"I'll be interested to meet them all at the party," Pandora said.

Winter let out a sound that might've been a laugh or a choking groan. "Oh, they'll be dying to meet you. Gussie in particular."

"Ah…I'm the infamous siren that seduced her son. She won't be exactly welcoming, will she?"

"Uh-huh. Don't expect a kiss on the cheek. Let's say harpy might be a more accurate word."

Pandora winced. "Not very flattering."

"Nope. But she won't make a scene. Too refined for that. She'll show her disapproval more subtly."

"Then Jessie and I will have to be very convincing."

Winter seemed to deflate at those words. "Don't worry. Jessie knows how to put on the charm. She's hard to say no to."

Pandora watched her closely as she asked, "You think I won't be able to resist her?"

"Just let's say I've seen her in action too many times."

"You've never had a crush on her yourself?"

"God no," said Winter in surprise. "Apart from the fact she's never indicated she's ever been interested, I've never been attracted to her. As a friend she's awesome, as a lover no way."

"Not even as a friend with benefits."

At this, Winter looked genuinely horrified. "I don't believe there can be such a thing. Even if a relationship is supposedly that casual, someone eventually ends up getting hurt. You can't have sex with someone long term and not have some intimate feelings for them."

"What about a one-night stand?"

"That's entirely different if you're into that sort of thing. You're not friends, so haven't a vested interest in the person."

Pandora eyed her curiously. "You don't sound like you do that either."

"I prefer getting to know someone and letting it go from there. I like sex to mean something." Winter turned to look her fully in the face. "Do you date anyone in particular?"

"No. Do you?"

"I haven't since my breakup. Why don't you, Pandora? I can't imagine you would lack invitations."

Pandora hesitated, taken aback by the question. It was her own fault for getting too personal. She struggled for an answer then merely replied, "I date of course, but not at the moment." Noting that Winter wasn't going to drop it, she looked around for something to change the subject. She pointed to a small building nestled amongst the trees. "What's that cottage?"

"It's just a guest bungalow."

"It looks cute. May I see inside?"

Winter stiffened and seemed flustered. "I'd…I'd prefer it if we didn't go inside. Maybe some other time." Then she strode off quickly, disappearing into the house.

"Of course," called out Pandora, hurrying to catch up. What the hell was that all about? The bungalow had clearly hit a nerve. She'd have to ask Jessie about it later.

In the lounge, Winter greeted her with a smile as if nothing had upset her. "Take a seat and I'll get us coffee."

"Sounds good."

When she returned with the cups and some chocolate cookies, Pandora eased back in her chair. "I guess we'd better discuss how this bogus romance with Jessie is to be played out. She'll be here soon."

Winter's face tightened a little. "I think we can leave that to her. She'll make it convincing."

Pandora had no doubt she would. She also knew Winter would retreat into herself with Jessie there. "She'll play the part admirably, I'm sure. It's right up her alley."

Winter plopped a spoonful of sugar into her cup, then looked up with a frank gaze. "Are we going to discuss the kiss last night or just ignore it?"

Pandora blinked, clearing her throat nervously. She hadn't expected that one. "Do you want to discuss it?"

"You know, Pandora, you are infuriating how you answer a question with a question. You're not avoiding this one."

"No, I guess I can't." She reached over and took her hand. "It did mean a lot to me. We seem to connect and I think you're terrific. But…well…I'm not in the position to take it further. If we have a night together, I sense it wouldn't be enough for us. Not for me anyhow. It's better to nip it in the bud before we start anything."

Winter gave a self-depreciating shrug. "Well, thanks. That's the gentlest blowoff I've ever had. And no doubt Jessie will be more your style if it's only casual you're after."

"That's not how—" The chime of the doorbell cut her off.

Winter rose abruptly. "That'll be her now."

Pandora could only watch in dismay as she hurried from the room.

Crap. She had really stuffed that up.

CHAPTER TWELVE

Great! Jessie looked spectacular.

Winter sucked in a breath. Gone were Jessie's careless outfit and nose studs. Today she looked classy: designer jeans, a frayed pocket shirt jacket, polished knee-high boots and a touch of makeup. When she slipped off her sunglasses, under her mascara-tipped long lashes her blue irises were sparkling. Done up like this, she was the very definition of a desirable alpha woman. Winter's shoulders slumped. Not only was she incredibly hot, she was a successful doctor. How the hell could she compete with that?

"Hi, babe," said Jessie, flashing her a broad grin.

"Hey. Come on in." She took the six-pack of beer tucked under Jessie's arm and moved aside to let her enter. "Pandora's in the lounge so go on through. I'll just put these in the fridge and get you a coffee."

When she returned, the two were chatting comfortably. She sank down in the chair, content to listen. It didn't take her long to realize Jessie was making an extra effort to be charming. It was also becoming clear to Winter that this was rapidly turning into a hopeless situation for herself. With Jessie at her scintillating best she was fast losing any chance with Pandora. Yet it was heartening to see her best friend actually showing a real interest in someone. However much it hurt, she figured it was probably for the best. No way she would be able to keep the interest of a captivating woman like Pandora for any length of time. She'd probably bore her to death.

Stop it! Delete that last thought. Don't dwell on Christine's bitchy words.

Twenty minutes later she excused herself to prepare lunch, leaving them to have a quick dip in the pool. Jessie always loved a swim—she claimed that having the pool installed was the only thing she'd liked about Christine. Winter positioned the chopping board on the bench in front of the window so she would have a view of the pool. Thankfully, Pandora had donned one of the spare bikinis in the change room and not gone in "au naturale" as she had this morning. The sight of her naked had sent Winter into a complete dither.

The woman had a fantastic body.

As she periodically lifted her head from the salad preparation to watch them in the water, she thought about Jessie. In the early years, she hadn't really given her behaviour much serious thought. They were young, focused on a good time rather than relationships. She was simply her best friend, the popular girl, the life of the party, who didn't—or perhaps in hindsight *couldn't*—commit to anyone romantically. She had always envied her for her easy success with women and followed faithfully in her shadow. Until she met Christine.

Jessie continued her wild life even as her friends began to pair off. But now in her mid-thirties, her behaviour seemed a little sad. She appeared driven to conquer, but after the sex the pursuit would end, and with the challenge finished, she moved on to the next.

Winter's overtures to encourage her talk about her childhood had always been fobbed off, though Jessie had let slip some scraps of her early life in foster homes. They weren't pleasant. Winter had given up asking when she began to date Christine and moved into different social circles. Now finally, when Jessie seemed to be actually showing more than a passing interest in someone, ironically it was a woman Winter fancied as well.

Life was a bitch sometimes.

Table set, Winter walked down to the pool. "Lunch is ready," she called out.

Pandora hoisted herself out, then sat on the edge with her feet in the water. "You use the room first, Jessie," she said, and patted the tiled space beside her. "Will you sit down with me while she changes, Winter?"

Without a word, she slipped off her sandals. As soon as she sank down to join her, Pandora began to sing softly. Enthralled, Winter sat quietly to listen. The tune had a natural, sweet melody that washed over her like a gentle shower of rain. It was just perfect.

As the moments passed, she became increasingly aware of Pandora's presence beside her: the woman's raw sensuality was causing an uncomfortable breathlessness and a persistent throbbing in her groin. She wriggled self-consciously, slightly off-centre, her skin tingling with want. Not allowing herself to linger on the smooth tanned body and toned muscle—and especially not on the generous breasts barely covered by the bikini top—she raised her head to focus on one sculptured eyebrow.

The eyebrow quirked and their eyes met. When Pandora gave her the briefest of nods, it took Winter a ridiculous amount of self-control not to reach up to tuck an errant curl back off her forehead. But the instant Pandora smiled, she could no longer contain herself and did just that. Afterward, she ghosted her fingers down her cheek. As she lightly stroked, they automatically swayed closer until their thighs were pressed together. She looked back up, becoming lost in the intensity of her gaze, and with their eyes still locked, Pandora reached up to take her hand to press the palm against her cheek. Winter squeezed her eyes shut to relish fully the feel of the cool, soft skin.

But in an instant the intimacy misted away when Jessie called out from the back patio, “I’ve finished.”

A pang of regret was like a soft punch as Winter felt the hand withdraw, the body move away. The loss was so acute she had to wait to gather her emotions before she climbed to her feet. Then steadying herself before she went back inside to the kitchen, she watched Pandora disappear into the change room.

After dressing the salads, she placed the bowls on the dining table along with the platter of cold meat.

When Winter joined her on the terrace, Jessie was deep in thought, leaning on the railing with a beer in her hand. Although Winter wasn’t short, Jessie topped her by an inch, but was no longer the lanky girl she had first known. Regular sessions in the gym had toned her body to super fit status. Jessie turned to look at Winter and raised the bottle. “I helped myself. You want one?”

“Not yet. I’ll have lunch first.”

“What did you want to discuss with me?”

“We’ll talk about it while we eat.”

“What’s with you and Pandora?” Jessie asked abruptly. “You’re very friendly all of a sudden.”

Winter lifted her brows in surprise. “I don’t know what you mean.”

“Come off it. Very touchy-feely for just acquaintances.”

“It was nothing.”

“Didn’t seem that way to me.”

“It’s hasn’t anything to do with you, Jess.”

“Someone has to look out for you.”

“Why? I’m a big girl.”

“Huh! Can’t you see Pandora wouldn’t suit you at all. You’re so bloody naïve when it comes to women and sex.”

Winter stared at her. Was there a challenge behind the words? Mockery? She frowned. “Just because I’m conservative doesn’t mean I’m stupid.”

"Really? Hell...you let yourself be Christine's doormat for years."

Affronted, Winter couldn't help but respond angrily. "I might have made the wrong choice there, but at least I made one."

Jessie glared back at her. "What makes you so damn self-righteous. I'll settle down one day, and when I do it'll be with someone who fits with me."

"Meaning what?"

Jessie gave a nonchalant shrug. "Meaning you're going for the wrong types. You need someone sweet, nice, with not too many expectations, not too sophisticated...like Linda."

Sometimes her attitude really ticked off Winter. She glowered. "Slightly dipsy, you mean?"

"Well...in the way...yeah. Someone uncomplicated."

"And you think I'd be happy with a partner like that?" Winter snapped, itching to wipe the smug look off her face. "You know, sometimes I think you don't know me at all. We've been best friends forever, but you've never seen past that awkward shy young girl I was when we first met. Believe it or not, I grew up. If you'd bothered to pay more attention to your friends rather than your next shag—"

She broke off, appalled at herself for letting Jessie get under her skin. She rocked back on her heels. "What are we doing? We never used to argue."

A small cough echoed from the open door. She whirled around, horrified to see Pandora leaning on the doorframe, watching them. Her expression was inscrutable. With a mumbled, "Sorry for that display," Winter brushed past her and headed inside. At the dining table, she called out, "Let's eat."

For once in her life, Jessie looked shame-faced when she sat down. She gave a feeble smile. "Well, that was awkward. Usually Winter doesn't bite back, but I guess I pushed her too far. My only excuse...I had a really shitty day yesterday."

Pandora's eyes ran over her face. "Something happen at work?"

"Two kids came in with severe respiratory problems. It took hours to stabilize them properly."

"You said you're a paediatrician."

"I specialise in respiratory paediatrics and I'm one of the Mater Children's Hospital's on-call specialists."

Winter ate, simmering as she listened to Jessie talk about her work. She probably should admire her—she had turned a demeaning situation into a point scorer. Busy doctor overstressed from saving children. And Pandora seemed to be hanging on her every word.

As the jumble of anger and hurt settled down, Winter forced herself to push past her resentment and be reasonable. Jessie's work *was* fascinating and heart-warming. And she *was* a good doctor who cared for her patients.

Damn! Facing the truth didn't make her feel any better, it only made her more depressed. She couldn't imagine anyone as vibrant as Pandora would be interested in listening to her waffle on about merges and acquisitions.

Silently she continued to watch morosely as the conversation moved to soccer, something else at which she had never excelled. On the other hand, Jessie had been a star, the captain of the university women's team, and still played in a local team on Saturdays when not on call. She was dragged into the conversation when Pandora asked, "Did you ever play, Winter?"

"She's not exactly a soccer babe," piped in Jessie with a hearty chuckle.

Winter tried to answer cheerfully but couldn't quite pull it off. "I seem to have two left feet when it comes to kicking a ball. They delegated me to be the water carrier." Then rankled by the continual smirk on Jessie's face, added defiantly, "I'm much better at golf."

"I love golf as well," replied Pandora, leaning forward over the table with a warm smile. "Perhaps we can have a round one day?"

"I'd like that," murmured Winter, lost in the smile. "There's a course attached to the local sports club down the road.

Afterward we could have a massage. The woman there has magic hands."

"Mmm. That sounds divine. Sign me up."

"Done," Winter answered, sinking back into a cloud at the thought of Pandora stretched out on the massage table.

She was brought back to reality by Jessie clattering her fork down on the plate. "Okay. Earth to Winter! Time to tell me why I'm here."

She pulled her eyes away from Pandora to study her friend, whose smug smile had dissolved into a pout. She felt a little burst of satisfaction—Jessie looked put out. "We want you to do something," she began.

"Go on."

Winter threw a questioning glance at Pandora who nodded her go-ahead. "As you no doubt noticed, Michael has a giant crush on Pandora."

"Yeah. He made that obvious the other night."

"Well…it's got to the point where he's practically stalking her and he can't seem to get it into his thick skull she's not interested. Gussie has asked me to do something about the infatuation."

Jessie stared at her. "Heck, Winter, it's nothing to do with you. Butt out. He's in his twenties."

"I know but tell that to his mother. She's really worried about him."

Jessie cast a discerning look at Pandora. "Haven't you told him to get lost?"

"I've tried to but it's not quite that simple," she replied with a grimace. "I'm expected to be pleasant to customers and he hasn't done anything that would warrant his being tossed out by the bouncers. It wouldn't be pretty. And quite frankly, I think he's too obsessed now to take rejection well. This has been going on for months."

"So…what are you proposing and how does it involve me? There's no way I'll talk to him if that's what you're suggesting."

"Of course not," Winter interjected. "We figured the best way to get the message across is for Pandora to be seen with someone else. Since she can't do that at the club, I'm throwing a party for my birthday and we want you to be her date. There'll be no dispute then that she's simply not available."

Jessie relaxed visibly, her face spreading into a wide grin. "Oh, that explains why you two have been so friendly. Sounds a good plan to me. I'd love to be your date, Pandora."

"No doubt you have a technique or two to show your interest in me," Pandora said lightly but there was a distinct gleam in her eye.

"You bet."

"Just so long as you don't forget we will be playacting."

"Maybe it'll be you that'll forget," replied Jessie with a wink.

Pandora laughed. "Perhaps. Who knows?"

"You wanna start practising?"

Pandora eyed her speculatively for a moment before she replied. "We probably should get to know something about each other to make it authentic."

Winter's heart sank. Jessie oozed sexual magnetism when in pursuit of a woman—she'd seen her moves often enough—and it was unlikely Pandora could resist her charisma for long. She'd read somewhere that people tend to take a partner who is roughly as attractive as they are, and both Pandora and Jessie were knockouts.

With a mixture of despondency and regret, she rose from her chair. To have to sit listening to their flirting would be too demoralizing. "You two go into the lounge, or out on the terrace if you prefer. It's a nice day to be in the fresh air. I'll clean up. Afterward, I have to email a document to a client. I shouldn't be too long. In the meantime, you two get to know each other and work out what you…um…have to."

Pandora cast her a look of surprise and rose quickly from her chair. "We'll tidy up…you did the cooking."

"No," said Winter firmly. "I've got this." She made a shooing gesture with her fingers. "Go."

Jessie climbed languidly out of her chair. "Come on, Pandora, let's sit on the terrace. When Winter uses that tone of voice you haven't a hope of changing her mind."

Pandora flicked a speck off her blouse. “Maybe you’ve never really tried.”

The cocky grin disappeared. “I think I know her a bit better than you.”

“No doubt, but sometimes old habits die hard. We all change as we grow older.”

Winter stared at her. Pandora wasn’t talking about the washing up, she was admonishing Jessie for the conversation between them earlier on the terrace. She’d clearly heard most of it and was standing up for her. Nobody had ever done that for her. Something shot through Winter, a warm feeling she’d never felt before.

With a sniff to fight back a tear at the unfamiliar rush of emotions, all she could do was smile before turning abruptly to seek the sanctuary of the kitchen.

CHAPTER THIRTEEN

With misgivings, Pandora watched Winter exit the room. She looked upset, which perturbed her much more than she was prepared to admit. The woman was getting under her skin. It had been a long time since anyone had come anywhere close to interesting her as much. Winter's face was intriguing rather than pretty. She loved the bump on her nose, the tiny cleft in her chin, how her wide mouth curved into a shy smile and the way her head tilted like a bird when she was asked a question.

Pandora had never put much score on looks. She had met enough drop-dead gorgeous women to know that beauty was not necessarily goodness. Maybe she was just jaded with the trumpery of the nightclub scene, but it was so refreshing to find someone genuinely nice who wasn't out to impress. A no-frills type of person—what you saw was what you got with her. Reserved as well, which made her just that much more alluring. But whatever it was that drew her to Winter was real. When she'd left the room, she'd taken all the warmth with her.

She turned her attention to Jessie, who sat relaxed in the brown rattan chair opposite, her outstretched legs crossed at the ankles. Her elbows on the armrests, Pandora quietly studied her. The doctor was sexy, charismatic, with a big soft spot for kids but no doubt had some personal issues.

"Tell me about yourself, Jessie," she said encouragingly.

Jessie looked at her with an enquiring smile. "You know about my work. What else do want to know? I'm a pretty laid-back kind of gal."

"If we're going to make this believable, it would be advisable to say we've been dating for at least a month. Otherwise…and don't take offence at this…Michael will presume I'm just one of your casual hook-ups. We have to make it plain it's much more than that. He's not to know we didn't know each other before your first visit to the club. You were sitting next to me."

Jessie flushed. "Righ—tttt." She drew out the word, plainly cautious now. "I'm not complicated. I like foxy women, fast cars, and hard rock."

"Well, that's putting it in a nutshell," said Pandora with a chuckle. "Favourite car?"

"Acura NSX."

Pandora gave a sharp whistle. "Wow! You have one of those?"

"Nope, but I'm working on it. The new model costs north of two hundred and fifty thousand."

"That'd take some serious saving. What about rock bands?"

"*Queen* is my all-time favourite…more modern, *Linkin Park.*"

"Good choices. I'm more into blues and easy listening, but I appreciate all music." Pandora gave a secret smile. "So…where do you usually take your…ah…foxy dates?"

"To dinner, dancing. To bed." Jessie's eyes flashed an invitation. "You think we should go on a date?"

Pandora's lips twitched. God, the woman was such a Fig Jam. "I don't think it'd be necessary. But if I change my mind, maybe we should start with dinner. I like to work up to the rest."

"Ah...you like to be chased a while," said Jessie, looking amused.

"Just let's say if I'm interested in someone, I prefer taking things steadily, making what follows count."

"Never could see the point of waiting. Sex is a fabulous way to relax and we all need it."

Ain't that a fact, thought Pandora as a mental picture of Winter naked on her bed appeared. She quickly hunted the image away to concentrate on Jessie. "I take it you don't like to get involved?"

"Everyone who goes home with me knows the score."

"Then you don't really date per se? You like meeting women at bars?"

"Occasionally I take someone out. But to this point I—" Her words trailed off and her expression changed from bold to uncertain in an instant. "Damn it, Pandora, you're making it sound like I'm some cold-hearted womanizer. I just like things uncomplicated and fun. What's wrong with that?"

"Hey. There's nothing wrong with that. I didn't mean to be critical. I'm just trying to understand a few things."

"What things?" asked Jessie, stiffening.

"For a start...why you spoke to Winter like that. You seem to think you have carte blanche with your own love life, but she shouldn't have choices. Seems to me she's a hell-of-a-nice person who deserves a bit more understanding from a friend."

Jessie opened her mouth, then snapped it closed. An angry flush spread across her face. "It's none of your business."

"Okay...point taken. I'm sorry if it sounded like I was prying, but I couldn't avoid hearing your argument. It seems to me like you've got some unresolved issues with Winter and her ex. Who exactly is this Christine?"

"Christine Dumont." The words were spat out. "She's a news reader on Channel Seven, and one of the hosts of their morning show."

Pandora stared at her. "*That* Christine! *She's* the ex?"

"Uh-huh. I take it you've watched her."

"Who hasn't. She's been around for years." Dumont was one of television's biggest stars, a striking, well-groomed woman who was an accomplished interviewer and very photogenic. The cameras loved her. She didn't appeal much to Pandora though, too narcissistic and pushy for her taste. One of those news commentators who thought they ran the country, constantly criticising politicians over frivolous matters. Certainly not a good fit for a woman like Winter. In fact it was hard to imagine them together.

She'd even met her once. About four months ago, Dumont had come to the Fox with some of the Seven network's crew for a celebration. What the occasion was she couldn't quite recall, but she remembered the TV star very well. Yuri, perpetually on the lookout for an opportunity to give the club a plug, had requested she join them for a few drinks after her last song. Late in the night, she was having a great time with the vibrant media crew when Dumont had made a whisky-soaked aggressive pass. After Pandora had prised the woman's grasping fingers from around her thigh, she ignored the expletive that followed and went off home.

She eyed Jessie curiously. "What was your problem with her?"

"They were never suited…right from the beginning the woman was an overbearing prissy princess. Then Winter asked her to move in with her. Shit, even when she was spending her money like water, she didn't toss her out."

"But she did in the end. Or was it the other way around?"

Jessie snorted. "That bitch wouldn't have left her cash cow. No, it was Winter who broke it off. She told Chris to get out when she caught her fucking the pool boy in the garden bungalow."

Pandora swallowed the lump that suddenly materialized in her throat. Poor Winter. She probably wouldn't have seen it coming either. Suddenly, the dynamics of the triangle began to take shape. Jessie was very possessive of Winter. What their friendship meant to her wasn't quite clear, but it must have hit her hard when Winter moved on with her life with another woman. She doubted Jessie harboured any sexual feelings for Winter, or vice versa, for there were no vibes they had anything other than a very close friendship. If she were to hazard a guess, she looked on Winter more as family.

Christine would have hated Jessie in return. She liked to control—that was obvious in her interviews—but there was no way she would have been able to manipulate this brash, confident doctor. The only way to dominate Winter was to take her away from Jessie's influence. And she would have done that subtly and methodically, without Winter even realizing it was happening.

"She sounds like your worst nightmare. Winter must have been devastated when she caught them?"

"Not really. Upset by the cheating naturally but was relieved to have a way out of the relationship. She told me after two years there wasn't much love left and Christine was very difficult to live with. I read between the lines that she was a bully. I had no idea things had become so bad."

Though Pandora felt a wave of empathy for Winter, she had difficulty ignoring the happy urge to smile at the news she wasn't pining for her ex. Then knowing she needed to get off the subject of Winter or Jessie would become annoyed, she said in a soothing voice, "You weren't expected to know, so don't beat yourself up over it. We all have to be responsible for our own choices. Now tell me about your family."

To her surprise, Jessie began to squirm in the seat, sucking in air like she was trying to stop throwing up. "I don't often talk about my childhood. It isn't—" She halted mid-track, then hesitated for a moment before she slowly drew her legs up until her feet were planted squarely on the floor. "Goddamn it—why the heck not? I'd really like to get to know you better, Pandora, so I want you to know where I'm coming from."

"I'd like to hear your story," she answered, then added in a warm intimate voice, "and I'd like us to be friends."

Jessie took a long steady breath. "I never knew my family," she began, her usual pleasantly deep voice rising to thin and reedy. "Apparently, my mother was brought into the ER, in labour and spaced out on drugs. After I was born, she disappeared. I became a ward of the state, shuffled through four foster homes until I ran away as soon as I finished high school. I'm not ready to tell what happened in that last home, but only that the father was an abusive violent arsehole. Believe me, living on the streets was a far better option than being in the same house as him."

With a burst of emotion, Pandora leaned forward impulsively and took her hand. "Geez, Jess, that's really shitty. How on earth did you manage to become a doctor?"

Jessie gave a crooked smile. "A fucking miracle happened! I won a scholarship to med school."

"How, if you were homeless?"

"My science teacher, Mrs Murphy, had persuaded me to apply in my last year of school. With all my drama I'd clean forgotten about it. I guess I just thought a person like me couldn't win something like that. Anyhow, she tracked me down to let me know. I used to think she was a funny old bird at school, but that woman was an angel. She took me home, cleaned me up and gave me some of her married daughter's clothes she still had in the cupboard. Then she helped me apply to Centrelink for the Youth Allowance, and got me a place in a residential college. The scholarship paid for the accommodation, books, and a few extras."

Jessie took another deep breath then continued. "That's where I met Winter...she was my first roommate and became the sister I never had."

Pandora could only stare at her, fighting hard to keep calm.

Never judge a book by its cover.

How true. She'd misjudged the woman completely. Who wouldn't have intimacy issues after a childhood like that? "Thank you for confiding in me. I understand now why you want to help children," she murmured, not able to stop her voice cracking.

"Yeah...well...kids are so vulnerable," Jessie said, the pink already on her cheeks deepening in colour.

"You're a very good woman, Dr. Drummond," Pandora said, squeezing her hand gently.

Jessie held it tighter, a tear on her cheek. She gave a gulp followed by a loud sniffle. "Sorry. I usually can handle my emotions."

Pandora reached up with her left hand to gently wipe the moisture away. "You shouldn't—" The sentence was forgotten as she caught a flash of colour out of the corner of her eye. She turned to see Winter staring at them from the threshold.

As casually as possible, she dropped the hand and sank back in her chair. "Hi," she said brightly. "Did you get the papers away?"

Winter responded with a brief "Yes."

An awkward pause followed. Jessie was still in her memories, while Winter's expression had changed from wounded to inscrutable.

"Jessie and I were getting to know each other," Pandora said, forcing a smile.

"I saw," said Winter. She flicked her eyes to Jessie. "You look like you could do with a drink. Would you like a beer or something stronger?"

Jessie nodded self-consciously. "A beer will do."

"Pandora?"

"The same, thanks."

When Winter disappeared back in the house, Jessie looked sheepishly at her. "Sorry about getting all emotional on you."

"Thank you for telling me."

"I wanted to tell you because I'd like to get to know you better. Maybe we could have dinner one night?" said Jessie earnestly, all swagger gone.

Pandora's stomach gave a lurch. Things were getting way too complicated. The last thing she wanted to do was to encourage her romantically but didn't want to hurt her feelings. She commanded more respect than that. She pulled on a sincerely regretful face. "That's nice of you to ask, Jessie, but I'm not in a position to date at the moment. In a few months perhaps, but until then—" She left the sentence dangling with a shrug.

"Until then what?" asked Winter from the doorway.

"Until then I have commitments," replied Pandora. "Now we'd better discuss how we're going to act at the party."

Winter handed them the beers. "Just remember Gussie as well as Michael will be watching you like a hawk. But then again, you two will be just fine. You're both experts at seduction."

"What's that supposed to mean?" growled Pandora.

"As if you didn't know."

"No, actually I don't."

"Pish!"

Conscious Jessie was looking at them perplexedly, Pandora forced a smile and a change of subject. "So what kind of party are you planning?"

Winter cleared her throat with a guilty look. "Um...yes... the birthday party. I thought laid-back—a barbeque in the back garden."

"That sounds great. That way is less catering. Everyone can bring a salad. Who do you want to invite?" asked Jessie, now her old self.

"The family for a start so Michael will be able to come. Then friends and some of my office mates. If you want to ask anyone else go ahead. I'll handle the food."

"There's a new girl in town. An anaesthetist. She might be more your style than Linda."

Winter shook her head. "Pleeease. Don't keep trying to be a matchmaker."

"Just trying to help. Pandora says I should be more understanding."

Winter's eyes narrowed. Anger glinted in them, like ice in autumn. "Did she indeed. She should butt out. I can look after myself."

Pandora tugged at the label on her bottle, avoiding Winter's gaze. Her stomach hitched in frustration. Jessie had deliberately thrown that one in, damn her. She would have known perfectly well Winter valued discretion. Now she was aware they had been discussing her. Pandora searched for words—it had been a long time since she'd been put so far on the back foot. "I'm sorry," she said simply, then looked at her watch. She'd better make a move or she'd be late for her appointment. "It's time I went home."

The anger fled from Winter's face. "You have to go?" she asked, more subdued.

"I have a few things to attend to."

"I'll give you a lift home," said Jessie immediately.

"Thanks all the same but I'll get a cab. I'll leave you both to plan the finer details of the party. That's what you came over for, Jessie."

"It's hardly a Gatsby party—just a barbie round the pool."

"I would appreciate your help, Jess," Winter piped up. "I plan to have it in two weeks, so we have to get the invitations out ASAP. I want it low key and no presents."

"But you gotta have a cake."

"Oh, all right. I'll organize one. But that's all. No speeches. Can you design an online invitation?"

"Okay," Jessie acquiesced good-naturedly. "I'll handle them while you prepare the menu. You know what my culinary skills are." She formed an O with her thumb and forefinger.

After Pandora ordered a yellow cab, she nodded in the direction of the staircase. "I'll have to go upstairs to collect my dress and shoes before I go."

"Go on up," said Winter immediately rising to her feet. "I'll get a shopping bag and follow you."

Dejected and a little desperate, Pandora ran up the stairs, trying to think how to repair the damage Jessie's words had caused. She was aware that if she didn't do something, it would be hard to mend. She shook out the wrinkled dress, folded it into a neat bundle and placed her shoes on top.

"Here," said Winter from the doorway.

"Thanks." She stuffed the clothes into the open bag and said politely, "I guess I'd better be going then. Thank you for having me. I'll send your clothes over next week."

She shuffled her feet, reluctant to leave things between them like this, but fresh out of ideas. With a sigh, she headed for the door.

"Pandora…wait," Winter said breathlessly, reaching for her arm as she slipped past. "I…I'm sorry for reacting so rudely."

"You were within your rights. I shouldn't have been discussing you."

"Don't go away mad. Please."

She looked so flustered and earnest that Pandora reached up to touch her cheek. Winter sidled closer as she automatically began to weave circles on the soft skin. They stared at each other, explanations forgotten. "Would you like to go out on Thursday night? I owe you dinner," Pandora blurted out without a thought.

Winter sagged with visible relief, then leaned in further until her face was barely a breath away. "I'd like that very much."

"You would?" Pandora stood mesmerized as she peered into her eyes. The irises had turned alive with dancing golden flecks.

"Uh…huh."

Pandora dropped her gaze to Winter's mouth. Her lips looked as soft as butter. Then when Winter poked out her tongue and slowly slid it across her bottom lip, a thrill jumped down Pandora's body to tingle between her legs. She wet her own lips—funny, she hadn't realized how dry they had become. Every bit of moisture must have gone south. Then all she could do was tighten her grip on the bundle in her arm when Winter reached up and ran her fingertip along her mouth.

Wow! She hadn't realized such a simple act could be so erotic. She was throbbing in places she hadn't felt before.

She had no idea how long they stood there, but it came as a shock when a cry echoed at the bottom of the stairs, "The cab's here."

Oops!

They hurriedly stepped away until they were no longer in each other's space. Pandora had no idea which one of them whimpered. It echoed in the silence like a seductive mating coo.

"I'll call you tomorrow," Pandora whispered and ran downstairs.

CHAPTER FOURTEEN

The city was grey, blurred by the heavy rain that had swept in without warning from the east. The cabbie followed her directions, turning off into a narrow side street fronted by a few tired shops and red brick apartment blocks with cramped front porches and tiny front yards. Vague figures hurried along the footpath, heads down against the weather. Pandora made a dash to a staircase in the recess jammed between a secondhand bookstore and a barbershop.

With a last searching glance around the area, she shook the water off her hair and jogged up the steps. When she knocked three times on the steel door at the top, it was opened by a tall muscular man dressed in work pants and a grey, collared shirt. At first glance he might be mistaken for a tradesman. His stance, alert eyes and the slight bulge of the shoulder holster told a different story. Agent Bart Finley was one of their top operatives, the security officer for their team. A former SAS soldier, he had joined their division of Home Affairs three years prior to this assignment.

"Hey, Colly. What's with the psychedelic shirt? You going all alternate on us?" he said with a grin.

She gave him a good-natured dig in his ribs. "Bugger off, Fin. The boss here yet?"

"He's in the office. I wasn't expecting you until tomorrow."

"Last-minute change of plan. I was out for lunch so figured it'd be wiser to come today. The rain was fortuitous…an extra screen."

"Something happen?" he asked with a frown.

"Things have become tense at the club, so I'm being extra cautious," she said as she stepped inside. All signs of the once dingy gym were gone. The space had been gutted, painted, and redesigned into a state-of-the-art surveillance centre. High-tech aids were at their fingertips: a portable biometrics lab, surveillance equipment, and five computer stations.

As she proceeded through, she nodded to the room's only occupant, a pretty blond woman in her late twenties who was tapping on the laptop keys at the far end. "Hey, Gail."

"Hi, Colly," she replied then raised an eyebrow. "Very decorative today."

"You wish," said Pandora with a laugh. The programmer loved bright clothes. She also hated working the Sunday shift equally as much—it interfered with her social life.

"See you when I get out," Pandora called out over her shoulder as she entered the office at the rear.

Captain Lance Milton was waiting at his desk, a takeaway cappuccino in his hand. There was nothing about her boss to suggest he was anything other than an average guy in his forties, with a wife, kids, and mortgage. He had a nondescript face, thinning sandy hair, wide-set guileless blue eyes, and a pair of old-fashioned wire glasses on his nose. Beneath the benign appearance though, lurked an astute intelligence officer with a keen mind and a take-no-shit attitude. Fair but tough. Early in Pandora's career, she had stuffed up and been on the receiving end of one of his reprimands. It was something she didn't want repeated.

"Afternoon, Captain," she said as she took a seat on one of the uncomfortable green vinyl chairs, a remnant from the gym.

"Colly, it's good to see you." He pointed to another disposable cup on his desk. "I got you a coffee. I thought you might need the boost." Then added with a wry grin, raising his cup, "Me too. I can't say I wasn't disturbed when you rang this morning. We're at the crucial part of the investigation…I was hoping you could stay undercover for another two or three months. How bad do you think this problem with Boris Anasenko is going to be?"

"Let's just say I was fortunate last night to get out of a potentially serious situation," she replied, curling her lips in distaste as she revisited the scene in the annex. "I'm not going to be so lucky next time, and it *will* happen again. He wants me and I doubt Yuri will have much influence stopping him, especially if the Melbourne thugs are with him."

Milton took a sip as he assessed her over the rim. "We'll have to have something more substantial for the director to justify an immediate extraction. We're at the crucial part of the investigation, so I can't just pull you out. We'll just move earlier than planned. How long do you think before he comes back to the club?"

"He and the mob turn up regularly every two months, though not always on the same day of the week. But next time you can bet it'll be on a night I'll be singing. Knowing the mentality of the men in this Russian family, it would have become a matter of pride. He'll be angry he lost face to a woman."

"Could you pinpoint the day as it gets closer?"

Pandora thought for a moment then nodded. "I'll be able to give you a couple of days' warning. The afternoon of a night's performance, I go across to the club to run through the program with Kurt. Yuri normally has a coffee with us to give us his instructions for the night. He doesn't interfere much—just when he wants me to socialize with particular clients or sing a special song for one of his family. Stuff like that. He's actually a good boss. A day or two before the heavies arrive, he's always on edge. He starts locking his office every time he steps out and gives his office girl four days off over that period. It's clear he has something very valuable in the safe to hand over."

"We know for sure now that the Silver Fox is key to the northern part of the Russian money laundering operations up here in Brisbane, so keep your guard up and continue as is. We'll discuss what's going to happen closer to the time."

He pulled a folder out from beneath a pile of scribbled notes and slid it across the table. "I need you to work here this afternoon. We've finally received the photos from the UN and Interpol of the people of interest. Apparently, their targets are camera shy and know how to get off the radar, hence the delay. Very few use commercial flights to enter the country."

Pandora flipped open the file. Inside was a stack of at least twenty A4 black-and-white snapshots. The top one she recognized immediately—a man in his sixties she'd seen a few times at the club.

"I want you to go through them and take out the ones you know have visited the club. We've tracked down most of the syndicate's northern criminal contacts, but the biggest fish is still out there. Take a look. I'm betting our man…or woman… is amongst them."

Pandora automatically glanced down at the folder. "You think the person is from overseas?"

"It's a distinct probability. We can't find anyone shuffling around really big dollars here," Milton replied, then leaned forward over the desk. "I want to know how many times you remember seeing them there, plus any other pertinent points you can remember. You know the drill."

She rubbed the back of her aching neck. "That might be a little difficult for all of them. I've been there nearly twelve months."

Milton gave her a shrewd, considered look. "This is the sort of stuff you do best, Colly. You've a good memory, intelligence, and instinct. That why you were picked for this op." His mouth twitched up into a small smile. "That and the fact you make a great lounge singer."

With a weak smile, she shuffled the photos back into the folder and rose from the chair. "Yes, sir. I'll get on to it immediately."

His next words stopped her mid-stride. "How did you get away from that bastard Boris? You never did say."

"A woman helped me. A patron at the club. She noticed I was being forcibly detained and that they were closing off the room. She intervened by pouring red wine on my dress, and insisted she take me off to the restroom to clean it off," she explained, not bothering to keep the pride for Winter out of her voice.

"Good lord. Maybe we should recruit her," he said, his eyes twinkling.

Pandora laughed. "We couldn't afford her. She's a corporate lawyer."

Back in the main office, she settled herself at a desk. Taking her time, she examined each photo thoroughly, siphoning off those she recognized into a separate folder. Some shots were perfectly clear, close enough to show any distinguishing markings. Others were poor quality, grainy or slightly out of focus, though still recognizable. In the end, she had nine people she knew she had seen in the club: eight men and one woman. Then she searched her memories, striving to recall the times she'd seen them there. After two hours, her head began to throb.

Eventually, when her vision became too blurry, she figured it was time to throw it in and report back to Milton. He looked up from his laptop with an enquiring glance. "That's the best I can do," she said, placing the two folders on the desk. "If something else sparks my memory, I'll shoot it through to you."

"Good. You'd better be off then. You look played out," he said, his face now more relaxed. "And Colly…be careful. I've just received word the Russians are tightening their security. Ditch your work phone and pick up a new one on your way out. If you have to send a message, go via Adriana…no direct contact with us here. No body wires, no tapes. We're nearly at the end of the assignment, so don't do anything to compromise yourself. Just lie low and observe. It'll be over soon and you can go home."

Home.

It sounded nice, safe, but she didn't know where that was anymore. Too many assignments in different places. She'd let her Sydney apartment go this time—too long away to be paying the rent. It was always a good break to visit her mother in Devonport, to catch up with her childhood friends, but she hadn't lived at home since she was eighteen. She needed to get off this carousel for a while, to make a life for herself. Unbidden, the image of Winter floated in and she pushed it away regretfully.

Once the operation was over, she would have to leave the city.

* * *

Pandora opened her fridge door and sized up the contents. Her already low spirits took another dive. A lone piece of stale pizza, two vodka lime UDL cans, a bottle of milk, and half a loaf of bread. *Crap!* With a resigned sigh, she pulled the tab off a can and sloshed the drink over a glass of ice. She took two long swigs to settle herself down, then emptied the rest of the can into the glass. After zapping the pizza in the microwave, she settled down in the lounge chair with her dinner to watch TV. She began to scroll through the channels absently.

There was nothing worth watching as usual—a couple of movie reruns, a hospital soapie, a cooking show, and a nature documentary about the breeding habits of an endangered African monkey. She'd seen the movies, couldn't cook, and there was no way she wanted to learn about a monkey's mating life when she couldn't get one herself.

Restless, she tossed the remote away and stared at the blank screen, wondering what the hell she was going to do now. It wasn't even eight thirty—she had no hope of sleeping. Normally she didn't mind being bored. After a rough day, a touch of tedium was welcome, giving her voice and body a chance to recharge. Sometimes she went home from the club completely exhausted.

But she needed to be occupied tonight, didn't want to dwell on the events of the past twenty-four hours.

Usually debriefing wasn't a problem. As an agent with nearly ten years' field experience, she had learned to recognize stress, absorb it and file it away, enabling her to function like the professional she'd been trained to be. But last night she had underestimated the danger and lost control of the situation. She should never had entered that room with those men. A big mistake. If Winter hadn't intervened, she would have been in serious trouble.

Winter—now that woman was becoming a real complication. She couldn't get her out of her head and was close to breaking rule one: never get romantically involved while on assignment. It was time to be more discerning. Casual sex was acceptable, but a relationship was not. After losing her singing dream, she wasn't prepared to jeopardise this career she'd carved out for herself. She had long since stopped thinking about the what-ifs in her life. What she had now was solid, exciting work, and if loneliness was a side effect, then it was a price she was prepared to pay.

With new determination, she rose to go to bed. On her way, she caught sight of her laptop on the desk. So far, she had shied away from looking Winter up, feeling it was a bit too much like stalking. Now she couldn't resist. Ignoring the pang of guilt, she eased down on her office chair and opened Winter's Facebook page. The fact there were hardly any entries, only reaffirmed what a very private person she was. It always amazed Pandora how indiscreet people were on social media. Didn't they realize whatever they entered was open to public scrutiny?

She surfed the Internet to learn more about their public split. They had stayed in the news for weeks, with pictures of the two women before and after the breakup. As a well-known media personality, most articles were about Dumont. From her point of view, she was the wronged and innocent party in their parting of ways. She might have sounded truthful, but the vibes were there it was a long way from the real version.

Winter had been remarkably quiet in the media about the whole business, only caught by the cameras with her head down trying to avoid reporters. She had never given an interview.

Two years later, a gossip columnist reported that there had been a substantial payout to Christine. It was also alleged that one of them had been caught with her pants down, but as this was only speculation, the affair eventually faded out of the news. Since the initial separation, the TV presenter had been coupled with at least three high-profile women. Jessie was right. Christine wasn't nearly good enough for Winter. And she bet the tabloid had been right about the de facto alimony. The bitch would have been viewing Winter as a poker machine, with the jackpot coming up whenever she pushed her buttons.

She brought up images of Winter and after enlarging the best one, she sat gazing at it wistfully until she came to her senses. Mooning over her picture was ridiculous. If she couldn't stop thinking about her, then she had to do something about it. She had another seven weeks to get her out of her system. Maybe they could have a bit of fun like Jessie would. Perhaps Winter wouldn't want anything serious after her last disaster.

Yeah, right. Like Winter is anything like Jessie.

Pandora shook her head, thinking that it would probably backfire on her as well. Who was she trying to kid anyhow? It had been years since she'd had anything that she could be remotely considered a romantic attachment, and she wanted one. Coming home to a lonely flat wasn't a way to live anymore. Merely an existence.

Her musings were interrupted by the phone.

"Hello."

"Pandora, it's Kurt. I heard Boris was a shithead last night. Sorry, I went out for a while and wasn't in the club to stop it."

She smiled into the receiver. At least *he* cared what happened to her. "Kurt. Thanks for ringing. I got out of it...just. One of the patrons helped me get away. I hope I don't have to go anywhere near that bastard again. Yuri will have to control him more when he comes to the Fox. The man's dangerous."

"I know. Just try to stay out of his way when he comes back. Call me if there's any more trouble next time. I'm glad you're all right. I'll see you Tuesday night then. Bye."

Pandora hit the off button with a snap. She doubted he'd be a match for Boris. Not with his accompanying goons. She was slipping the phone back into her pocket when it rang again.

"Hello," she answered gruffly.

There was a pause for a moment on the other end, then Yuri came on the line. "Pandora. Hi. I'm just ringing to see how you are. I've rung a few times today, but only got your voicemail."

She shot up straight, focused now. No wonder she hadn't heard from anyone at the club. With all the drama, she hadn't checked her messages. "I thought it wiser to spend the night with a friend after what happened. My phone's been on the charger."

"I heard what happened."

"Then you know Boris went too far."

"He and the boys were only wanting to let off a bit of steam. Just having a bit of fun."

"I wouldn't have called it amusing for me. The bruises on my wrists tell another tale," she snapped.

"Come on...Boris just got carried away. They'd had a bit to drink. He asked me for your address so he could apologise this morning."

Pandora nearly choked. As if that swine would apologise to a woman. Then it sank in that he had gone to her apartment. She shivered, imagining what would have happened if she'd been home. "I just want him to leave me alone. I told him I wasn't interested, but he wouldn't take *no* for an answer. Is he still at the club?"

"They flew out at three." There was a long pause before he added, "You'll still come in on Tuesday?"

"Yes, I'll be there."

An audible sigh echoed in her ear. Good, he was worried. But his next words made her heart sink and demolished any hope that he'd support her in the future. "Be nice to him next time, Pandora. I know he can be difficult, but he is family."

"I'll be pleasant, but I don't intend getting too friendly."

"We'll discuss it later. He won't be back for two months." After that, he went off on another tangent, discussing at great length the various Russian families who had come out for the celebrations. Usually a man of few words, she knew it was his way of apologising.

When he finished the call, she stared at the phone thoughtfully. She was under no illusion now—Yuri couldn't control his brother. Boris was by far the stronger personality and there would be no protection for her next time. She would definitely have to be gone by then. One good thing—he'd confirmed it was going to be in eight weeks.

CHAPTER FIFTEEN

Winter found herself staring into space again, her mind wandering back to Pandora. Despite the pile of work on her desk, the outing tonight had her too keyed up to concentrate. God knows why—she was hardly a teenager on her first date. But she couldn't deny that she had never felt quite like this about any woman. She made her feel so many things on so many levels. But then again, what could she really know? Christine had been her one and only long-term relationship, so she hardly was an authority on the affairs of the heart. Watching Jessie with women wasn't a good yardstick on which to base anything either.

After battling on for another half an hour with her latest client's deal, Winter gave up and clicked Save. Then on spec, she rang her favourite salon, figuring that not only would some pampering help her relax, it would also keep her mind off the coming date. Much to her delight, they managed to fit her in for a massage. With renewed energy, she packed up her things and cast a last glance around her office before opening the door.

Nancy looked up, her eyes widening in surprise when she saw the handbag. "Are you going out, Winter? I thought you were preparing the Valcourt merger this afternoon."

Winter searched for an excuse. Not that she had to answer to her—she was her boss—but she always found Nancy McCaffery a wee bit intimidating. Not far off her sixtieth birthday, the perceptive, no-nonsense PA had been a fixture in the office long before Winter joined the firm. A stickler for protocol, Nancy always wore immaculately tailored business suits, her greying hair fashioned back in a neat bun, and she couldn't remember ever seeing her without makeup. When Winter joined the firm, it had taken her a lot of cajoling to make her drop Ms. Carlyle and call her by her first name. Finally, she merely said, "I'm not feeling well so I'm taking the afternoon off."

"Oh, dear. It's not like you to take a sick day. If you like, I'll prepare the documents and have them ready for signatures."

Winter smiled at her gratefully. Nancy knew as much about corporate law as anyone in the building, partners included. She didn't know what she'd do without her. "Thanks. I'll be fine. Just an upset stomach. I'll see you in the morning."

Feeling like a truant schoolgirl, she hurried off with a spring in her step down the corridor to the lift.

The rest of the afternoon passed so pleasantly, she wondered why she didn't do it more often. After a relaxing Swedish massage, their beautician did her makeup as well. With only just over an hour to spare, she sailed off home feeling like a million dollars. What to wear proved a little taxing. Since Pandora had rung saying not to get dressed up, she had to scrounge in her cupboard for something casual but decent. She hadn't realized how much of her wardrobe comprised of work suits and after-five wear.

Eventually—after a minor panic attack—she found her Paige denim jeans packed away in the bottom of the cupboard. Relieved they still fitted, she pulled on her nicest top, a grey silk ruffled blouse, then peered critically at her reflection in the mirror. Not too bad—at least her makeup was flawless. Remembering Pandora had liked her hair free, she brushed it out of its French twist, then added a bright necklace, a few dabs of perfume and she was ready.

The chime of the doorbell brought butterflies to her stomach, which she dismissed as thoroughly irrational. The sight of Pandora on the landing brought them fluttering back. She involuntarily clenched her thighs as Winter's gaze travelled over her. Gone was the slinky feminine singer from the stage. This woman was bold, strong, edgy with a hint of swagger. Someone who took charge. She stood at ease, her black leather bomber jacket open to the evening air, revealing a clinging blue T-shirt and a glint of gold on a chain. Low jeans hugged her hips, biker boots covered her legs, and her dark hair curled in luxurious waves over her collar. Winter nearly groaned aloud.

She was in so much trouble.

Pulling herself together, she smiled over-brightly. "Hi."

Pandora dipped her head, mirroring her smile as she passed over a box tied with a pink ribbon, together with her borrowed clothes. "For you. I hope you like chocolates."

"Love them, thanks," she murmured, her eyes welling up at the gesture. It had been a long time since anyone had given her a present other than at Christmas and on her birthday. Just another thing that had been one-sided with Christine. Though she often gave her gifts in their dating days, Christine had never reciprocated. Embarrassed at her unexpected show of emotion, she turned quickly to place the box on the table in the hallway. "I'm ready," she said over her shoulder.

"Great. Let's go then."

Winter followed her to the silver RAV4 in the driveway, charmed when Pandora opened the door for her. The trip into town passed pleasantly, the conversation easy and light. Then instead of going to one of the uptown eating venues, they made their way to a suburb popular with people living more alternate lifestyles.

"This is as close as we're going to get," said Pandora as she eased the car into a parking spot on top of a hill above the busy streets.

When they alighted, Pandora immediately took her hand and laced their fingers together. They stood in the semidarkness to enjoy the view of the city lights before they strolled down to the main hub. The streets were crowded with revellers enjoying the night life. Always reticent about showing public affection, Winter relaxed when she realized they weren't out of place from the number of same-sex couples walking hand-in-hand. After a few blocks of window-shopping, Pandora made her way down a side street to a recess next to a dress shop.

"We're dining at The Blue Peacock. It's in the basement," she explained as she led the way down a flight of steps. They passed through an archway into a cosy restaurant lit by round Turkish mosaic lamps hanging from the ceiling.

Winter took note of her surroundings. The décor was bohemian, woven rugs hanging on the walls, and lots of cushions and throws. The room was filled with chunky wooden tables, the bench seats arranged to face a small raised stage at one end. The place was packed with an odd assortment of patrons: all sizes, all ages, very multicultural. Clothes varied from jeans to flamboyant caftans, with no suit brigade in sight.

They were greeted by a slender woman with dark brown hair tied back with a scarf, dressed in a vibrant loose top and flared bell-bottomed pants straight from the seventies. She engulfed Pandora in a tight hug. Before she pulled away, she mumbled something in her ear that Winter didn't catch.

Her dark eyes swept over Winter curiously. "I've reserved the table for two in the left corner for you."

Pandora introduced her as Adriana Flavus, though Winter had no idea how close a friend she was. The hug seemed possessive. Maybe they had a thing in the past? She hated to admit it, but she was more than a little jealous at that thought, especially when Adriana rubbed Pandora affectionately on the shoulder as she said, "I have a few things to attend to, so have fun."

Pandora smiled fondly at her. "I'm sure we will."

Winter slid onto the bench seat, her pulse not quite steady as she wriggled to get comfortable. It was very cosy, their thighs touching lightly. She could smell Pandora's perfume mixed with her distinctive musky scent, feel the heat radiating from her body. Her voice felt oddly thick as she said, "You and Adriana seem…um…good friends."

"We've worked together for years. She's a remarkable woman and a great singer."

Winter winced. *That'd be right. Hard to compete with.* "What type of songs?" she asked. Adriana didn't appear at all like a sultry blues singer. She was attractive, but in a home-spun sort of way, as if she belonged behind a potter's wheel or a weaving loom.

"Folk mainly…Joni Mitchell, Joan Baez, Tracy Chapman. She's singing tonight."

"Oh? She's the entertainment?"

"Yep. Wait 'til you hear her. You'll love her," said Pandora and handed her a menu. "The Spanish tapas are superb."

"Then let's order," replied Winter.

And they were delicious. They were finishing the last dish when a stool and a microphone were brought out to the small stage. The restaurant began to buzz with anticipation and excitement. The lights dimmed except for the mosaic lamp above the stage, and Adriana walked out to a burst of applause. After she settled in front of the mike with one foot on the stool rest and a guitar cradled on her lap, she plucked a few cords before beginning her song. She began with Joni Mitchell's "River," her attractive cameo face calm, though her eyes were intense as her fingers strummed restlessly over the strings. Held captive by the sweet tone of her voice, Winter sank back to enjoy the show.

"Big Yellow Taxi" came next, followed by a bracket of Tracy Chapman's songs. As they listened, they wordlessly leaned closer together until finally Pandora put her arm around her shoulder. Winter sank against her, shaken by the strength of her desire. Then in the anonymity of semi-dark corner, Pandora lowered her head and brushed her lips up the inner shell of Winter's ear. She nearly moaned aloud, her nerves racing, her heart thudding.

Pandora ran a fingertip down the side of her neck, lightly touching the hollow of her throat, a gesture that was at once innocent and erotic. "I want to touch you," she whispered.

"Please…please behave," Winter whispered back. But she found the words, like her pulse, a bit unsteady. She had no wish for her to stop, no strength to refuse the caress.

Pandora claimed Winter's hand and brought it to her mouth, pressing her lips to the centre of her palm. "Does this," she whispered, "feel good?"

Winter swallowed, unable to think of anything but the heat rushing to her centre. The lips were filled with promise, gentle and warm as a summer's breeze. Her ordered disciplined mind swam out of focus as Pandora moved her hand down under the table to stroke her thigh. Gradually the stroking became more insistent, and closer to the seam between her legs. If she kept going, Winter thought she would explode.

Then out of nowhere, a voice called out, "Pandora. Would you sing a duet with me?" Startled, they straightened to attention. Winter looked up to see Adriana looking at them, her stare piercing.

"Damn," said Pandora in a barely audible whisper. She let her arm slide off Winter's shoulder and moved to the side to put a space between them. "Okay," she called out. "Why not?"

Later, Winter thought, at some lonely dark hour, she'd explore her reaction to Pandora's caresses. But now all she could do was watch the two women enviously as they sang in perfect harmony. Their three songs were steeped in regret and lost love, which made Winter wonder again about their history. When they finished with "You Don't Bring Me Flowers Anymore," Winter had to remind herself that this was showmanship, not reality. The women were consummate performers. Still, to her, Adriana looked genuinely upset. But when they both burst into smiles after the finale, she revised that thought, figuring it was all in the act.

When she returned to the table, Pandora seemed tense, avoiding Winter's eye as she slowly stirred a spoonful of sugar into the small cup of black Turkish coffee. Uneasily, Winter watched her over the rim of her cup as she sipped. She looked less assured. When she glanced up and their eyes met, Winter flashed her a reassuring smile. Pandora tilted her head, giving an answering smile, though she still appeared wary.

They filled the next half an hour with strained small talk, and she was relieved when Pandora announced, "I guess we'd better be off. Would you mind if I had a quick word with Adriana before we go? I won't be long."

"No probs. I'll go to the loo while you're away."

Dejected, Winter watched her stride away and disappear down the back. Clearly, Pandora regretted what happened between them. And who was she kidding anyhow? She was totally out of her element with someone like Pandora. Not when the talented, vivacious Adriana seemed to have a thing for her.

Suddenly, Winter just wanted to go home. She had no place here.

CHAPTER SIXTEEN

"I hope you know what you're goddamn doing," hissed Adriana.

Pandora managed to suppress a scowl as she met her eyes. "There's no reason I can't go out. I've been discreet."

"Bollocks! You're supposed to be undercover, not carting some woman around the town."

"So what? No one expects Pandora not to have a social life. In fact, it's only natural a woman my age dates. It's probably more suspicious that I don't. Anyhow, I don't know what you're worrying about. This place is completely off the radar from anyone who visits the Silver Fox. Different clientele altogether."

"I know that, otherwise I wouldn't have asked you to sing. That's not what I was referring to. Who the hell is that bimbo on your arm, and—" Adriana waved her hand irritably at her, "—what does she think of this transformation? Have you looked in the damn mirror? You hardly look like a lounge singer."

Pandora's anger flared. "Winter is *not* a bimbo. She is a highly intelligent woman who would be mortified to hear you call her that. As for this outfit," she continued, in a more reasonable tone, "I wanted one night to relax and not have to pretend. Even if Winter thinks it's odd, she won't say anything."

She ignored the little voice in her brain as she spoke—*Pride is one of the deadly sins!* What was wrong with wanting Winter to see she was a woman in charge and not just some sexpot?

"Yeah—right," said Adriana with a toss of her head.

"You don't even know her so don't be judgemental. She knows how to be discreet."

"Then I'll have to take your word for it. What's with you and her anyhow to risk jeopardizing your cover? You're always so circumspect when it comes to your work."

Pandora pretended to consider the question for a moment. "I'm not compromising my cover. She's a friend who did me a good turn…I'm returning the favour by taking her out to dinner. No harm in that."

"For Christ sake, Colly, I wasn't born yesterday. You can't keep your hands off her. I've never seen you like that with anyone. You always play so…so hard to get."

Something in her tone made Pandora study her closer. She tried to read her. Adriana sounded really peeved that she'd turned up with a date. She was acting completely out of character. "Rubbish. I date."

"Yeah. You do, but they never last. More like interludes."

"So? I'm never in one place long enough to have a long-term commitment. What's got into you tonight? I actually came here because the boss wanted me to give you this." She reached in her pocket and handed her an envelope. "Since the Russians are supposed to be tightening their security, I've been instructed to pass on anything through you. Phone calls have to be kept to a minimum."

Adriana huffed out a breath, then snapped into professional mode. "Right. How often do you envisage you'll have info to pass on?"

"It'll depend. Probably quite a lot in the coming weeks. They've given me photographs of persons of interest. I'm to keep my eyes open if I see any of them in the club. They're pulling me out in about seven weeks."

"Then it'll be less noticeable if we meet in different spots. We'll use our own code, not the standard company one, to relay where and when we meet."

Pandora nodded. "Good plan. Now I'd better get back. Winter will be wondering what's happened to me. I'll be in touch."

Adriana caught her wrist as she turned to go. "Do you intend to keep seeing her?"

Pandora froze, then slowly but firmly pulled the hand off. "Maybe. That'll be up to her. But whatever happens, it's our business. Besides," she said, softening her voice. "Dating her could be the perfect cover to meet you in places I wouldn't normally frequent."

"I guess," said Adriana. "But for shit sake, dress in character in future."

As she exited the dressing room Pandora pushed back her annoyance. She went over their exchange to make sense of what just transpired, concluding that it wasn't her outfit that had Adriana so het up. She knew perfectly well that Pandora wouldn't take unnecessary risks. No, it was about Winter. Why did she care who she took out anyhow? Hell, Adriana had had her share of lovers, and they'd been friends for ten years.

Pandora had met her at a bar one Friday night in Sydney, when she was celebrating her graduation from the Australian Institute of Music and Adriana was doing a gig with the band. They had clicked immediately. Following a drinking session, they'd ended up in bed. After spending the weekend together, Adriana was keen to take it further. Pandora had shied away from a repeat, for although the vivacious singer was fun, she had no time or inclination for a relationship. Not while she was trying to establish her career. Even though Adriana hadn't taken the rebuff well, they eventually put it behind them and became firm friends. But they had never gone back to being lovers.

A year later, they were approached by Adriana's uncle, a director of a covert department in Home Affairs, to join the organization. Though she would never had considered it if she'd had time to establish her musical career, circumstances forced her to consider the offer. Her widowed mother had fallen seriously ill, and virtually overnight, Pandora became the breadwinner of the family. So reluctantly, she put her ambitions aside and filled out the form.

Pandora had never forgotten that first interview.

On a grey wintery August morning, she and Adriana had set off in a taxi for their aptitude and psychological tests. She didn't really know what she had been expecting, but it had come as a surprise when the cabbie let them out in front of a plain building that looked more like a warehouse than a government office block. At their first knock, a man in green and brown army fatigues appeared at the door and led them silently down a long corridor to a small room. The walls were a stark white, the only furniture four chairs and a table. A harsh bright light flooded the room. Not a place designed to alleviate anxiety. Then a strict security check was performed by two stern-faced women in black suits, who scared the shit out of her.

Once they had been examined thoroughly, they were shown into a room where ten equally nervous men and women sat waiting. It was obvious that all had military or law enforcement training. As she nervously took a seat, she had wondered why they were so keen to recruit two female performers to this closeted organization. They lacked experience in anything remotely dangerous. In retrospect, she realized that Adriana's uncle wasn't a fool—a singer was the perfect cover in this cloak-and-dagger world.

The eight-hour testing had been so arduous that only six of the twelve applicants went on to the next stage. Surprisingly, both she and Adriana had passed. Physical trials came next: four days of gruelling courses. As they both were natural athletes, they passed with not too much difficulty. Bootcamp training lasted eight weeks, a hectic and taxing regime. Pandora surprised herself by flourishing in the environment. She turned out to be a natural. As well as survival training, martial arts, and weaponry instructions, the director had insisted they continue professional singing lessons.

The sight of Winter standing at the doorway, brought her mind back to the present and she flashed her a smile. She looked younger, more vulnerable with her hair down. Pandora felt a flare of desire and a simultaneous protective twinge. There was no use denying that the woman was getting a hold on her and it was beginning to concern her. The only way to stop the attraction would be to burn it out—she'd never remained interested in a lover after a few weeks. In fact, she was beginning to think she was incapable of sustaining any lasting attachment. Though—and this was worrying her—she'd never been so taken with anyone before. It was a mystery why. Winter had done nothing to try to gain her attention or go out of her way to flirt, yet there was this sense of inevitability that they would be together no matter what.

"Ready to go?" she asked.

Winter nodded, a polite smile on her lips and a faint frown on her brow. "I'm ready."

Pandora stopped and placed a hand on her arm. "You're angry."

"Not angry, more feeling out of place. I'm beginning to think I'm the third wheel."

"You're worried about me and Adriana?" Pandora said, eyeing her incredulously.

"You seem…well…very close."

"Of course we are. I've known her for ten years and she's one of my best friends." Then catching the sceptical look on her face, added, "Nothing more."

Winter raised her eyebrows. "Come on, Pandora. She clearly has a thing for you. It was plain as day from where I was sitting."

"Nonsense," she replied gruffly. "There's nothing between us…you have an overactive imagination."

When Winter just shook her head, Pandora linked their fingers. "No more of this rubbish. Just let's enjoy what's left of the evening together. There's a great café at the end of the next street that serves the best hot chocolate with whipped cream. You wanna have one before we head home?"

Winter squeezed her fingers. "Sounds perfect."

* * *

It was after midnight when Pandora turned into Winter's driveway. When she switched off the ignition, Winter brushed her hand against her arm and murmured, "I had a great time tonight."

Pandora flexed her hand on the steering wheel, feeling suddenly shy. "I did too." Then slightly dizzy with want, she tugged open the car door and followed her up the steps of the house.

As she waited on the front porch for Winter to find her keys, she let her gaze wander over her body: from the flare of her hips, to the swell of her breasts, to finally rest on her face. Winter lifted her head as if aware of the scrutiny, and they stared at each other for a long moment. The look of tenderness in the autumn-brown eyes caused Pandora's breath to hitch. She slowly reached up and cradled her face in her hands, then brushed a gentle kiss on her temple. Ever so lightly, she fanned her breath over her cheekbone, and kissed the tip of her nose before she dropped her head lower to claim Winter's mouth.

Bolts of sensation zigzagged straight to Pandora's chest when their lips touched. With a strangled gasp, Winter buried her fingers into her hair and pulled her in closer to deepen the kiss. Immediately, Pandora dropped her arms around her waist, locking their bodies firmly together. Long fingers began to knead the nape of her neck, sending tingles of pleasure down her spine. A moan escaped from Winter. The sound filled Pandora with a feeling that was at once sweet and wild, and she purred deep in her throat. She slipped her tongue into the wet, warm mouth, her lower body tightening at the feel of the tongue stroking against hers. Then Winter captured her tongue with her mouth, sucking it in and out in a steady seductive rhythm.

Shivery sensations cascaded through Pandora—she felt like a fireball. Lost in a haze of desire, her hands slid up under the blouse and fondled the side of a breast. Encouraged by another breathy groan, she cupped the soft globe and squeezed it lightly. Then through the bra rubbed her thumb over the nipple. It immediately hardened into a small nub. Pandora lowered her head to suck the tender hollow at the bottom of her neck as she began to work down the bra to free Winter's breast.

"You taste so good," she murmured.

"Do I?" whispered Winter with a quiver.

"Like rich dark chocolate and wild strawberries."

A hitching breath escaped from Winter, and her fingernails dug erratically into Pandora's back.

But when Pandora eased her thigh in between her legs, Winter stiffened. It was like flipping a switch—one moment her body was loose and receptive, the next it tensed like a rubber band. Slowly, Winter pulled away with a throaty half sob, half laugh. "Pandora, if we don't stop now, we won't be able to."

At the sudden loss, she reached for her again, then blinked when Winter took another step backward. "Stop?" Pandora asked in a daze.

"I think we should. It was really great tonight, but I don't want to rush into anything. Not until it means something and I really like you a lot."

"Oh, God, you don't know what you do to me."

Averting her gaze, Winter began to tuck her shirt into her jeans. "I'm sorry," she said simply.

Pandora forced a smile, though her whole body was taut as a drum. "Me too." She took a step away awkwardly. "I guess I'd better be going then," she said. She fisted her hands at her side, trying to keep her voice light and not sound too pathetic.

The embarrassment and disappointment must have been evident because Winter looked at her anxiously and said, "You're upset."

"Of course not," she replied, striving to sound gentle but the words seemed to come out sharply. "I don't want you to think I was trying to hurry you into anything."

"No. No. I love that you want me and I found it difficult to stop. But let's go a little slower, enjoy getting to know each other."

"You just make me feel so much."

"Me too. But I've been hurt and I can't help being cautious," Winter murmured and touched her cheek. "Now it's time I said goodnight. Drive home safely and thanks again for the lovely night." Then she turned and disappeared inside the house.

"Goodnight," echoed Pandora, and for a long moment stood dazed, staring at the closed door. What had just happened? Then it sank in—she had been emphatically, albeit nicely, rejected.

Sonofabitch! How could she had been so stupid? What had she expected? That Winter would be agreeable to have sex? She knew that she'd been hurt badly, but it had never entered her head that she wouldn't want to go to bed with her. It should have. Winter was cautious and logical in all the other aspects of her life, so why would her love life be any different?

Despondent, Pandora slouched down the stairs to her car. She was getting out of her depth, she knew. Her feelings for Winter had taken yet another turn tonight. The rush of arousal had been intense, but the overpowering tenderness that had accompanied that rush was a red flag waving frantically at her.

She sighed wearily.

Too late. She was hooked.

CHAPTER SEVENTEEN

Winter pressed against the hallway wall, listening to Pandora's boots thudding down the stairs. Stepping out of the embrace had been hard. As much as she knew emotionally it had been the right thing to do, so much arousal hummed through her body that it was beginning to physically hurt. She'd never been so keyed up. She drew in a shaky breath, trying to get her head around the unfamiliar feelings. What she had felt for Christine when they were first dating wasn't anything like this. That had been sedate, cool, calculated. This was giddy, heady, fierce.

And totally addictive.

As soon as she slipped under the sheets her mind automatically zeroed back over the night. It was clear Pandora had an alter ego—her true personality, she suspected, was the woman who took her out tonight. The lounge singer persona was an act, which probably wasn't unusual in show biz. That was what she was paid to do—go on stage, look gorgeous. But there remained a niggling feeling that this transformation was unusual, the gap too great. Although she still remained feminine, tonight she had been bold and capable. A woman who could kick ass.

One thing she did know—this new Pandora was even more exciting.

She really rocked.

Winter punched the pillow, trying to stop the depressing thoughts. Why did she have to be so damn precious about her feelings? She'd acted like a prude and blown any chance she'd had with her. *Me and my scruples.* Why couldn't she have Jessie's attitude and just have sex because it felt good? Why the hell did she always expect it to mean something more than that? No one else seemed to think like that. Pandora certainly wouldn't. She could have anyone she wanted and wouldn't be used to knockbacks.

The sound of the text alert cut short her gloomy thoughts. Quickly, she rolled to the side to reach for the phone on the bedside table. When she opened the text, she sagged back with relief. Pandora.

I had great time tonight.

With a happy face, she tapped back.

Me too.

A few moments passed, then a reply came.

R we ok???

Yes, of course.

Can I see u again?

Winter hesitated for a sec, then took the plunge.

Want to come with me to a garden party Sunday arvo?

What's it for?

Fundraiser—Children's Hospital. I'm a board member.

Winter waited anxiously until the answer flashed onto the screen.

Love to. Pick you up?

She thought for a moment. A little late would be better if she was bringing a date. Like any closed community, the hospital fraternity loved gossip. They could just slip in unnoticed.

Meet me 2pm at front gate. Botanical gardens.

Dressy?

A bit.

Right. Sleep tight.

With a satisfied sigh, Winter settled under the covers. Asking Pandora to the garden party was a spur-of-the-moment thing and it felt just fine. But on second thoughts, she mused, maybe it wasn't. She'd forgotten Jessie would be there, which would make the date awkward. She'd just have to make it clear Pandora was with her for the afternoon.

"Best of luck with that one," she groaned. "Jessie will be straight on to her like a bear to a honeypot."

* * *

The weather was perfect for an outdoor event—a barmy afternoon with a light breeze blowing under a clear blue sky. When she sighted Pandora waiting outside the gate Winter tidied her hair and straightened her top a little self-consciously. Yesterday, she'd bought a dress with a split up one side especially for the event. Usually her dressy outfits were on the conservative side—what her aunts would describe as "nice." From Pandora's appreciative look, she was pleased she'd splurged out.

Pandora was back in her lounge singer image, dressed in a three-quarter floral form-fitting dress. Her hair was swept up in a chic messy style that accentuated the graceful curve of her neck. She oozed class.

"Hi," Winter said a little bashfully, but any lingering embarrassment faded when she was engulfed in a hug. She sighed happily as she breathed in the fragrant perfume mixed with the enticing essence that was distinctly Pandora.

"You look lovely," Pandora murmured.

"Thank you." Winter smiled, flattered. *Yep, the expensive dress was worth every cent.* She gestured toward the entrance. "Shall we?"

They followed the music to find the garden party in full swing. The air was filled with a sweet grassy bouquet, with a hint of flowers and warm earth. Brightly coloured bunting festooned the lawn which was dotted with tables and chairs under blue and white umbrellas. A marquee was set up with a buffet table laden with food, and a violinist was playing quietly in the background on a small podium. A bevy of young people in crisp black and white uniforms carried drink trays amongst the guests.

Winter swept her gaze around, recognizing most of the people talking in groups: hospital staff, city dignitaries, and sponsors who had donated to the building fund. As her firm was their financial and legal advisor, they had a place on the Board and she had been relegated the position. Not that she had particularly wanted it, but it came with the youngest partner's territory.

Before they could get a drink, she was immediately claimed by the Chairman of the Board. Terrance Baker was an accountant of a city firm, a stooped ponderous man in his mid-sixties. Earnest and knowledgeable, he dominated any conversation. Or, as Winter's mother would have said, he "liked the sound of his own voice." Caught, she smiled resignedly and introduced Pandora. After a few minutes of listening to his lecture about the share market, Pandora excused herself to look for a drink. Winter looked longingly at her back as she wandered off, then forced herself to carry on with the conversation pleasantly. Or rather, made small observations when he paused for breath.

Eventually she was rescued by her good friend, Fay Cooper, an orthopaedic specialist. A lively woman in her late forties, Fay was a fellow Board member and a thorn in the side of the Chairman. "Winter. Just the person I want to see. You won't mind if I whisk her away will you, Terrance?" Not waiting for his answer, Fay took her firmly by the arm and bustled her to a quiet spot out of his earshot.

Winter smiled at her with delight. "I owe you one."

"He can be such a dreadful bore. He had me cornered for ages when I arrived," Fay replied, with a twinkle.

"I always find it difficult getting away from him. He has such a thick skin," Winter said, looking around idly. "There are the usual 'who's who' here. Anyone new?"

"A few. The local pollie who won the by-election. Smooth type. That's him over there in the grey suit with the polka dot tie. Then there's the author who wrote that book about the drug trade...she's that earnest-looking woman in the blue slacks and short blond hair at the buffet. And I believe the press will be here shortly to interview the hospital hierarchy about the proposed new wing. The rest are the same old ones." She tilted her head, peeping at her with a distinct gleam in her eyes. "Now tell me what is going on with you. Who is that lovely lady you brought with you? Are you finally dating again?"

"She's just a friend."

"Ah...but a *very* good friend, I'd say. You look blooming. And that dress. Wow!"

"Oh, hush up, Fay. We haven't known each other long, but we get on well. She's smart and good company," Winter said, then cast her eyes around to find Pandora. Her mood soured somewhat when she saw her chatting with Jessie and a group of the hospital staff by the side of the marquee. "Come and I'll introduce you," she said, inclining her head in their direction.

"Then let's go," said Fay with a chuckle. "I wouldn't leave her too long with Jessie Drummond if I were you."

Winter chose to ignore the comment, but silently agreed. Jessie was leaning into Pandora far too closely for comfort. Quashing the niggle of jealousy, she took a glass of wine from the waiter who appeared beside them, then walked off through the crowd. It was slow progress, saying the necessary quick hellos as they moved through the press of people. Nearly there, she could see one of the hospital's most influential patrons, Ellen Jamieson-Ford, approaching directly toward her and quickly side-stepped behind a group sitting under an umbrella.

A chuckle from Fay echoed in her ear. "Skilfully done, my dear. You've perfected the art of avoidance."

"She might be a big donor, but I don't like the woman."

"I don't imagine you do," replied Fay with a gleam of sympathy. "Not with her views on same-sex relationships. Though she has been quieter since her daughter Lindsey married a woman."

"Couldn't have happened to a better person. But let's don't waste any more time even discussing her. Bigots make their own bed to lie in," Winter growled as she crossed over to Jessie's group.

The look of tender warmth on Pandora's face made Winter feel a little dizzy. She answered with a ghost of a smile before she waved a hand. "Hi everyone."

"Hey. You too, Fay. You're both looking very smart," Jessie said, giving Winter's low cleavage a raised eyebrow.

Fay gave a soft laugh. "Very smooth as always, Jessie."

"Where's your better half?"

"Alan took the boys to the footy. This isn't his scene."

"Right. Then let's get you a drink," announced Jessie, regarding the small woman with amusement. "It's about time you let your hair down, Cooper."

"Ha. You wish. But I will have a glass of that champagne," she said drolly. Immediately Jessie signalled to one the waiters who was hovering nearby.

Winter cleared her throat. "Fay, I'd like you to meet a friend of mine. This is Pandora."

"Hello," Fay said, looking at her speculatively. Winter wrinkled her nose. Could she be any more obvious?

With a smile, Pandora raised her glass.

"Since we're doing introductions, I'd like you to meet Veronica Randall, Winter," Jessie interrupted. "She's the anaesthetist I told you about."

A curvy woman with jet black hair and olive skin that set off her green eyes, stepped forward with a smile. She looked of Mediterranean descent, with a wide mouth, small straight nose and full face—more intriguing than pretty. "Lovely to meet you, Winter. Jessie has been singing your praises," she said, her voice low with a slight lilt.

"Jessie's always inclined to exaggerate. You'll learn, Veronica, she's quite the bullshit artist," said Winter dryly.

Fay gave a chuckle. "She's got your measure, Jessie. Now what say we get something to eat and find some seats. I'd like to get off my feet."

Low murmurs of agreement followed that proposal, and after commandeering a large table, they adjourned to the buffet.

Winter wandered off to the toilet first, and when she arrived back with her plate, found the seat left for her was between Fay and Veronica. She flashed a glance at Pandora who gave her a shrug of apology. Fay, looking uncomfortable, muttered, "Sorry," as she settled into the chair.

Winter fumed. *Damn!* She'd been outmanoeuvred by Jessie yet again.

She forced a pleasant smile and began to eat while the two women engaged her in lively conversation. Veronica turned out to be fun and Fay had a sharp wit. Every so often though, Winter couldn't help flashing a quick glance at Pandora. Most of the time, she had her head down, intent on what Jessie was saying. But there were a couple of moments she caught her eye, which made her heart flip-flop. Maybe it was her imagination, but she looked just as wistful as Winter felt.

Then three male medical residents joined the party. One, a buff guy in a smart sports coat, spent the next half an hour trying to get Pandora's attention away from Jessie. Pandora didn't look fazed in the slightest, handling them both with ease and amusement. Winter stifled the pangs of jealousy, having to be content that Pandora threw her a fleeting smile every so often. But then as she watched, the truth set in with a jolt. What she was experiencing now wasn't exactly jealousy, more possessiveness. When had her feelings taken this turn?

Shit! This had heartbreak written all over it.

She pulled herself together and concentrated on what Veronica was saying. Plenty of time later to obsess, worry, overthink.

As time passed and more champagne was consumed, jokes began to fly around the table. Winter sat back quietly, letting the comedians hold the floor. Fay was a natural. Her wisecrack about her mother-in-law elicited a wave of giggles, and when she went on to relate a story about her family at Christmas, the punchline brought roars of laughter around the table.

Winter chuckled. "You can pick your friends—"

"But not your relations," someone behind her interrupted. "How is your mother, Winter?"

She froze at the voice. *This can't be happening!*

But it was—she couldn't mistake that perfume wafting over her shoulder. Her entire body began to clench in a combination of horror and embarrassment. The group fell into sudden silence. Conscious she had suddenly become the centre of attention, she couldn't help flicking a glance round the table. All eyes were locked on her. Those who knew her story looked sympathetic, but Jessie was frowning angrily. Pandora had an odd look on her face that she couldn't read.

Winter's composure scattered like leaves in the wind. Her legs began to tremble and she pressed her hands down on the top of her thighs for control. Very slowly, she rose to her feet and turned to face the woman who stood watching her with hooded eyes.

"Hello, Chris. What on earth are you doing here?"

CHAPTER EIGHTEEN

As usual, Christine Dumont looked elegant and self-assured, a woman completely in control. "We're running a segment about the proposed new wing," she said in her distinctive well-modulated accent. A voice that had made the TV presenter a household name. A voice that Winter had once admired, but now only grated.

Then Christine did something that surprised her. She began toying with a strand of hair. The gesture was all too familiar. It meant she was nervous. For a fleeting moment, Winter wondered why she should be, then wondered why she even cared. The woman meant nothing to her now. It was strange that she had always dreaded the moment she'd meet her again, but now she had, she felt absolutely nothing. A blank. Not even anger. It was as if any emotion she had ever felt for Christine had been expunged with a scrubbing brush.

"Ah…yes. I'd forgotten about that. The hospital will be pleased with the publicity. Sponsors are becoming harder to attract," she said distractedly.

Christine made an impatient clicking sound with her tongue. "Always the money maker, Winter. That hasn't changed. I didn't come over to talk about fundraising, I came to say hello and see how you were going." She swept her eyes around the table and gave an off-handed wave. "Hi, folks." Then turned back to Winter with pursed lips. "Perhaps we should move somewhere else to continue this in private."

Winter's initial reaction was to tell her to get lost, that she wasn't interested in talking, but she knew Christine wouldn't take no for an answer. And she had no intention of becoming public gossip ever again. With a frown to make her irritation plain, she agreed. "Okay. There's a bench over to the right under the trees."

They moved off, Winter trailing a little behind as usual. Things hadn't changed. When Christine sank down, she did so as always, with effortless grace. Watching her closely now though, it was evident that in the nearly three years, she had aged. Even her carefully applied makeup couldn't disguise that. She looked—for a better word—a little used. Winter wondered if this came from the vodka bottle rather than time.

"Well, I have to say you look very well. You've clearly moved on with your life," Christine said as she eyed her closely.

"I'm happy. And even after what you did, I hope you are too. It doesn't do anyone any good to hold a grudge. I've learnt that for my peace of mind."

Christine turned her body round to face her and peered at her intently. "Do you ever miss what we had together? There were a lot of good times."

"Are you serious? We barely spoke to each other without fighting the last couple of years. And what happened in the bungalow can't be undone…it wrecked whatever good memories we had. It took me a while, but I've moved on with my life. Now that's all it is: the past. So…to answer your question…I don't miss it, in fact I don't even think about it anymore."

"You wouldn't want to give it another try?"

The way she was watching her like a lion ready to pounce, made the hairs on Winter's neck twitch upright. Was the woman actually suggesting they get back together? "No. I definitely wouldn't," she muttered.

Christine spread her arm over the back of the seat and leaned in closer. "I've learnt my lesson, honey. I want you back. Why don't we go out to dinner…see what happens? We won't rush it."

Winter stared at her. *Unfuckingbelievable!*

With a reflex action, she moved further forward until she could barely keep her balance on the bench. "I'm not interested. Haven't you been listening to what I've been saying?"

Christine crowded her head closer until she could feel her breath on her cheek. "Come on. All I'm asking for is a chance. One date. You name the place."

Winter flinched. She knew full well that tone of voice—it always preceded an argument. Was Christine going to make a public scene? Surely not. She took a deep breath and forced herself to speak in a low calm voice. "No. Now I'm going back to my friends."

Christine's hand dropped onto Winter's shoulder. "We should—"

"Hey, babe. They're taking photos and they want one of us," Pandora's voice echoed above them.

Winter nearly wept with relief. It took all her willpower not to jump up and kiss her. She swelled with emotion and said huskily, "Hi, sweetheart. We've finished here, but before we go, meet my…um…ex, Christine Dumont."

Christine sat stock still, staring at them incredulously.

Pandora edged down onto the seat. "We already met at the Silver Fox four months ago. Hello there, Christine," she said pleasantly, then circled Winter's waist and pulled her until their bodies were pressed together. The hand was hastily removed from the shoulder.

Taken aback, Winter exclaimed, "You know her?"

"I joined her party for drinks one night after I finished my act."

"I was there with my crew after a shoot," said Christine curtly. Winter wondered why she had paled.

"I hadn't realized you'd met," Winter said a little grumpily, feeling like she'd been broadsided.

"You know entertaining guests is my usual routine," said Pandora soothingly. "Though I think I left earlier than I had planned to that night. Christine may remember why."

Ignoring the remark, Christine looked directly at Winter. "How long have you two been an item?"

"Long enough to know what a treasure I have," Pandora cut in.

"Really?" Christine stared at her with dislike and said with a tinkling laugh. "I would never have described Winter quite like that. But then again, taken literally…"

Winter bristled. "What's that supposed to mean?"

"Your greatest attribute has always been your ability to make money. A veritable treasure trove."

"You should know. You spent enough of it."

Another brittle laugh came. "And you were certainly counting."

"Go to hell," Winter said quietly.

Pandora abruptly rose from the bench and stretched out her hand for Winter. "Shall we? The others are waiting."

Winter looked up at her, a lump in her throat. She took the proffered hand, feeling the warmth against her palm. Firm, safe. Quickly she ducked her head, desperate to hide welling tears. Pandora gave her hand a comforting squeeze and moved off. Before she followed, Winter took a deep breath and turned to look down with dislike, and a smidgeon of pity, at the woman who once shared her life. "Goodbye, Chris. I hope you find what you're looking for," she muttered, then hurried off quickly before she could reply. She had no wish to prolong the contact or see the woman again.

Instead of going straight back to the table, Pandora led her to the back of a large bush on the perimeter of the lawn. "I think we should have a quick word before we go back."

"I know that was gross for you, and I'm sorry. But I'm eternally grateful you came over."

"No...no. That's not what I wanted to talk about. I intervened because I could see you needed support."

"She wanted me to go on a date with her. Can you believe it?"

Pandora narrowed her eyes. "She wanted to get together with you again?"

"Yes, and I have no idea why. But what Christine wants, she expects to have. She can turn nasty if she doesn't get her own way," Winter said, shivering with misery as she remembered.

"She bullied you?"

"She likes to manipulate people. I was constantly criticized, particularly when I tried to curb her spending. I'm not mean, but she was going through my money like water. I was never much good at handling her mood swings...I hate confrontation which makes me weak I guess."

"Don't make excuses for her. You were a victim. Plain and simple. You're well rid of her."

"I know," she replied, but couldn't help wondering what Pandora's real views were on her failed relationship. Underneath, she probably thought she lacked guts. She couldn't imagine Pandora taking shit from anyone—she seemed so in control. With an effort, Winter pulled herself together and asked, "What was it you wanted to talk about?"

Pandora rubbed the back of her neck and cleared her throat. "Well...I presume some of the people here will be invited to your party."

Winter nodded, silently waiting.

"Then it probably would be wise if I pretended to like Jessie, considering our plan is for us to be a couple when we come next Sunday. It's going to look strange if you and I go home together, then I turn up holding her hand."

Ouch! So much for her date.

It made sense of course—she hadn't thought it through. She had forgotten all about Michael and his damn obsession. It was a pity his mother had spoilt him rotten, she snarled to herself. But venting her anger did nothing to erase the sinking feeling that Pandora had lost interest in her. Her drama with Christine would frighten anyone off, and Jessie had had all afternoon to weave her charms. Winter swallowed hard, suddenly finding it difficult to speak. "You're right. I don't know what I was thinking when I asked you today. It was a spur-of-the-moment thing…a brain hiccup." Then added after a pause. "Maybe I should pay more attention to Veronica as well."

"If you want to, but it won't be necessary," Pandora said with a stiff shrug.

Winter forced out a chuckle. "It wouldn't be a hardship. She's actually good value, loads of fun and really nice. Jessie said she's not dating anyone at the moment."

"Let's get back then," Pandora said gruffly.

Winter followed her to the table and took her seat without a word. Fay handed her a glass of wine. "Here. You look like you need this."

"Thanks," she said gratefully, though didn't elaborate.

A phone ringing suddenly pierced the air. Fay rose quickly. "Excuse me for a second. I've been expecting a call."

Winter took a gulp of wine as she watched her go. Then turned around when Veronica asked with concern, "Is everything all right?"

She mustered a smile. "I'm fine. Just a bit shaken. The woman I was talking to was my ex and we parted under not so pleasant circumstances."

"You were with Christine Dumont?"

"For five years. We parted nearly three years ago."

Veronica patted her arm. "I know what it's like. My breakup was different…not acrimonious…but it hurt badly when it was over. Joanne was a violinist in the London Symphony Orchestra and we met when I was doing my post grad in the UK. I stayed for two more years after I graduated to be with her, but I was committed to come back to Australia. Her career would have stalled over here, so she wouldn't come with me. What we had together gradually fell to pieces when I returned. It was impossible with the distance to maintain the connection."

Winter's heart went out to the woman. It was one thing for a dysfunctional relationship to break up, but infinitely more tragic if circumstances forced you apart. "I'm so sorry," she murmured.

"Don't be. It was, like you, around three years ago when we called it quits. Time does heal wounds. I'm ready to move forward now." She looked pensive for a moment, then added with a sad smile, "In retrospect, I have come to realize we both didn't try hard enough. Neither Joanne nor I were prepared to put our careers second."

"You'll never rekindle your romance?"

"No. She's found someone else. Someone more suited to her lifestyle…a musician."

There was a moment's awkwardness before Winter spoke. "Looking back, although Chris and I had bigger problems, I was guilty of putting my work first as well."

"I won't be making that mistake again. Now enough of being maudlin," said Veronica. "I have a question, which I'd very much like an answer to. Are you dating Pandora?"

Winter cleared her throat, feeling slightly sick at the dilemma she faced. How she hated being put on the spot. But there was only one way she could reply. "No. She's just a good friend. Jessie is probably more her style." She took a gulp of her wine at the pleased expression on Veronica's face. Christ, she felt like a Judas.

"I'm very happy to hear that. Would you care to join me for lunch on Thursday? I've only patients booked in the morning."

"I'd like that." She looked at Veronica curiously. "You and Jessie must see each other all the time. You've never been interested?"

Fay, just back from her phone call, answered her query with a chuckle. "No one in their right mind at the hospital would get tangled up with her. She has no idea what fidelity means. I doubt if she can even spell the word."

Winter suddenly felt an overwhelming urge to defend Jessie. Though what was said was true, it was also incredibly sad that her reputation had reached this level. "She just likes a good time, Fay. Prefers to keep her life uncomplicated and she's a kind, caring person. In fact, truth be known, she's probably the happiest of the lot of us."

"Sorry. I forgot you were great friends. That remark was out of line," Fay said with a wry smile.

"No," said Winter with a sigh. "It's me who should apologise. I didn't mean to snap at you. I just worry about Jessie sometimes. She really needs someone in her life."

Fay looked over to the other end of the table thoughtfully. "Maybe Pandora might be the one. Jessie's different with her, more...I don't know...more attentive than usual. Not so full of herself. What do you think?"

Although it was the last thing she wanted to comment on, Winter pretended to study the two interacting. It tore at her insides watching them laughing together. Then as soon as she could, she averted her gaze. "Perhaps. We'll just have to wait and see. Now I think the speeches are about due to start."

"Who are the speakers?" asked Veronica.

"The CEO will outline the planned new wing, and then the Chairman is saying a few words," replied Winter.

Fay let out a snort. "Only a few? That'll be a first."

Winter chuckled. "No doubt he will be riveting."

The last word was soon out of her mouth when the PA system blasted over the grounds, introducing official party. Three quarters of an hour later with the formal part of the afternoon over, Christine and her cameraman could be seen interviewing Terrance. Winter hoped he'd bore her to death.

The crowd began to drift off home and Winter issued an invitation to everyone at the table to her party as they rose to go. Only then did Pandora appear at her side. "Will you be all right finding a cab?" she asked. "I'm going to head off with Jessie."

"Alan's picking me up. He'll drive Winter and Veronica home," Fay called out.

"Then I'll see you all next Sunday."

"Bye," Winter said with a fixed smile. She watched her walk back to Jessie, wondering how the afternoon could go so ass-up so quickly.

And why, amongst friends, did she feel so very alone?

CHAPTER NINETEEN

Her boxing gloves curled into fists, Pandora pounded the heavy cylindrical punching bag that dangled from the ceiling by three chains. The black leather had seen better days, battered shiny and thin by the constant abuse.

Jab, hook, uppercut—pause—jab, hook, uppercut—

She had done this routinely for years. Today it meant something. Too many damn thoughts, too many damn feelings. Whenever they crept back into her head, she hit harder.

Whack—Destroy—Whack—Defeat.

Simple and repetitive—no time to think, to dwell. Her bunched muscles began to burn as she continued to punch with methodical blows. She embraced the pain as the jolting impacts shocked up her arms and down her legs. It seared everything out of her brain. Perspiration trickled over her face, dribbled down her neck, stained the tank top under her arms. She paused only to swipe her forearm over her face before moving on to the speed bag. After a long flurry of punches, she finally took notice of her aching body and eased back.

Exhausted, she slid down onto the hard floor against the wall and pulled off the gloves. As she took a long drink of water, she took stock of the room. It was filled with basic equipment: punching bags, free-weight benches, dumbbells, floor mats for the kickboxers and martial arts and a small boxing spar ring in the far corner. Built down by the docks in the 1930s, O'Hara's was one of the few genuine historic gyms left in the city. It had produced three welterweight and two featherweight Australian champions, but those days had long gone. For years now, any boxer with potential was snaffled up by more modern, wealthier clubs.

Ten in the morning, the place was nearly full, noisy with the thud of fists on punching bags. She could feel the testosterone bouncing off the walls. The air smelt musty, tinged with the acrid odours of stale sweat, menthol and seawater. Three women in Ts and shorts were on the free-weight benches against the wall—toned tough women who knew how to take care of themselves. The rest were male, most heavily muscled, some shirtless. Though it was a far cry from the trendy health and fitness clubs popular in the city, the gym was exactly what she wanted. Private, safe, and anonymous.

She had registered herself simply as Dora. No one asked questions here.

"You practising to fight some bastard, slugger?"

She looked up at the man above her and gave a noncommittal shrug. "Nah, Ray, just working off a few frustrations."

"Right. Take ten minutes, then I'll put you through your kick-boxing paces. Half speed, no full blows today. The mood you're in, I prefer all my parts to be intact when we finish. We'll work on your technique."

"Okay," Pandora said with a wry chuckle. As if she'd be able to get anywhere near him. Ray was owner and chief instructor of the gym, a very fit bear of a man who had nearly made it to the heavyweight titles in '95. His father had owned the gym before him, and his father before that.

She finished off the water bottle, then flexed her fingers. They were sore and a little bruised. Serve her right for letting her emotions to override her good sense. To allow her personal feelings distract her from her work was serious. Once undercover, she needed all her wits about her—the people she was dealing with were dangerous.

But she couldn't get Winter out of her mind. She should never have accepted the date to the garden party—neither of them had thought it through. It had only made the simmering attraction worse. First, she had to fight back the urge to give Christine Dumont a tongue lashing, then had no option but to sit with Jessie, while Veronica chatted up her date all afternoon. And then they had gone home together in the same car.

But what really hurt—and completely ticked her off—was when she texted Winter asking her to lunch, she had replied that she already had a luncheon date with Veronica.

A booming voice interrupted and she filed the thoughts away for later. "I'm ready when you are, Dora."

She looked over at Ray who stood waiting with crossed arms at the kickboxing square. "Right," she said, and with a heave, climbed to her feet.

At the edge of the foam floor mat, she flexed her muscles and prepared to vent more of her anger. They sparred at half speed for several minutes, then she shot a swift kick at his abdomen which he just barely deflected. A follow-up punch and another snapped kick, and he took a more cautious stance. Noting the defensive body position, she began a barrage of attacking moves with a combination of kicks and punches. When he began to puff, she applied more pressure relentlessly. She shoved hard and went for a chin shot. When he countered, she gave an extra burst of speed and tensed her body, ready to launch at his torso.

The next was a blur. With a swift lunge, he grasped her arm, swept her off her feet and it was all over. She was on the floor, pinned under him with her face pressed hard into the mat.

Crap! She'd walked into that one.

"Slap the mat and I'll let you up," he ground out into her ear.

Resigned, she gave it a tap with the palm of her free hand. The other was pinned awkwardly beneath her.

Surprisingly, he wasn't angry, more solemn when they got to their feet. "You okay?" he asked.

She nodded. Her pride was hurt, but that didn't count in a place like this.

"Good. You behaved like a bloody amateur today. You fought with your temper, not your brain. Haven't you been listening to me all these months. Stay in control. If you're angry, you'll have to channel it properly or you'll get yourself killed." She must have looked as dejected as she felt, because he continued in a kinder voice. "That's enough for today. Get yourself cleaned up, then buy yourself a long cold beer. Whatever's got you so frigging worked up will look better in an amber glass than a sparring ring."

She laughed, the ball of tension dissolving away. "That's probably the best advice I've had for years."

* * *

For a Saturday night, the Silver Fox was much quieter than normal. The River Fire celebrations and the fireworks extravaganza were the main attractions in the city tonight. Absently, Pandora gazed across the tables, not concentrating much on her songs. She'd performed them so often, she could have sung them in her sleep. Her act had become too routine, too predictable to keep her interest. She'd be so relieved when this assignment was finally over. Quite frankly, she was sick of playing Pandora the Siren. She really didn't know how women liked the life. She had wanted to be a singer, but not on these terms. Being a pinup babe didn't equate to talent.

But most of all, she was bored with the bar scene. Though most faces changed, the behaviour didn't. With no dance floor, they either came to the club to drink, to see the floorshow or to meet someone. She had become adept at recognizing those who wanted a fun night out, the serious drinkers, and those who trolled for sex.

Only a certain clientele were regulars at the Fox: those who could afford to pay for the overpriced drinks. Because of the floor show and its upmarket setting, the club was usually filled with people socializing in a crowd or celebrating an occasion. They were Yuri's bread-and-butter customers, and she normally stayed with these partygoers for a while after the show. It was all in the "club experience" for them. And they were the ones who spent the most at the bar, usually sloshed by closing time.

Tonight, there were no loud revellers. The tables were filled with small groups of older patrons who sat and applauded quietly. Lawrence Partridge, sitting with two men, was staring at her while she sang. Pandora ignored his attempts to get her attention. She'd only seen him in the place once after his run-in with Winter, and, thankfully, the flowers had stopped. She'd hoped he'd disappeared for good, but no such luck. Here he was tonight, back like a bad penny.

Halfway through her last bracket, her gaze fell on a couple sitting in a small shaded table in the far corner. If she hadn't been so bored, she wouldn't have paid them any attention. There was nothing unusual about them: he wore a dark grey suit with a white shirt, no tie, while the woman was dressed in a blue dress with a high neckline. Both appeared to be in their fifties. But as her eyes idly passed over them, something stirred in the back of her mind. He looked familiar, though she was sure he hadn't been at the club before. She snuck another glance a few minutes later and then it came to her. His photo had been in the original pile from Interpol.

Michael hadn't appeared. In fact, there weren't any young people at the tables or bar. Very strange. The hairs twitched at the back of her neck and she snapped into cautious mode. Something was definitely going on. Before she came on, Yuri had appeared in her dressing room, insisting she was due for an early night and to go home straight after her performance. What had seemed like concern for her welfare, now took on a different light. He wanted her gone.

As nonchalantly as she could, Pandora smiled at the audience as she furtively began to study each person. Her attention immediately focused on a tall silver-haired woman at the bar. Another person of interest. Hilda something-or-other from

Brussels—the last name escaped her. She moved on quickly. By the time she'd finished, she'd recognised at least eight people from both photo folders.

Her pulse pounded. Something was definitely going down tonight and she had to get a message to Adriana. They needed to get a surveillance crew outside ASAP. It took all her willpower to relax through the rest of her performance.

When she finished her last note, she replaced the mike on the stand and as she waved to acknowledge the applause, a cold feeling crept up her spine. Where the ambient gleam from the ceiling lights had been inviting and intimate, it now seemed chilly and grey. Spooked, Pandora leaned over to Kurt with a whispered, "I'm off, now. I'll be fine getting home."

She turned immediately to walk backstage to her dressing room. She didn't hurry, conscious her movements were being recorded. And there would be surveillance cameras in her dressing room. If the Russians had tightened their security, then her every move would be recorded there too.

With a straight face, she stripped off her clothes and forced herself to stretch upright before tugging on her jeans and sweatshirt. She could just imagine some creepy lowlife salivating over her naked body as he watched the video. But she couldn't afford to have her disguise compromised. She put it out of her mind, tidying the room as she always did, before exiting via the back door. Keeping to her routine was essential.

Kurt was waiting outside in the alley when she appeared. "I'll walk you to the street," he said with a fatherly pat on the arm.

Gratefully, she walked out with him. Then was heartily sorry she'd hadn't taken up his offer to accompany her right home. The two blocks to her apartment felt like four as she walked briskly along the shadowy footpaths.

When at last home, Pandora closed the door, leaned back against it and let out a long puff of breath. She needed to maintain her cool. So far, Yuri wasn't suspicious of her and she had to keep it that way. Thankfully, she didn't have to return until Tuesday.

Without pausing, she immediately took out her phone to text Adriana. Five minutes later, her coded message was sent and her job for the night finished. She was only there to observe and report—the rest of the unit took care of it from there on. The captain would send in a squad to stake out the club tonight. With the information, the net would close tighter around the Russian syndicate. When arrests were made, there had to be enough evidence for a conviction.

She made herself a cup of coffee, wishing she had someone with whom to talk things over. When the police went in, Pandora the lounge singer would have quietly disappeared. Any hope she could stay in Brisbane was only a pipe dream. They'd alter her appearance and send her on a long holiday overseas. Her next assignment would be somewhere far away.

She put the events at the club out of her mind to concentrate on the plan tomorrow. She wasn't relishing meeting Winter's family. It was probably going to be far more stressful than the Silver Fox tonight. At least there she had done what she had been trained for. The party was a complete unknown—she hadn't a clue what might happen. On paper, it all sounded fine, but best laid plans were known to crash.

Then there was the added problem of being Jessie's pretend girlfriend. It wasn't looking as straightforward as when Winter had first made the plan. The signs were quite clear now that Jessie viewed Pandora as more than a casual flirtation. She had become a little too attentive. Underneath the swaggering good-time-girl façade, she was a very sensitive woman who was likely to get hurt in the subterfuge.

Plus, there was the fact that Pandora had a thing for Winter, who had just had lunch with the very eligible Veronica. And not forgetting Michael, who had a giant crush on her, nor his mother who thought Pandora was a harpy cougar.

Fuck!

It was beginning to sound like a second-rate soap opera.

CHAPTER TWENTY

A persistent buzzing dragged Winter out of another heated Pandora dream. Knowing there was no ignoring the infernal alarm, she groped at the nightstand until she located the phone. Squinting at the screen, she groaned when she saw it was Gussie. Before she answered, she coughed a few times, trying to clear her throat of the effects of her erotic dream.

"Hello," she said huskily.

"Did I wake you up, Winter?"

Winter peered again at the screen. 7:00. Of course, she damn well did. Saturday was her chance for a sleep in and her aunt knew it. "No…no. I was just getting up. What can I do for you?"

"I'd like to go through what you've planned for the party." Her tone had slipped from casual to businesslike.

"It's all under control. There's no need for you to do anything."

"You know I hate surprises."

"I've organized the salads and sweets from a caterer, and Dad has offered to do the barbeque. I've hired tables and chairs and decoration lights, which the hire place will set up. All you have to do is come along."

There was a pregnant pause at the end of the phone, then a clipped reply came, "That's not what I was referring to, as you well know. Have you organized the other business?"

Winter clenched her jaw. "I have."

"And?"

"It's all taken care of. Pandora will be coming with a date."

"Who is it?"

"Someone suitable," Winter replied vaguely.

"Humph. I hope he's her age and plays his part properly. Being an actress, *she* won't have any trouble."

Winter just shook her head and bit back the grumble of frustration. It served no purpose in pointing out that Pandora was a singer, not an actor. Her aunt in protective mother mode was deaf to everything. "Don't worry. Once Michael sees them together, he'll know he hasn't a chance with her."

"You better be right. But just to be on the safe side, I've organized for the son of a friend of mine to come along as well. He's apparently quite a catch."

Winter shot up straight in the bed. What the hell was Gussie thinking? The last thing they wanted was some blind date pursuing Pandora as well. "You've done *what*? I told you I was organizing it," she snapped into the phone.

"There's no need for that tone of voice, Winter. I thought it best to have all our bases covered."

"You're just complicating things."

"Nonsense."

"What does this guy do?"

"He's a musician in a band, so they'll have plenty in common. He's around her age, so she won't have to cradle snatch," Gussie replied.

Winter ignored the dig. "Just make sure he doesn't get in the way. Pandora won't be interested in him, so I suppose it won't do any harm if he comes along."

"I wouldn't be too sure of that. Tracey said he's hot...her words not mine. Now, I'll let you go and I'll see you tonight," Gussie said cheerily and with a touch of finality.

"Goodbye," Winter said testily. As if her cousin was an authority on men. What was her aunt thinking? Crossly, she threw the phone on the bed. But then she chuckled when she visualized Gussie's reaction to Pandora holding hands with Jessie. She wouldn't have seen that one coming. So much for the spunky musician.

Her mood improved, she slipped through the shower and headed for the kitchen. With a bowl of muesli and fruit, she retired to her study for a few hours on her portfolios. The party supplies were ordered, so all she had to do was wait for everything to arrive. Unlike most people, work was a therapeutic way for her to relax. However, as much as she tried to concentrate, her mind kept wandering.

Frowning, she drummed her fingers on the desktop in a jittery tattoo. Lines were beginning to blur—she was having difficulty separating her professional life from her personal one. Something that had never happened before. For the entire week she had tried to focus on work, but every so often, numbers and words morphed into body parts that entwined in the most delightful ways.

An hour later she gave up, powered down the computer, and after making herself a cup of coffee, wandered out onto the patio.

As soon as she stretched out on a reclining chair, Jinx appeared. Meowing loudly, he rubbed himself against her leg, refusing to be ignored. With a little smile she gave in, picked him up and cradled him in her arms. When she tickled him under his ear, she was rewarded with a string of contented purrs. Then he sprawled across her and promptly shut his eyes. She gazed down at him fondly—there was something about the way he took possession of her lap that brought everything into perspective. He didn't wait to be invited, he simply went ahead and claimed his space.

So—maybe instead of sitting back daydreaming about Pandora, she should follow his lead and give her a ring.

They hadn't been in contact after she'd asked Winter out to lunch, an invitation she had hated to refuse. She'd teed up with Veronica to have lunch in the city that day—just her luck. Her mind wandered back to that date. The anaesthetist had proved to be a pleasant dining companion: bright, interesting, and easygoing. As well as a charming woman, she was professional, capable, and smart. They had got on like a house on fire, parting with a promise to get together again. And it would be nice to have her as a friend to have a meal with occasionally.

She rubbed her thumb restlessly over the rim of her cup. She couldn't ignore the fact that Veronica, with her light-hearted flirting and fleeting touches, had made it obvious she wanted more than friendship. Winter, though, hadn't felt even a smidgeon of attraction. Why she couldn't fathom. Veronica was the exact type of woman she'd always liked. Another professional woman committed to her career.

Winter took a gulp of coffee, knowing she needed to ask herself the question she should have addressed years ago. Was that preference simply to fit into her lifestyle? To remain in her comfort zone?

In her heart of hearts she knew that it was. It was no use denying it any longer. She had always been afraid of letting go, of losing control. She never leaped until she had somewhere to land. And always the job—her secure haven. The thought of letting herself go completely, to be vulnerable without a safety net, was utterly terrifying.

The uncomfortable truth made her squirm. What she felt for Pandora wasn't safe or controlled. She wanted to rip the woman's clothes off and whisk her off to bed. Regardless of the consequences.

Good God! What is happening to me? When have I become so sexual?

Winter clenched her jaw against a fresh surge of awareness—her feelings were way past the interest stage. She had become smitten with the woman.

Yeah, right. Join the queue.

Her head a mess of conflicting thoughts, she dug her phone out of her pocket and tapped in the number before she could change her mind. When "Hello" sounded in her ear, her stomach gave an involuntary lurch.

"Hey, Pandora. I just thought I'd touch base before tonight. Everything's prepared on my end. All my family are coming, including some of the cousins I haven't seen for yonks. According to my mother, no one intends to miss the only party I've thrown for years. So much for a small crowd. I..." She trailed off awkwardly. Damn, she must sound like a jabbering idiot.

A soft laugh came. "Hi, Winter."

"Oh. Sorry, I'm babbling. I actually just rang to say hello."

"I'm glad you did. I missed you this week."

"You did?"

"I've been thinking about you."

Warmth spread over Winter and her toes curled. "Me too. I'm sorry I couldn't have lunch with you the other day."

"How was Veronica?"

"She's nice. Really good company and we have a lot in common. Um...how did you go with Jessie after the garden party." Winter gulped. Damn—why did she blurt that out? She had foot-and-mouth disease today. What Pandora did with Jessie was their affair.

"We went to a fantastic steak house for dinner. Best fillet steak I've had for years."

Winter's heart sank. Wining and dining her dates at the top restaurants, was a true-and-tried seduction ploy for Jessie. Swallowing her resentment, she said brightly, "You're making my mouth water. Jessie always knows the best places to eat. And it was...um...good practice for you two for tonight."

Pandora laughed. "Jessie doesn't need any practice."

At that, Winter could only manage a morose, "No, she doesn't. She can get anyone she wants."

"Not everyone," said Pandora a little sharply. "Now, let's forget about Jessie and talk about you. Tell me about you and your family."

"I'm not particularly interesting. I'm an only child, but with plenty of cousins. Mum's mother is still alive...eighty-eight this year. My father owns an electrical store and my mother's a financial adviser for a superannuation fund. They're talking about going on a three-month holiday next year."

"Where to?"

"The UK first..." Winter sank back in the chair, languidly stroking the soft black fur in a slow steady rhythm as they talked.

Time flew by as they went from one topic to another easily, like old friends. Winter had never meshed quite so comfortably with anyone before—Pandora seemed to understand her. And she couldn't help comparing her to Christine, who had been only prepared to talk about things that interested *her*. And as they talked, it reiterated the feeling she'd already formed, that Pandora's real self was far removed from the glamorous temptress she portrayed on-stage.

It was only the sound of a truck pulling up outside that she thought to look at her watch. With a shock, she saw they had been talking for nearly an hour and a half. Regretfully, she wrapped it up. "I'll have to go, Pandora. The crew are here with the tables and chairs. They're stringing up some decorations for me as well."

"Then I guess that's my cue to say goodbye. It was really nice talking to you, Winter."

"Ditto to that. Au revoir," she murmured, then went to meet the truck.

A small smile tugged the corner of her mouth.

She couldn't wait to see Pandora tonight.

CHAPTER TWENTY-ONE

"I'll help you butter them when I finish these," Joyce Carlyle called out when Winter entered the kitchen carrying a box of bread rolls.

She nodded to her mother who stood at the bench, her sleeves rolled up, transferring the gourmet salads from their containers into bowls. Even at sixty-six, she still had a trim figure, due mainly to the eighteen holes of golf every Sunday, weather permitting. She was a few inches shorter than Winter, her face fuller, her hair much fairer. Though in the last few years, her strawberry blond seemed to be even lighter, due to the increasing silver among the gold.

A smile hovered on Winter's lips as she began buttering the freshly baked rolls. This was so different from when she and Jessie had flatted together years ago in their cramped little two-bedroom apartment. They had thought the place so cool, despite its mishmash of ill-assorted furniture, and a stove that didn't heat properly. They entertained frequently with cheap wine casks, paper cups, Sao biscuits and cheese slices, and if anyone was really hungry, there were always packets of two-minute noodles in the cupboard.

God, she hadn't thought about those fun times for years.

Her mother's voice cut through her nostalgia. "You've done wonders with the house and the yard, dear. Gran would have been proud of you."

"Thanks, Mum. I love the place."

"Well, it's a credit to you," Joyce replied as they stacked the rolls on the buffet table. Then added, "It's a relief the rain has cleared away for a while."

"I'll say," Winter agreed. In fact, she couldn't have asked for a better day for an outdoor party. It was an idyllic spring evening, the air pleasantly warm with a mild breeze. The garden looked spectacular with the flower beds an array of colourful blooms. Strings of fairy lights would turn the backyard into a shining wonderland after dark.

Thirty minutes later, with a satisfied smile Joyce dusted her hands on her apron. "Right. Everything's ready. Time to go upstairs and dress. Your father and I will meet you downstairs at six."

Winter glanced at her watch. The three hired waitresses were due at six, and the guests at six thirty.

Once showered, she slipped on her black slacks, yet to decide on her top. She vacillated between the pretty blue, and the vibrant black-and-white cold shoulder blouse with the low neckline. The cleavage won, though it seemed a tad too low. But what the heck—she needed to get out of her comfort zone. After applying her makeup, she shook her hair out of the French twist, letting it fall free. A satisfied glance in the mirror, and she went downstairs.

When Winter walked out onto the back patio her mother's initial quick gaze became a stare. "Well…well. Don't you look nice. New clothes?"

Winter nodded self-consciously. "I went shopping this week."

"For someone in particular?"

"I needed to upgrade my wardrobe," Winter replied gruffly.

Joyce gazed at her with a gleam in her eyes. "You can't blame me for asking. It's not your usual style and you've a certain radiance about you tonight. I'm just hoping there's a lovely lady involved in the transformation. You deserve someone nice."

Winter didn't comment. Her mother had disliked Christine, but she wasn't sure that Pandora would be viewed as any more acceptable if Gussie had shared her worries with her.

Winter wasn't surprised to see the first guest was her aunt. She swept in and immediately commandeered her. "Happy birthday, Winter. The place looks marvellous. You've outdone yourself." She lowered her voice. "What time is *she* coming?"

Winter bit back a sharp retort, determined not to let her get under her skin. "I imagine about seven. Is Michael with you?"

"He'll be here shortly with Tracey. I'll see you later then. I can see Phyllis coming in," she said, then disappeared into the crowd who were emerging from around the side of the house.

For then on, Winter was busy greeting the flow of guests and accepting their best wishes. As expected, virtually all her relations turned up, and there was soon quite a crowd on the lawn. Michael appeared, looking very cool and smart, plainly going all out to impress tonight. Tracey, on the other hand, had made no attempt to tone down her gothic look, oblivious of the raised eyebrows. She greeted Winter with a, "'Lo, Cus," while her brother avoided her gaze.

While she was mingling through her relations with the obligatory small talk and polite smiles, she caught snatches of the whispered conversations. It didn't take her long to realize what they were discussing. She tapped her foot irritably, rather shocked. It seemed all the rellies knew about Michael and were avidly waiting for Pandora to appear. She felt like throttling Gussie. Her aunt, on the other hand, was showing no remorse as she greeted everyone as if she were the hostess.

Most of Winter's work colleagues had arrived, and when she spied Veronica and Fay, she headed straight over.

Fay gave her a peck on the cheek. "Happy birthday, hun. Everything looks great."

"Thanks. Where's Alan?"

"Over at the bar having a drink with your father."

"I'll catch up with him later. Hey, Veronica."

Veronica gave her a warm hug immediately. "Hi. You look great." Then instead of letting go, she tucked her arm through Winter's.

"Have I been missing something?" asked Fay, regarding them with amusement.

Winter felt herself blush, at a loss to know what to do. Veronica had obviously read a lot into their luncheon date. "We went out to lunch," Winter said lamely, trying to keep the defensiveness out of her voice. Then before she could say another word, she caught her mother making a beeline straight for them.

Damnit! Nothing escaped her.

"Winter," said Joyce, eyeing Veronica with interest. "Your father wants to know when you want him to start the barbeque."

Yeah, right. Good one, Mum.

"I told him to start cooking at eight," she said, squinting her eyes pointedly. It didn't faze her mother, who hovered expectantly. Could she be any more obvious? "I'd like you to meet Veronica Randall. Veronica, my mother Joyce," she said, quashing down the niggle of annoyance. Sometimes her mother tended to forget she was in her mid-thirties and her love life was her own affair. Selective memory loss and a desire for grandkids. Another reason her mother had disliked Christine. She hadn't wanted children. Thank goodness.

Veronica looked a little uncomfortable and slipped her arm away. "It's a pleasure to meet you, Mrs. Carlyle."

"Please, call me Joyce, Veronica," she said, beaming. She turned to greet Fay, chatted for a moment and then bustled off.

Immediately, Gussie descended upon them with a handsome man in tow. "Winter, this is Cain Wilding," she said with a tiny wink. Winter presumed this meant he was the backup plan. She studied him with interest. She had to admit that Cain was as hot as Tracey had claimed. He was over six feet tall, with a strong symmetrical face and a sculptured well-formed body. Several days' growth stubbled his lower face and his dusty blond hair was spiked stylishly. A tattoo wound its way down his left arm giving him an edgy look. He also had a predatory gleam in his eyes as he peered blatantly down her front.

"Hi, Cain," she said politely, then recoiled from his beer breath as he leaned in closer.

When she introduced him around, he flashed a practised smile of someone used to adoring fans. Where exactly he belonged in the music world, she had no idea. She'd never heard of him. She made a mental note to look him up tomorrow. As Gussie talked on, he didn't say much, his gaze every so often flicking back to her cleavage. Veronica began to look annoyed. Thankfully, he eventually wandered off to find another drink. With a last wink at Winter, Gussie left too.

"Thank God he's gone," muttered Veronica. "I was ready to tip my drink over him if he looked down your front one more time."

Winter just shook her head with a wry smile. "He was harmless enough."

"Not much up top, if you ask me," Veronica growled.

"Bet he's hung like a Brahman bull downstairs though," said Fay with a snicker.

Winter poked her with her elbow. "Ugh! Now I'll be drawn to look at his crotch."

Gales of laughter exploded from Fay. "Poor man. You'll get him worked up for nothing. He probably has no idea he's barking up the wrong tree there."

"Behave yourself," she growled back with a chuckle.

Then a voice echoed behind her, "What's the joke?" and she turned to see Linda, accompanied by Dana holding Frankie's hand.

"Just Fay thinking she's being clever," she said, shuffling around to make room for them.

But as they talked good humouredly, it wasn't quite so much fun for Winter. Linda kept frowning at Veronica who had her hand resting lightly on Winter's arm. She tried to ignore the tension, aware that Fay was watching the rivalry attentively. Winter snuck a look at her watch—they should be here any minute. As if on cue, the chattering around the yard died to whispers, and Jessie and Pandora walked around the side of the house, hand-in-hand.

Winter's eyes widened. *Holy shit!*

Jessie was dashing in black jeans, and blue shirt with a grey waistcoat. But Pandora looked fabulous. Tight hipster slacks and a red silk sleeveless blouse that ended below her ribs showing her well-toned stomach. Her hair was swept up on top of her head, loopy earrings dangled to her shoulders and a diamond twinkled in her navel. Pandora looked hot enough to combust. Winter swallowed and shot a look across at Gussie. Her mouth sagging open, she was staring at Pandora.

"Jessie won't let that woman go in a hurry. She looks smitten," muttered Fay in her ear.

Winter stared at her longingly. *Who wouldn't be?*

And she also eyed Pandora with respect. It was perfectly clear to her that she was making a statement. And her message wasn't hard to read. She wasn't going to take any shit from Michael's mother.

Then out of the corner of her eye, she could see Michael heading toward them.

Winter forced a smile. "Excuse me, I'd better say hello to Jessie and Pandora."

"I'll come with you," said Veronica quickly, taking her hand firmly as she moved off.

Her mind on the impending drama, Winter barely registered the clasp as she wove through the groups of people who reluctantly moved to let them pass.

When she reached the two women, Jessie's eyebrows waggled as her gaze wandered to her chest. "Damn me, birthday girl. You're looking very…sassy tonight." She threw Veronica a knowing lopsided grin.

"Hello, Jess," Winter said ignoring the remark, then added with a shy smile, "Hi, Pandora."

"Hey there. Happy birthday," she replied in her low husky voice. When her gaze dropped to their clasped hands, she stiffened imperceptibly. But then her body relaxed again, and she smiled affably. "Nice to see you again, Veronica. We must be the last to arrive. Is Michael here?"

"To the right…closing rapidly," muttered Jessie in her ear, then threw her arm around her shoulder.

Pandora immediately sank into the embrace, tilting her head for a quick peek over her shoulder. Like a man on a mission with a determined look on his face, Michael was striding toward them from across the yard. Winter blinked at him. She'd expected him to watch the two women from afar and retire to lick his wounds. No such luck. She'd underestimated him entirely. This had all the makings of a major scene, and in front of his relations. The whole lot had turned to watch the drama. She had no idea how this was going to play out, or how to prevent a blowup.

Their plan was beginning to appear very shaky.

As he neared, Winter moved forward to take the brunt of his anger but was stopped by a restraining hand on her arm.

"Let me," Pandora whispered and walked in front of her. "Hello, Michael. I was hoping to catch up with you tonight," she said in a friendly low voice.

His steps slowed, watching her cautiously, though his face was alive with anger. He jabbed a finger at Jessie. "What are you doing with her. I don't understand."

"No, I imagine you wouldn't," Pandora said, and touched his arm lightly with her fingers. "I was hoping to see you, because we're overdue for a frank talk. But let's go somewhere private for that. It's our business, no one else's. Not even Jessie's, and especially not your mother's. This isn't the time or place to make a scene."

He looked hesitant for a long moment then replied stiffly with a reluctant, "I suppose I could."

"You can use my office," Winter offered.

He whipped his gaze to her. "Bugger off, Winter. Everything was all right until you meddled." Thankfully, he had the presence of mind to keep his voice down.

"Don't be ridiculous," Winter snapped. Then bit off a scathing remark about his being a spoiled brat, when Pandora shook her head urgently at her.

Pandora calmly took his arm and with infinite patience, somehow managed to steer him through the guests and into the house without him protesting. Winter was left feeling foolish but relieved.

Ignoring the interested stares, she stuck her chin in the air and called out, "The barbecue's ready, so get a refill before dinner, folks. I've a very nice champagne if anyone would like a glass."

"That's it, babe. Ply them with alcohol and they won't care who's shagging who," whispered Jessie in her ear.

"How true. Everyone in the family loves free booze."

"Let's hope Pandora can talk some sense into the little shit."

"I think he's got the message. But at the moment we've got a bigger problem. Gussie is heading our way and she doesn't look happy."

Jessie winced and took a swig of her beer. "Fuck!"

"What was that all about?" Veronica asked, eyeing them curiously.

"I'll tell you later. Would you do me a favour and get us another drink. Jessie and I want to speak to my aunt alone."

"Do we?" Jessie squeaked.

"I'm not facing her by myself."

Jessie huffed resignedly. "Okay."

Veronica smiled. "I'm off. Pity though. I'm dying of curiosity."

As she started to the bar, Gussie swept by her and gestured to the side of the house. "Come with me. I want a word with you two."

Winter wondered why her aunt suddenly felt the need for discretion—she'd already told the world. But she didn't argue, dutifully following. Out of earshot, Gussie put her hands on her hips. "Really, Winter. Was Jessie the best you could come up with?"

"Hey," protested Jessie.

"Nobody in their right minds would believe that…that hussy is a lesbian. She's a man-eater. And the way she's dressed. Flaunting herself in front of the boy."

Winter narrowed her eyes. "Her name is Pandora, and she likes women."

"Rubbish. She's just experimenting. Tracey says a lot of girls do that nowadays."

Winter had to quash the impulse to shake her aunt. "As if Tracey would damn well know. And what does it matter? Now he's seen them together, he'll have to give up his obsession."

Gussie made a dismissive motion with her hand. "That's my point. He's not going to believe she's a lesbian, so he'll think he still has a chance."

For shit sake!

There were a few times in her life when Winter wished she could just let go and scream. This was one of them. Instead, she forced a pleasant smile and said, "Pandora is having a talk with him now. We'll see how that pans out."

"He's alone with that hussy?"

"That's a bit rough. She's my girlfriend," piped up Jessie.

Gussie gave her a withering stare.

Really angry now, Winter had had enough. She straightened to her full height over the smaller woman and said with authority, "That's quite enough, Aunt. No more. Pandora is a friend of mine, so stop bad-mouthing her or you'll have me to contend with. She's speaking to Michael, so we will wait and see what happens. Do you *understand*?"

Gussie shrank back in surprise and said meekly, "Yes, Winter. I'm just worried."

"Then give him a little credit and stop interfering in his life. We have this under control."

Gussie sighed and shook her head in resignation. "If you're really certain."

"Good, then let's get back to the party."

"When they come out, you won't mind if I introduce her… ah…Pandora to Cain, will you?" Gussie asked, eyeing her warily.

Winter just shook her head.

Unbelievable!

CHAPTER TWENTY-TWO

Pandora settled down in the swivel chair at Winter's desk and indicated with her hand to the seat opposite. "Sit down, Michael."

He did so cautiously, perched on the edge as if ready to storm out if provoked. She watched him closely, aware she had to move carefully. She had been trained in the art of persuasion, but she was going to need all her skill here. He wouldn't be easy to reason with.

"It's about time we had this talk. This crush of yours has been going on too long, and I've never given you any indication that I'm interested in you," she began, keeping her expression neutral, her voice scrupulously calm.

"But I thought you really liked me that night we talked."

"That's what I'm paid to do, Michael. Entertain guests…to make them feel comfortable and to have a good time."

"Then why did you single me out. What was I expected to think?" he asked truculently.

She held his gaze calmly. "You were supposed to think it was fun, a mild flirtation with the hot singer to boast about to your mates. It was my fault—I thought you needed to be brought out of your shell, but I miscalculated. I didn't realize you'd take it so much to heart, so I apologise for that. But now I'm asking you to stop."

He looked at her, wide eyes pleading. "But I love you, Pandora."

"No, Michael, believe me when I say you don't. What you're feeling isn't real. You're infatuated with a fantasy woman." She shook her head slowly and said emphatically, "You've got your whole life ahead of you, so don't waste it on someone who can't love you. And never will."

"Why? Because you're with Jessie now?" he asked, with a belligerent pout. "It's all Winter's fault for introducing you."

Pandora held her temper with an effort. "This has nothing to do with Winter and you know it. I've been into women long before I met Jessie."

"You really *are* a lesbian? Shit, you had everyone fooled at the club," he said, eyeing her more now with curiosity than anger.

She gave a half smile. "Yes, I am. I play a role on stage. It's a fake. So, don't look at this as rejection, just think it never could have happened."

"That arsehole Lawrence Partridge is going to get a shock. I see him looking at you all the time."

Pandora couldn't help chuckling. "I'd like to drop him that clanger, but I can't. I'd lose my job." She leaned over the desk, lowering her voice to a quiet serious tone. "I want you to promise me you won't come to the Silver Fox anymore."

"But—"

She interrupted him impatiently with a wave of her hand. "It's nothing to do with me. I've heard things, bad things. Boris, Yuri's brother, has ties to the Russian underworld. They're after young men like you and because you frequent the club, they've noticed you. Once you're recruited—and you won't have a say because they'll threaten your family—you'll never get out."

While the explanation was rubbish, there was also some truth in there too. If he continued, the club could be a dangerous place for a boy as unworldly as Michael. And when the raid did go down, he'd be brought in for questioning if he'd been there recently. They'd been monitoring who frequented the club now for months, and his face would be on file.

He turned pale and slumped back in the seat with a squeal. "Fuck!"

Satisfied that she had scared the living daylights out of him, she went on in a more conciliating voice. "This is the real world right here, Michael, not the club. You have family and friends who care about you. You should hang out with people your age. A place like the Silver Fox is great for one night out, nothing else. I've seen a lot of lonely people there, people who sit and drink all night, or come to pick up someone."

Even though she was aware she was laying it on too thickly—most his age wanted alcohol and sex—Pandora knew from her own perspective, that there was truth in what she was saying. She, too, wanted more than drinks at a club and a lonely apartment. Then she couldn't resist asking, "Why do you dislike Winter so much?"

He looked at her, puzzled. "I don't dislike her. She's like a big sister. When Dad died, she helped Mum set up her finances and to buy the house. She's the one Mum calls when there's any trouble."

"Oh. I misunderstood by the way you talk about her."

"She's bossy, that's all. Likes to tell us what to do, especially about our credit cards." Then he added with a hint of genuine apology, "I guess I must have been a bit of a nuisance with the flowers and all."

Understatement of the year!

"Forget about it. Now, let's go and talk to Winter and Jessie. Show your rellies you don't give a damn what they think."

"Okay, but Mum's on the warpath."

"Just leave your mother to me, Michael," Pandora said, pursing her lips.

As they walked out together, she hoped she'd gotten through to him, though it would be foolish to assume it would be instantaneous. He'd been wanting her for too long to shed his obsession that easily. But that was his problem now, not hers. She was confident that he would accept the rejection without doing something rash. Or self-harm. Being afraid to come to the Fox again would be the best thing to damp his ardour. Out of sight, out of mind.

In the starry night, the party was in full swing. After he disappeared into the crowd, she skimmed the groups for Winter.

She wasn't far away, with Jessie and Veronica at the drinks' table. When their eyes caught, the smile that blossomed made Pandora immediately feel hot and needy. She craved to connect with her so much it hurt. She pointed to the door to the house. Winter nodded and turned to speak to the two women. Veronica inclined her head after a quick glance in her direction, but Jessie clutched Winter's arm, muttering something in her ear. Clearly annoyed, Winter shook her head with an unmistakable air of authority and pulled her arm free. She ignored any further protest, her attention focused on Pandora as she moved off to where she waited.

A calm slid over Pandora as the brown eyes gazed into hers.

"Let's go inside," Winter murmured. And without another word, she reached down to firmly interlace their fingers. When they'd moved into the house, she kicked the door closed.

The thud caused Pandora's heart to give a little stutter. "Michael got the message," she forced herself to say, but talking about him was the last thing she wanted to do. Not with Winter standing so close and looking at her with such quiet intensity. She was desperate to close the gap, to take her in her arms. Done trying to restrain herself, she reached out to run her knuckles gently over her cheek. The fragrance of a heady perfume mixed with Winter's unique scent flooded her senses as she took a steadying breath. Somewhere at the back of her mind a warning sounded that this was not the time or place, but she was beyond reason now.

Winter looked just as out of control, her heavily lidded eyes smouldering. "Come with me," she whispered hoarsely. "There's a room down the hallway."

Pandora followed her past the lounge to a door next to the stairs. Winter flicked on the switch, lighting up a cosy vintage-style bedroom with floral curtains, a tiffany lamp and antique polished wood wardrobe and drawers. The queen-sized bed was covered by an embroidered white bedspread and a number of multicoloured throw pillows.

"Nice," she murmured.

Winter gazed at her, her irises dancing with golden highlights. She clicked on the lock. "It was the maid's room years ago, now a guest room. Please kiss me. I haven't been able to think about anything else for days," she said huskily.

Nipples tight in anticipation, Pandora shivered. With a low hum, she pressed close to Winter and brushed her mouth over her temples, her eyes, the hollows beneath her cheekbones. She worked her way down until finally, possessively, she claimed her mouth.

At once Winter responded eagerly. Her fingers buried into Pandora's hair, the tugging sending little tingles down Pandora's spine as the kiss deepened. Pandora pulled back a little to stroke her top lip with her tongue, and then the bottom before she teased it inside her mouth. When Winter groaned, she pushed it in deeper, filling her. Then with a steady rhythm in sync with their rocking bodies, she slipped her tongue in and out. Heat surged through her as the ache in her groin intensified.

Soon though, the room began swimming and Pandora realized she'd forgotten to breathe.

Coming up for air, she said, "You taste so good. So good."

"So do you," purred Winter. She grasped the back of her neck to pull Pandora's lips to hers again.

On fire, Pandora devoured her mouth, pressing for more bodily contact. When Winter began to scrape her nails on the exposed part of her back, goose bumps sprang over her skin. Relishing the tingling sensation, she ran her hand over Winter's shoulder to her chest and cupped a breast. It made a perfect handful. Through the silken material, she could feel the nipple tightening. She pinched it and rolled it between her fingers.

Her hand itched to pull off the dress and feel the skin underneath, to touch her all over. But this wasn't the time or place. When they went to bed the first time, she wanted it to be memorable. Wanted her to feel special. Pandora buried her face in her neck and whispered. "I want to make love with you but we can't now. Not here."

"I know," murmured Winter. "Let's lie down and just cuddle for a while. I really, really want to kiss you again."

Without any more words, they stretched out on the bed. Winter inched forward until they came flush together and then they became lost in their kisses.

When Pandora pulled away to stroke her face, Winter's gaze locked on her lips again. "You're such a good kisser."

Pandora needed no second invitation, lowering her mouth again. When Winter began to run her palm over her upper arm, Pandora couldn't help flexing her muscles.

"You must really work out. You're so hot," Winter said as she melted into her.

"Uh-huh," Pandora murmured, slipping her hand to the curve of her breast.

Suddenly, a text buzz sounded.

They jerked apart. Pandora peered at her watch, then winced. "We've been here nearly three quarters of an hour."

"Damn. That'll be someone wanting to know where I am," Winter exclaimed.

"Calm down. Just say you were showing me through the house and we got talking."

Winter pulled a face as she rifled through her pocket for the phone. "Yeah…right! I'm going to have to go out there with lips like puff balls and we were *talking*?" She pulled it out and looked at the screen. "It's only Mum. She wants me to cut the cake before Grandma goes home."

"There…see. No one even noticed we've been gone."

"Jessie would have," Winter said morosely.

"And Veronica."

Winter gave her a sideline glance as she slipped off the bed. "You're not jealous of Veronica, are you?"

"Maybe a little. She obviously likes you."

"Don't be. If I haven't made it clear enough it's you I prefer, then I don't know what we've been doing for the last three quarters of an hour."

Pandora captured her hand and brought it to her lips. "Next time I want you to spend the night with me. Would you like to come to my place tomorrow night for dinner?"

Winter looked at her with a shy smile. "I'd love to."

"Then it's a date. I guess we'd better get back."

"Wait a minute," said Winter, opening the door a fraction. "I'll just have a peep to see if the coast's clear."

Pandora watched with amusement as she poked her head outside. It had been years since she'd had to creep out of a girl's room.

"All clear," said Winter with a touch of relief in her voice. She grasped Pandora's hand and squeezed. "Come on."

When the back door came into view, Winter turned to face her, her eyes bright. "One last kiss before we go? I shall hate seeing you with Jessie."

Inhaling deeply, Pandora caught her in her arms. She didn't want to go back outside—she wanted to go back to the room with Winter. Kissing hadn't been enough—her body was craving more. She closed her eyes and crushed her mouth to hers with all the pent-up emotion she carried inside. Winter sank into her, returning the kiss with equal fervour. But when they broke apart, she felt Winter stiffen in her arms. She turned her head to follow her gaze.

Standing at the door was a woman who had to be Winter's mother. She was dressed in a coffee-coloured dress that fell over her trim figure to mid-calf. Her silvery-blond hair was gathered in a loose bun just like Winter's, and her facial structure was much the same, only fuller. This stylish woman was Winter in thirty-some years.

But she wasn't looking at her daughter with any maternal pride at the moment. She was staring at her as if she'd grown three heads.

That wasn't the worse of it. There was another woman standing at her side, with a furious expression on her face. If looks could kill, Pandora would be dead.

This one she recognized.

Michael's mother.

CHAPTER TWENTY-THREE

"Not you too, Winter?" Gussie cried out.

Winter groaned, hurriedly stepping forward in front of Pandora. *Shit! Just her luck!* She schooled her features into nonchalance and ignoring the remark, smiled as they approached. "Hi, Mum, Aunt. I was just coming to see Grandma. Where is she?"

"On the patio talking to Fay and Veronica. You know how she enjoys hospital gossip. Your father's going to take her home shortly," her mother replied, her expression now more curious that incredulous.

Winter couldn't help chuckling. Her mother's mother, a former nurse, would be in her element with the two doctors. Then she was brought back to earth when her mother cleared her throat and looked over her shoulder at Pandora.

"I'd like you to meet Pandora," said Winter, remembering her manners. "Pandora, this is my mother Joyce Carlyle, and," she flicked a nervous glance at her aunt who was looking frostily at them, "Gussie Hamilton, my aunt."

Pandora seemed perfectly comfortable as she gave them a friendly smile. "Hello, ladies. It's lovely to meet you both. I can see where Winter gets her looks, Mrs Carlyle. And Michael too, Mrs Hamilton. Now if you'll excuse me, I'd better get back to the party and leave you three to talk." She gave Winter's arm a squeeze, "I'll see you later," and then without another word, disappeared out the door.

Winter blinked at the speed of the departure. Talk about deserting the sinking ship.

"Well," said her mother, eyeing her speculatively. "You're full of surprises tonight. I thought she was with Jessie."

"I'm not going to discuss it, Mum. It's my business."

"Of course it is. I'm just glad you're finally having a social life again. And what an exciting life it is. Both women are lovely."

Red spots blossomed in Gussie's cheeks. She looked like she was going to have a stroke. "You call that slut lovely, Joyce? She not only has her claws into my son, now she's got your *daughter* in her snare." She glared at Winter. "I thought you would've had more sense."

To Winter's surprise, her mother crossed her arms and glared at her sister. "That's enough, Gussie. If anyone was a nasty woman it was Christine Dumont. I've waited years to see Winter happy, so leave her alone. As for Michael. You've spoilt the boy and he needs a good talking to. Anyone can see he's far too immature for a woman like that."

Gussie's mouth thinned. In the awkward silence, Winter realized it was up to her to smooth things over or there would be a row. Both sisters were as stubborn as each other. "It's fine, Mum," she said, making calming gestures with her fingers. "Pandora had a long talk with Michael, and he's not going to the Silver Fox again. He's also promised to leave her alone."

Gussie gave a harrumph but didn't comment.

"That's a relief," said Joyce. "Thank goodness she was able to talk some sense into the boy. Now let's go outside. It's time to cut that cake."

Grateful for her support, Winter headed for the door. "I'll get Grandma."

The old lady was leaning on her walker with Fay and Veronica next to her. "Winter. Everyone's been looking for you," she said.

Winter coughed self-consciously as all eyes focused on her. "I had a few things to attend to, Grandma," she said vaguely. "You're nearly ready to go?"

"It's my bedtime, dear. Your father is dropping me home. It's was a wonderful party." She looked at her with a twinkle in her eye. "You're certainly glowing tonight."

Winter grimaced. There was no putting anything over the old girl. With an ingrained sixth sense she seemed to know exactly what was going on with every family member. She hoped she didn't catch a whiff of Pandora's scent as she pecked her on the cheek.

A small smile played on the old lady's lips as she patted her hand. "Come and have morning tea with me one day soon, my dear. I'm sure you have lots to tell me. Now, cut that cake."

After her father did the honours with a few words and she thanked everyone for coming, Winter sliced through it with a flourish to the raucous chorus of "Happy Birthday."

Then after she helped him shepherd her grandmother down the pathway, she took the glass of champagne Fay offered her with a grateful, "Thanks."

"I saved a bottle. The whole lot went in no time at all."

"It's a very nice champagne," Veronica said. "I don't think I've tasted one so crisp."

Winter acknowledged the compliment with a smile. "I can't claim credit for the choice. It was a gift from a client who owns a vineyard in the Barossa Valley. I'm not much of an authority on wines, but he certainly was an expert. It's delicious. I've been saving the bottles for a special occasion." She looked across at the crowd who had launched into exuberant party mode and said dryly, "It looks like it went down well."

"Champagne always gets the crowd going quicker than any other alcohol," said Veronica. "It's the fizz. The carbon dioxide in the bubbles speeds up absorption in the digestive system."

"Spoken like an anaesthetist," said Fay with a chuckle. "Have you had something to eat, Winter? We've had ours."

"No. I'd better get a plate before the sweets are brought out. Shall we join Jessie's table over there?" She perused the yard as she sipped her drink. "Where's Alan?"

Fay flicked her head at a group of men near the bar and smiled fondly. "Discussing football of course. What else? He'll come over when he's ready. I'm dying to sit down."

"Okay, I'll join you all in a minute," Winter said and headed to the buffet.

Focused on the assortment of dishes, her heart gave an almighty leap when a familiar voice purred in her ear, "Dinner looks great. I've already had a scrumptious entrée."

Winter choked, nearly dropping the plate. "Shush, Pandora!"

The reply came back barely louder than a breath. "But I'd prefer ice-cream to lick."

So would I.

"Behave. You're getting me worked up again," she admonished in an urgent whisper.

An eyebrow arched. "Am I now?"

Noticing that a couple of curious faces had turned their way, Winter shifted a respectable distance apart and said louder, "Try some of the egg pasta salad. It's one of my favourites."

"Right," Pandora replied, heaping a spoonful on her plate, then lowered her voice again. "How did the inquisition go?"

"Coward. You certainly disappeared quickly enough."

"I call it a tactical retreat. I'm neither brave nor a fool."

Winter tried to suppress the laugh, but it still came out in little snorts. "I don't blame you. They can appear intimidating if you don't know them. Wait till you see all five sisters together."

Pandora screwed her face up in horror. "That sounds totally scary."

"Nah. They're harmless, though they do like to gossip. Tell one something at breakfast and the lot will know it by lunch."

"So…you haven't answered the question. What did they say?"

"Mum was fine. She never pries, in fact, she stood up for you."

"Really?"

"She just wants me to be happy."

"And she actually approves of me?"

"Just let's say any woman will seem a saint after Christine. She didn't like her."

Pandora stopped ladling out the rocket salad and gazed at her with compassion. "When we're alone again, I'd like you to tell me all about that relationship."

"Some things need to be forgotten," Winter replied firmly. She imagined it was the last thing Pandora would want to hear about. There were a few things she had never told anyone and it would be too hard dragging up the past.

"Hmmm. Maybe…but it's also therapeutic to talk about things," said Pandora. "What did Gussie have to say?"

Winter shrugged. The last thing she wanted to do was to repeat the words and upset Pandora, so she merely said, "As much as I'd expected. She still harbours resentment, but she'll get over it."

"Then I'll avoid her for the rest of the night."

"Don't worry. She won't come near us, but I expect my mother will join us for a chat at some stage. She won't be able to resist." She gave a little snicker. "She thinks I'm interested in Veronica as well as you."

Pandora gave a curt, "Huh!"

"How was Jessie?" Winter asked, trying to sound casual, but knew she failed miserably.

"She noticed," said Pandora in a different voice, the banter gone. "I think we miscalculated there."

"I know. She's going to be hurt," agreed Winter morosely. She collected a knife, fork, and serviette. "Come on. If we linger here any longer it'll make things worse. Would you sit with Fay and Veronica for a while? I'd like to talk to Jessie."

Pandora nodded, pulling in a seat between the two doctors when they reached the table.

Winter dragged up a chair next to Jessie. "Hiya," she said brightly.

Jessie swung around to face her, and leaned closer to mutter crossly, "It's about time you turned up. Where did you and Pandora get to? You were gone for ages."

"Hey, Jessie. Ease up, will you," Winter said with an equally low voice, stifling her annoyance. "You're my friend, not my keeper."

"Sorry," said Jessie, flushing. "I guess that came out a bit abruptly. I just didn't expect you would go off with her for so long. I thought the whole idea was for Pandora to be with me."

"She is with you," Winter said soothingly. "But that doesn't mean she can't be sociable and mingle. Anyhow, it worked... Michael knows definitely now she's not interested. She had a talk with him."

"And now you expect me to do *what* exactly? Forget I'm the girlfriend?"

"Well, for a start, tone down your flirting. You got the message across."

Jessie stiffened and ground out, "Since when have you been an authority on romance? Women like flirting. And what were you doing with her in the house for so long anyhow?"

"We got talking and lost track of the time. She wanted... um...a bit of financial advice."

"Why are you so flustered?" Jessie asked, staring at her.

"I'm not flustered," Winter said, taking a bite of her steak.

Jessie's eyes narrowed. "Is there something going on I don't know about? Are you trying to get rid of me?"

Winter quashed down a desire to flee. Things were getting so muddled. It was a long time since she'd seen her friend this annoyed. "No, we're not."

"Hang on. What do you mean *we're*? I was referring to you."

Winter's mind went into crisis mode. At some stage soon, Jessie would have to be told the truth. But here was not the time or place. The nerves in her stomach twitched as she fumbled for a reply.

Then respite came from an unexpected quarter.

Gussie bore down on them with Cain in tow. Winter pursed her lips. Meddling woman. But then conceded if nothing else, she'd have to give her top marks for persistency.

Everyone rose awkwardly to their feet when they hovered at the table and made no move to sit down. Gussie homed in on Pandora, who was swaying from one foot to the other like a gazelle ready for flight.

"Cain wants to meet you, Pandora," Gussie said, brushing a piece of lint off his sleeve.

Winter cringed. Could her aunt be any more obvious?

Pandora nodded at him. "Hi, Cain."

"Pandora's a singer," said Gussie, and added with a hint of censor, "at a nightclub."

Winter frowned at that unnecessary information. For pity sake, as if he hadn't been told who she was.

"Really," he said, slipping his gaze over her appreciatively. "Perhaps we could sing a duet?"

Winter swayed back on her heels. *Pleaseee!*

But to her surprise, Pandora eyed him thoughtfully and nodded. "Sounds like fun. What do you sing?"

"I'm in a rock band now, but I used to do the pub circuit. I know most of the popular ones."

"Pity we haven't any music," mused Pandora. "Maybe we can rig up something from an iPod."

"Better still...my guitar's in the car. What do you say?" he asked hopefully, suddenly appearing boyish, less assured, and for the first time, genuinely enthusiastic.

"I'm game." Pandora looked across at Winter, her eyes telling her she wanted this. "Would you like us to?"

She nodded, realising it was Pandora's way of gaining her family's acceptance. "That would be fantastic." Then catching the frown settling on Gussie's forehead, she said disarmingly, "Thanks, Aunt. How fortunate you brought Cain to the party. It'll be such wonderful entertainment for everyone."

Gussie spluttered, but to her credit, didn't argue as Cain dashed off to his car. As they carried their chairs closer to the patio, everyone was talking at once.

"Winter, there you are," called out her mother, who had appeared as soon as the rearranging began. "What's happening?"

"Pandora and Cain are going to sing," she said with a proud smile. "You'll just love her, Mum. She's really great."

"Ah. I am glad you've found someone to put the sparkle back into your eyes. It is obvious now who that is."

Winter's eyebrows twitched but she didn't deny it. Couldn't. She was mad about her. She nudged her mother with her elbow with a sly grin. "Aunt Gussie isn't too pleased she's singing."

"For an intelligent woman, she can be remarkably tunnel visioned."

"She is at that. Later though, she'll probably take the credit for the entertainment, seeing she brought Cain," replied Winter with a touch of narkiness. "Ah…here he comes back. You'd better find a seat. The pool crowd are coming over."

After her mother went off to get a chair, Winter retreated under the trees to view the show in private. After Cain strummed out the first chords on his guitar, Pandora slowly raised her hands and began to sing a modern rendition of "Happy birthday." Her voice carried easily over the crowd, the noise gradually tapering off until there was silence. When Cain joined in with a vibrant baritone, they sat hushed, as mesmerized as she was. Hidden in the shadows, Winter watched with raw emotion.

After the song ended with a string of wistful chords, the audience burst into spirited applause. Winter smiled as she took in the performers' body language: clearly the two of them were having fun. Their voices harmonised perfectly as if they had sung together for years. She was forced to revise her opinion of Cain—he was definitely professional when it came to his music. And had a great voice.

After two more songs she rejoined her table of friends, though would have liked to remain listening by herself. It seemed more intimate that way. The duo sang one song after another, and it wasn't until one in the morning that they announced the next was their last. At the end of the finale, her mother appeared at her side. "That was incredible. She's a very talented woman."

"Yes, she is," Winter replied.

"They certainly look good together," remarked Joyce. "Gussie must think so by the way she's fussing around."

Winter glared over at her aunt but refrained from commenting. Instead, she pointed to the people milling around the pathway to the street. "I'd better get over there...everyone's ready to leave. Any other night the oldies would have gone by now, which is the best indication how popular the concert was. I'll catch up with you later, Mum."

When the guests had said their goodbyes, she headed over to Pandora, who had managed to extricate herself from Winter's starstruck cousins. She was preparing to leave with Jessie, who had her arm loosely around her waist. Winter ignored the stab of jealousy, pleased when Pandora moved forward to hug her. She took a second to breathe in the familiar scent, relishing the embrace. "Thank you for the wonderful show. It was fabulous. I don't know how to thank you."

"I can think of a way," Pandora whispered in her ear, and Winter nearly jumped when she felt the tip of her tongue flick across her earlobe.

She gave Pandora a furtive dig in the ribs as she pulled slowly out of the hug. "Do you want me to call you a cab?"

"I already have," Jessie piped in. "Great party, girlfriend."

"We'll be off as well, Winter, thanks for the delightful night," said Fay. "We're giving Veronica a lift home."

Veronica's soft touch on her arm brought Winter to attention. "If you're not busy next Saturday, would you like to come to the opening of an art exhibition at the new Patrice gallery."

Taken aback, Winter couldn't think of a single excuse. "Umm...that would be nice," she murmured, resisting the temptation to glance at Pandora.

"Good. I'll see you there at seven."

And then they were all gone, leaving Winter alone with her thoughts.

CHAPTER TWENTY-FOUR

Pandora gave a last discerning glance around the apartment before answering the doorbell. Even though she had bought flowers to brighten the room, it still looked sterile. The small dining table and vinyl lounge had been cheap and looked it. She wished now she'd at least gone to some trouble with the paintings, instead of the two generic landscape prints she'd picked up at Kmart. It wasn't that she didn't care, but the budget for an undercover assignment was modest. She'd never minded—it wasn't a good idea to become attached to temporary accommodation, and the clean-up crew donated the furniture to charity once an agent moved on.

When she opened the door, all thoughts of the inadequacy of her home disappeared. Winter painted an alluring picture. In low faded jeans and a pink scalloped blouse that hugged her breasts, she looked sexy as hell. Without hesitation, Pandora wrapped her arms around her waist and pulled her in tightly.

Winter immediately relaxed into her, her cheek brushing against her ear. Then she took Pandora's face in her hands and kissed her sweetly. When they broke apart, she murmured, "Hi."

After stealing another kiss, Pandora took her hand. "Hey yourself. Let's go inside." She shuffled from one foot to the other as she watched Winter peruse her home. "I didn't go to much trouble with the interior design," she said self-consciously.

Winter looked back at her with a quizzical expression. "It's a cute apartment, but I get the impression it's not intended to be permanent."

"No. One day I'll have to go."

"*Have* to go? That sounds like you have no choice." Winter chewed her lip as she studied her profile. "I think it's time you told me something about yourself. We're hardly just casual friends anymore."

Pandora took a deep breath. Winter was within her rights to ask and it was unfair not to share something of herself. "No, we're not. Would you like a glass of wine or a beer before I order the Thai takeaway?" She flashed a sheepish smile. "Cooking isn't one of my fortes."

"Ah, so you do have some weaknesses?"

Pandora quirked an eyebrow. "Really? You think I don't?"

Winter's eyes darkened, a naked look of want unmistakeable in their depths. "I was beginning to think you were superwoman."

"Is that right," Pandora said, feeling a flush of pleasure that morphed quickly into desire. She reached for Winter, anxious now to reestablish the connection. "Come here."

As soon as she pressed against her, Pandora's libido spiked. She swung Winter around until her back was against the wall and began to work the blouse out from under the waistband of her jeans.

"I want you so much," Winter murmured in her ear, then nuzzled her mouth into hers.

Amid kisses, Pandora managed to pull off the top, and after quickly unfastening the bra, tossed it aside as well. At the sight of the perky stiff nipples, wetness lodged between her thighs. Wow, they were gorgeous. She bent her head to take one into her mouth. With a groan, Winter grasped behind her neck, cradling her head as she suckled.

Pandora raised her eyes to hers. "Come into the bedroom. I want to do this properly."

"Mmmm. Hurry. I want you so badly."

Without another word, she led Winter through, shedding her clothes as she went. By the time they reached the bed, she was down to her thong and Winter's jeans and knickers were on the floor. When she reached down to slide off the thong, Winter grasped her wrist. "Let me, Pan."

Ever so slowly, she eased it over her hips, sensuously sliding her fingers across her skin as she guided the fabric down over Pandora's feet. Then she sank to her knees, grasped her hips and kissed her mound. Her heart racing, Pandora's stomach flip-flopped when Winter pushed her legs further apart and kissed up and down her inner thighs then moved agonizingly slowly to her folds. She played there for a while, nibbling, sucking, and tickling with her fingertips until Pandora whimpered. "Please, babe. I need you. Please."

When Winter finally snaked in her tongue and licked with long delicious sweeps, Pandora sighed ecstatically. With her tongue still stroking steadily, Winter edged her backwards until the back of her legs hit the end of the bed. She pushed her gently onto it. Thighs spreadeagled, Pandora could only clutch the quilt with both hands as the clever tongue and mouth worked their magic, ravishing her sex until she shattered into a wrenching climax.

"Fuckkkkk, Winter," she wailed, arching upward as the waves of bliss crashed through her. When the last ripple ebbed away, she flopped back glistening with sweat and completely spent.

A satisfied smile on her face, Winter rose to her feet, slid onto the bed and brushed back the wet strands from her face. "I loved how you called out my name."

"That was incredible," Pandora panted out. They rocked together quietly for a few moments, content. After a last squeeze, she crawled up the bed to the pillow. "Come up here, you. It's my turn to make you scream out *my* name," she said, gesturing with a hooked finger.

Winter wriggled up until their hips and breasts were pressed together, their legs entwined. She nibbled her way up Pandora's neck until she captured her mouth. Fire spread through Pandora's belly. She flipped Winter under her and began to rub her body over hers in a constant rhythm. When Winter grabbed her ass and began to massage, she grazed her teeth over the nipples, nibbling, teasing.

As whimpers echoed in her ears, something foreign rose up in Pandora. Her pent-up feelings exploded. She didn't want to be soft and gentle. She wanted to claim her. They stared at each other, Winter's expression radiated both need and insecurity. Instinctively, she knew that Winter desperately wanted Pandora to take her. To possess her. This wasn't just about sex for Winter, this was about cutting the shackles of the past. A renewal. She wondered fleetingly what her sex life had been like with Christine, but all thoughts vanished in the maelstrom of passion.

"Hold on, babe," she whispered. "I'm going to make you come like you never have before. It's going to be a wild ride."

She reached up to tangle her fingers in Winter's hair, testing the strands with little tugs before she brought her lips to hers in a crushing kiss. Insistently, she explored every crevice of her mouth with her tongue. When she moved down to her breasts, Winter pressed her chest against her hungry lips. After sucking each nipple until they were hard and swollen, she moved downwards, nipping the tender flesh of her abdomen.

Marking.

Desire was an electric current, sharp and vibrant, making her more alive than she had ever felt. She entered her with two fingers and began a steady, slow stroke. Winter grasped her by the shoulders, pumping in time with the thrusts. She begged for more. Pandora went harder, deeper, intoxicated by her scent. Winter dug in her fingers, urging her on. She hovered on the edge, her body slick with perspiration as she strained for release. Pandora vibrated her thumb hard against her clit, lightly nipping her breast as she drove her to orgasm. Winter's body stiffened as the pressure continued. Then the dam burst. With a shudder her muscles contracted and she screamed out, "Oh, my, God…Pandora."

When the waves finally abated, she collapsed back onto the bed.

But once she had settled down from her high, with a teary sniffle she pressed her face into the soft flesh of Pandora's throat.

Concerned, Pandora cuddled her in closer. "Did I hurt you, babe?"

"Hurt me? Don't be silly. I've never felt so loved in all my life," Winter said with an odd choking sob.

"Then what's wrong?"

"Nothing. I…I never imagined it could be so good."

Pandora nuzzled her face into Winter's hair and held her firmly. "You never came like that with her?"

"No. It's…it's always been hard for me to climax during sex."

Pandora propped herself up on an elbow to study her face. "So your love life wasn't really good with Christine?"

Winter turned her head to silently look out the window for a moment. When she turned, she curved a hand around her throat as if to physically control the tremor in her voice. "No, it was an unequal relationship. She liked me to pleasure her, but only occasionally would she reciprocate." She audibly swallowed. "Damn it, this is really embarrassing. I shouldn't be telling—"

"Shush," Pandora interrupted softly. "It needs to be said so you can move on. She was a selfish lover. That wasn't your fault."

"Maybe it was in a way," Winter said, turning back to face her squarely. "I realized we weren't suited in bed. I was never the aggressive lover she wanted. But I let it ride."

"I take it then you didn't spend a lot of quality time together when you were dating?"

"When we met, I was wrapped up in my career and moving up the corporate ladder, while she was equally as busy establishing herself at the TV station. We saw each other a couple of times a week, but our dates were mostly parties and dinners with important people. She was a very sociable person."

"I get the picture. So you let things slide, thinking things would get better?"

"Yes. She was a demanding lover and impatient with my needs. To my shame, it was easier to fake an orgasm than to beg for more," Winter said, her voice dropping to a whisper.

"Why on earth did you ask her to move in with you?"

"You have to understand what my life was like in my early twenties. I was quiet, studious, and lacked confidence when it came to sex. I mostly ended up being the third wheel around Jessie…all the girls loved *her*. I had casual dates, but no one special. When I graduated, I left the bar scene to concentrate on my career. A few years later, I met Christine at a party thrown by one of my clients. I was bowled over by her. She was bright, attractive, a sought-after TV personality. Really interesting to be with."

"Was she a considerate lover in the beginning?"

"Not really. We were always partying late in the night. Mostly too tired for anything but a quickie when we got to bed. But I was happy…she opened up a new world for me. I was starstruck. I thought when we lived together and had more time, that things would get better in bed. But they didn't," Winter said, her voice thick with misery. "My performance anxiety got worse, so I retreated more into my work. She probably had a string of lovers I didn't know about."

For a moment Pandora felt a surge of outrage but managed to keep her voice quiet as she said, "Listen to me, babe. We all make wrong choices but believe me when I say you're a hell-of-a-sexy woman. And you can't tell me you faked that orgasm."

"God, no. I even felt it in my bones," Winter exclaimed, then added with a shy smile, "I never wanted her like I want you. Not even close."

"Come here," said Pandora huskily, tracing the soft contours of her body. She cradled her breast as she pressed her lips down the side of her neck, then moved upwards to catch her bottom lip with her exploring tongue. As Winter opened her mouth to admit the teasing tongue, she idly swirled fingertips over Pandora's abdomen. Without any urgency this time, they stroked and kissed each other as they absorbed the essence of their mutual attraction. Their bodies shivered with arousal and sweat coated their skin.

Finally, Pandora felt the warning twitches of Winter's impending climax. She entered her with firm thrusts, riding her thigh as she pumped. Almost incoherent, Winter sobbed out her name as she went over the edge. Pandora climaxed immediately with long exquisite waves that rolled and rolled through her pelvis.

They lay silent, lost in the languid aftermath. Winter placed her head on her shoulder and fell asleep. Pandora draped her arm over her stomach, closing her eyes too.

Pandora lifted her head to glance over at the clock on the side table, trying not to disturb Winter who was snuggled under her arm. Five thirty in the morning—the city was beginning to stir. Already traffic sounds echoed in the distance. She cast her eyes over the naked body pressed into her, lingering on the soft swell of the exposed breast. Desire welled up in her again, but she bit back the temptation to stroke it. After another session of lovemaking in the middle of the night, Winter needed her rest. And she didn't need to catch up on many of her missed orgasms in a single night. What a selfish idiot Christine had been not to realize Winter was a passionate woman who needed to be brought patiently into her sexual awakening.

She raised her head to find Winter's eyes focused on her, the beginning of a grin on her lips. "Good morning."

Pandora brushed her mouth over those lips. "Hi. I didn't mean to wake you. It's still early."

"What's the time?" Winter asked, rolling over onto her back with a lazy stretch.

"Half past five. Do you have to go to the office this morning?"

"Unfortunately, I have a meeting at nine which I can't put off. And I have to get dressed at home, so I'll have to get going by seven thirty at the latest." She wound her arms around Pandora's neck. "I wish I could stay and make love all day."

"Me too. What say I join you in the shower before I get you some breakfast. You must be starving after no dinner last night."

"Come on then, you gorgeous thing you," Winter said with a little chuckle. "I am hungry, but not only for food."

Pandora cupped her between the legs. "You're insatiable. I've unleashed a sex fiend."

Winter undulated against the hand, her eyes squeezed shut. "I think you have," she purred.

"Then get thee into the shower, wench."

Pandora slipped on her dressing gown, leaving Winter to dress while she prepared breakfast. She emptied a can of baked beans into a saucepan while she fried up some bacon. After popping bread in the toaster, she made two cups of coffee. When Winter wandered into the kitchen moments later, she handed her a cup. "It's instant. Sorry…no coffee machine."

"Great with me." She leaned over the stove and inhaled. "I'm ravenous and the bacon smells divine."

"Grab two plates and some cutlery. It'll be ready in a sec."

"Good. And while we eat, you can tell me all about yourself. We still haven't got to that."

Pandora cringed. How much could she say? She was bound by a strict confidentiality clause not to disclose any information pertinent to the operation, but she owed this woman some facts about herself. Any relationship had to be built on trust, and even though she would have to leave Brisbane, it was clear she and Winter were no longer casual. Last night sealed that. She would give anything to be able to date her like normal people and explore the attraction much further. But all she had left was six weeks—a lifetime commitment couldn't be made in that time.

"My father was in the army, which meant we moved every couple of years," Pandora began, images flashing through her mind like a video clip. Townsville, Cairns, Canberra. Different cities, same closed community life. "When he went on a tour overseas, we would be left for six months at a time."

"Have you any siblings?"

"A sister, Emma, and a brother, Derek. I'm the eldest." Pandora took a deep breath to go on to the next part. "When I was fifteen, Dad was killed in an accident. Nothing related to his work, just one of those random things. In the wrong place at the wrong time. Someone ran a red light and collected his car. He died instantly."

Winter reached over and grasped her hand. "I'm so sorry, Pandora."

"Yeah…well. It was a long time ago." She pushed a piece of bacon around her plate, collecting her thoughts. *A long time, but it still hurt.* "My parents had savings, so we were fine for a few years. My mother moved us to Tasmania where she had been left her great-aunt's house. She applied for a job in the bank. When I finished school, I went to Sydney to study singing at the Conservatorium of Music. I had been graduated for just over a year, trying to make a name for myself in the music world when the shit hit the fan. My mother was diagnosed with bowel cancer. My brother was still at high school and my sister studying first year physio, which meant I had to find a regular income to support the family when Mum went to hospital. Emma took a part-time job as well at a pizza parlour. We managed until she was on her feet again."

A little frown creased Winter's forehead, her eyes filled with compassion. "So you gave up your dream?"

Pandora ignored the clinging tendril of self-pity and shrugged. "I didn't have any option. It was what it was."

"How is your mother now?"

"She had surgery and chemo, and thankfully has been cancer-free since."

"It's wonderful that you're back singing. You're really talented," Winter said with a smile. "I take it Pandora is your stage name?"

"It is," Pandora replied, knowing where this was heading. She was in a quandary now. No way she could divulge her real identity, yet Winter deserved something. She fell silent, waiting for her to ask.

Surprisingly, she only looked at her, her intelligent eyes veiled, searching. Then when Pandora didn't offer anything more, she said in a quiet voice, "I'm not stupid, Pandora. I've already worked out you have secrets. And I imagine there are other people involved, so you have to exercise discretion. I won't pry…when you're ready though, I'd like to hear the rest of your story."

"Thank you," Pandora murmured, profoundly grateful. "Not many people would be so understanding."

"I handle sensitive material all the time. I know what it's like to have to keep things to myself." She cracked a smile. "But that doesn't mean I'm not dying of curiosity."

In spite of herself, Pandora grinned. "I bet you are. Now eat up…it's nearly time for you to go."

"That's your fault for keeping me in the shower."

"Ha. I didn't hear you complaining."

"God, no. Best shower I ever had."

Pandora chewed her toast absently as she watched Winter. Like everything she did, she ate economically and neatly. Her gaze drifted down to her breasts, feeling a soft warm glow inside as she remembered last night. Deep pleasure radiated in her depths and her voice turned husky when she said, "I'd like to see you as much as possible in the next six weeks."

Winter's expression sobered, her eyes growing distant. "And after that?"

"After that I don't know."

"We're going to get hurt."

Pandora winced at the stark statement. "I know. Do you want to stop?"

"No. I'll take whatever time we have." Winter stopped abruptly and moaned. "Damn, I forgot I promised I'd go to that art thing with Veronica on Saturday."

"I'm working Saturday, so go."

"Okay. It'll give me the opportunity to have a talk with her. She's too nice not to tell her to her face that I'm not interested." She cocked her head at Pandora, studying her face. "You have to say something to Jessie."

"I took care of it last night."

"How did she take it?"

"She was hurt."

Winter looked a little sick. "Then I'd better have a word with her this week. She won't be happy with me." She cast a quick glance at her watch. "Now if I don't go now I'll be late. This client is a grumpy old fellow and a stickler for time."

"I'll walk you to your car."

"Not in this you won't," she said with a smile, tugging the tie of her dressing gown. When they reached the door, she rested her head on Pandora's shoulder. "You've changed me, Pan. After last night, I feel a different woman. Like I've turned into some exotic butterfly."

"You always were one, you goose. I won't be able to wait until I see you again. I'll text you before I go to work," Pandora said, pulling her close.

With a smile, Winter kissed her briefly on the lips, then disappeared down the stairs.

Her mind in a jumble, Pandora stared out over the railing.

Six weeks didn't sound like a lot of time.

CHAPTER TWENTY-FIVE

For the next two days, Winter's body was in a state of hypersensitivity. The numerous flirty texts from Pandora didn't help. Very disconcerting to have erotic thoughts pop into her mind at inopportune moments.

A little before five on Thursday afternoon, she powered down her computer, impatient to be home to prepare for her date. When she exited the office with her handbag over her shoulder, Nancy tilted her head in surprise. "Are you off home already? I thought you were finalizing the Goodwin's portfolio."

"Um…I'm busy tonight. It's not due until next week, so there's plenty of time," Winter replied, hating how she always felt the need to defend her actions to her super-efficient PA.

"I'll see you tomorrow then," Nancy replied, then added with a knowing smile. "Have a lovely time."

Winter grumbled as she headed for the lift. *Brilliant.* Could she have been any more obvious she had a date?

When she eased the Lexus into the parking bay, Jinx was waiting to greet her in the garage. Normally selective when doling out affection, he had been shadowing her every move since the party. This evening was no exception, dogging her heels as she changed, then following her to the kitchen. Finally, tired of nudging him aside, she gave him an extra tin of food to get him out from under her feet. As soon as he finished, she shooed him out the door. With a plaintive *meow*, he flounced off with his tail in the air.

The menu was an old favourite: sizzling Moroccan prawns, followed by citrus-poached pears. At the party, she'd taken note of Pandora at the smorgasbord, pleased to see she wasn't a fussy eater. The opposite really. She'd piled up her plate with gusto, commenting when she saw a dish she liked.

Her thoughts drifted back to their lovemaking. Pandora was a great lover, sensing just what she had needed. Winter should have been mortified discussing her problem with her, but strangely, after the initial confession she had been pleased to get it off her chest. Suddenly, she felt really angry. For all those years, Christine hadn't even attempted to help her. Instead, she'd added to Winter's anxiety and misery with her self-indulgence and complete lack of empathy.

She should have left her well before she did. She grimaced. *Right!* Easy to say now. The woman had been a time bomb ready to explode if crossed.

Then she shook her head in disgust. Why was she even thinking about her ex? She was out of her life. Conjuring up an image of Pandora, she went back to cooking. Crooning happily, she made the marinade, put a good handful of peeled prawns into the mixture and put the bowl in the fridge. Satisfied, she went upstairs to shower. Once dressed, she looked in the mirror, giving herself a once-over before heading back downstairs.

She was putting the finishing touches to the dining table, when a knock sounded at the door. "It's open," she called out.

Pandora entered carrying a bunch of yellow roses and a bottle of wine. "Hi," she said, smiling as she handed over the bouquet.

"That's so sweet of you," Winter said, and planted a quick kiss on her lips. She didn't hide her admiration as she perused her outfit. Pandora looked superhot, a woman in charge in a white shirt unbuttoned to her cleavage, low slung jeans cinched with a leather belt, ankle boots, and a bomber jacket. Winter waggled her eyebrows. "Oh my. In that outfit you might score tonight."

"Huh! You better feed me first, woman."

Laughing, ridiculously happy, Winter replied, "There's an opened bottle of wine in the fridge. Could you get us a drink while I get the couscous ready, please? Or a beer if you'd prefer. We'll relax in the lounge before I put the prawns on. They won't take long."

"Okay," Pandora murmured, stroking her lightly on the shoulder as she slipped past.

Winter dampened the urge to reach for her, determined tonight they were going to enjoy a relaxing meal instead of rushing off to bed. It was so long since she had prepared dinner for a real date, she wanted to savour the experience. She took the armchair opposite rather than join Pandora on the sofa. Her libido would take over if they touched, and she wanted to learn more about this beautiful woman.

"I take it if you have to leave Brisbane, then it's not where you call home?" Winter began tentatively.

"Sydney has been my base for all my adult life. Most of my good friends are there. What about you? Were you brought up here?" Pandora replied, seemingly happy to share some information.

"Born and bred in Brisbane," Winter replied, and relaxed back in the chair. So far so good. "Um…any exes back in Sydney?" When Pandora raised an eyebrow, she continued hastily. "Sorry…that sounded like I was prying. I was just wondering why you're still single. You're…well…such a good catch…so complete."

Instead of laughing it off, Pandora blushed. "I'm not perfect by any means, Winter. No one is. I've plenty of faults."

"Have you been in a long-term relationship?"

"Not really long term…no. I've dated plenty, but I've yet to find a woman I want to settle down with. That special someone who completely suits me, if you know what I mean."

"I know perfectly well what you're saying," replied Winter. "You have to want the same things, be on the same wavelength to be really happy. My past relationship was a living testament of that. What we had was superficial and became toxic quickly enough. We weren't a good match at all."

"I travel a lot, which makes it difficult as well."

"In Australia or overseas?"

"Both. Have you seen much of the world?"

Winter eyed her thoughtfully. Pandora had moved off her personal info quickly enough, which left Winter even more curious. Why did she travel so much? Pleasure or work? And why so secretive? She bit back the questions on the tip of her tongue, and replied mildly, "I backpacked across New Zealand with a friend after I finished uni. That's the extent of my overseas experience. I'd love to see Europe, maybe Canada and the US. What's your favourite place?"

"I'm going back to Paris one day. It's the most romantic city."

Spellbound, Winter watched the light of excitement in her eyes as she described the French city. Then when she moved on to other interesting places she'd been, she made Winter feel she was there seeing it with her. She had a way of taking her out of the commonplace with words alone. Winter wished for once she could just chuck work and go on a long holiday. Travel with Pandora to exotic places, share all the wondrous experiences together. To laugh and make love under some foreign sky, swim in an ocean on the other side of the world, walk the Great Wall of China, see the pyramids of Egypt, to have a *life*.

A hollow sadness seeped through her. Pandora would be gone soon enough, leaving her with only memories to keep her warm at night. She would be back to walking alone, *being* alone. But this time it wouldn't be a relief, it would be purgatory.

"Hey," said Pandora with concern. "Where did you drift off to?"

"Just imagining us travelling together," Winter replied, not even attempting to keep the wistful tone out of her voice.

"It would be fun. Really nice."

"Yes, it would."

"I..."

"Don't. I know it's impossible. Come into the kitchen while I cook dinner."

After getting another round of drinks Pandora perched on the kitchen stool. She sipped her beer, watching as Winter made the couscous then dropped the prawns into the hot oil. "That smells great," she said enthusiastically.

Winter smiled, her dejection dropping away at the words. Regret could come later—she'd face that when she was forced to. Pandora was here for another six weeks and that was all that mattered. Tonight they would have a delicious meal, maybe watch a movie, then go to bed and make love. Everything was perfect.

They talked random subjects as Winter tossed the sizzling prawns around in the saucepan for four minutes. Then after she spooned the couscous on the plates, she scooped generous portions on top, and decorated the food with a few sprigs of parsley.

"Right. Let's eat," she said. She gestured to Pandora to sit while she lit the candles.

"You've cooked this dish before," Pandora commented when she took a bite. "It's sooo good."

Winter couldn't help being flattered at the little tics of enjoyment Pandora was making as she ate. "I like to dabble in different recipes and spices. It's one of my favourites."

"Hmmm. It's wonderful."

Then Pandora did something Winter least expected. In the middle of a second helping, she began to talk about herself. The real Pandora emerged. She went back through her childhood: what it was like being an army brat, their homes, her siblings, their yellow Labrador, the time she nearly drowned in the creek behind the house, the school concert when she first sang in front of an audience. She elaborated on her close relationship with her father and his sudden death. How it devastated the family, and the battle they had to pick up the pieces and move on. And lastly, what she had felt like when her mother had become ill, forcing her to abandon her singing career.

When the words stopped abruptly at the loss of her dreams, Winter reached over the table and took her hand. "Thank you for telling me, Pan."

"I don't usually discuss my personal life. It always seems easier not to say anything."

"Sometimes it's good for peace of mind to talk to friends?"

"I know. But I've never met anyone I've really wanted to tell before."

Pandora looked so lost that Winter's heart went out to her. "I'm so glad you did. I'm honoured you think enough of me to tell me."

Pandora pushed the remaining food around on her plate. "You're different from the people I knock around with. And the women I usually go out with."

Winter absorbed this without replying, waiting for her to say more.

"My friends...well...come from a different sort of environment," Pandora said after a long silence.

Winter gave a sigh of frustration. "Sweetheart, I'm not a fool. I'm well aware you have another life. I can't imagine any feminine singers would have muscles like yours. They're like bands of steel. You don't just jog, you seriously work out. That commitment would hardly be necessary for someone in the music industry. But I won't ask, and you can be assured I won't be discussing this with anyone."

"I wish I could say more, but I can't."

"I know and it doesn't matter. But...I would like to know about the women you usually date."

Pandora let out a chuckle. "I wouldn't exactly call it dating. More episodes."

Winter raised an eyebrow. "Really? You're like Jessie?"

"Hell no. Exact opposite. I'm too fussy...and I like to get to know someone before the bedroom. But then I lose interest. I can't seem to help myself. So when I need...ah...relief, I usually hook up with women who know the score."

"The score?"

Pandora cleared her throat. "Um...women who have no expectations it'll go further."

"No strings types, you mean. If there is such a person. I always think that's a bit of a front for insecurity."

"There are women out there just looking for a good time. Or too busy, or whatever other reason, for anything more than casual. It's hardly your lifestyle, so you wouldn't know," Pandora said, her voice lowering into defensive mode.

Winter studied her thoughtfully. Did she believe what she was saying? Maybe young adults weren't looking for long-term commitments, but later on it was only natural to want someone constant in your life. "Believe me, I know all about it. I've watched Jessie in action for years, flitting from one woman to the next. And I've had her sobbing rejects crying on my shoulder too many times to believe what you're saying."

When Pandora didn't answer, she asked softly, "Am I different, Pandora? Is what we have different?" Then she wondered why she was persisting. Did she really want to know the answer? Was this all just an *episode*? One in a list?

"Yes. This is different, you're special to me."

"Yet it has to end," said Winter sadly.

"I don't want it to, but I'll have to go. Can't we enjoy what we have?"

"I suppose a couple of months is a bit more than an episode," said Winter dryly.

"Come on, babe. Don't let's argue. Won't you believe I care about you?"

"I'm sorry. I'm acting like a teenager and I can't stop myself. Put it down to lack of self-confidence, a legacy of my past. Of course I know you care about me. You've made that perfectly clear. But it's early days, too soon for either of us to declare anything but interest. This attraction will probably have burnt itself out like a burst of fireworks by the time you're ready to go," Winter said, determined to put her insecurities aside. She flashed her a sultry smile. “In the meantime, let’s eat our dessert in the lounge so we can cuddle on the couch.”

“Good idea. I’ll put these in the dishwasher,” Pandora said, rising to clear the table. “But maybe we can have dessert later. After that second helping, I shall have to let my stomach settle.”

“Okay. Would you like a movie? I’ve Netflix. *Brooklyn* is a good romance,” Winter said, heading for the living room. Once settled on the couch, she reached for the remote.

“I haven’t seen that one,” replied Pandora. She motioned for Winter to move over, then took off her boots and slid in next to her.

The feel of her warm body was enough to make Winter forget the movie. She placed the remote back down and turned to face her. “You’ve got too many clothes on.” Then one by one, she undid the buttons of her shirt. She looked up to meet Pandora’s gaze.

She met Winter’s eyes and smiled.

CHAPTER TWENTY-SIX

Winter loved art galleries. They suited her organized personality. Quiet, structured, and pristine spaces of peace and tranquillity filled with soothing colours and forms. But a part of her also liked that art was full of contradictions: from the sublime, the symbolic, to the sometimes incomprehensible "masterpieces." Over the years, she had made time to view a visiting exhibition or a particular artist's display. It was one passion she and Christine had shared, and over the years they had attended many opening nights.

The Patrice was a contemporary gallery in the cultural hub of the city. Privately owned, it had an impressive catalogue of renowned artists and held regular changing exhibitions. In recent years, it had included a diverse range of international art in its three showing rooms. Winter was very interested in this exhibition. It featured works from two artists: an established floral painter, Grace Hartwood, whom she liked, and a young male contemporary abstract artist hailed as an exciting new talent.

When she alighted from the cab, Veronica, dressed in a mid-length black cocktail dress, was waiting for her on the footpath. She welcomed Winter with a hug and murmured, "Hello. You look very smart."

"Hi there. You don't look too bad yourself." She returned the embrace a little guiltily. The doctor was a genuinely nice person, and she dreaded the frank talk with her later.

They made their way through the foyer into the spacious front room, where each exhibit was subtly lit. The walls were filled with huge floral paintings, so lifelike that Winter could nearly smell the perfume and touch the dewdrops. Entranced, they carefully studied each canvas before moving to the next. As they browsed along the opposite wall, a slender stylish woman appeared beside them. She kissed Veronica with a, "Lovely to see you again, Roni."

Winter looked at her quizzically. When Veronica introduced her, she added with a smile. "Brenda is the director of the gallery. She and I are old friends."

"Cut out the old bit," said Brenda with a chuckle. "Come on and I'll give you a tour. There are a few more of the florals in the next room."

They moved on through the crowd, a mixture of serious buyers in conservative clothes, interspersed with arty types in flamboyant outfits. Winter recognized quite a few people, mostly the art connoisseurs who were the gallery's bread-and-butter customers. First-night showings were popular—there were always a few bargains to be picked up from emerging artists. Brenda gave a running commentary on each piece as they strolled through the room. When they reached an almost ethereal painting of white orchids, Winter paused. She'd been looking for something for her sunroom and this would look spectacular.

"A slight deviation from her usual style," Brenda murmured beside her. "But I believe Grace intends to do more with this technique in the future. It's beautiful, isn't it?"

"It's fabulous," enthused Winter, studying the canvas closely and checking the catalogue. She never hesitated buying good artwork, even those on the expensive side. They only increased in value. In fact, she always encouraged her clients to invest in art.

"Is it perhaps something you would be interested in?" asked Brenda smoothly.

"Definitely. I've always admired Grace's work and I love this one. I would like to buy it."

"Wonderful. She will be so pleased."

"I'll come over tomorrow to finalise the sale."

"Excellent." Brenda twirled a long, manicured hand at her assistant and pointed to the painting. "She'll put on a red dot. Now, let's cement the deal with a drink."

They followed her up an internal staircase to a room which was discreetly closed off from the public. Two waiters carrying chilled champagne and exotic finger food immediately appeared in front of them. Brenda handed them both a flute. "Enjoy, ladies."

They both murmured their thanks.

"Oh dear," exclaimed Brenda, her eyes focusing on a young man in an ill-fitting suit, listening with a pained expression to a buxom woman in a flowing kaftan. "I'll be back in a little while. My poor artist needs rescuing."

Veronica nudged her with her elbow when she moved off. "Only her most valued clients are asked up here."

"Then I've come up in the world," said Winter with a grin. She plucked a caviar canape from the tray. "And the food is definitely better than the cheese and wine they usually serve at these things."

"You're an art collector, Winter?"

"Only for my personal pleasure. If I like something, I'll buy it. That floral will go wonderfully well with the cane furniture in my sunroom."

"I'm renting an apartment at the moment. It must be nice to have a house to decorate," Veronica said wistfully.

"Are you planning to settle—"

At the sound of the familiar laugh across the room, Winter choked on the sentence. She turned her head automatically, then wished she hadn't. Christine Dumont looked up at the same time and their gazes locked. Winter caught the surprise in her eyes before Christine's elegant features hardened. She turned back to see Veronica regarding her with raised eyebrows. "My ex is over there," she said, subdued.

"Really? That's bad luck. Let's just ignore her, shall we."

"I'll try."

"On second thoughts," Veronica murmured, entwining an arm through Winter's with a suggestion of a laugh. "What about we give her something to think about."

"You don't want to annoy her, trust me."

"Oh, I think I can handle her," whispered Veronica into her ear.

Winter took a gulp of her champagne as she felt the hot breath on her lobe. Veronica had no idea what she was doing. It was suicidal to prod the tiger—Christine was capable of making a scene at the least provocation. She glanced over at Brenda who was talking earnestly to the woman in the kaftan. No help forthcoming from that quarter.

"Perhaps we should go back downstairs," muttered Winter.

"Nonsense. You can't possibly let the woman intimidate you."

"You're right. I guess it's a force of habit to be wary around her."

"Okay," said Veronica, slipping closer. "What say we compromise and adjourn to the balcony. You can tell me all about your art collection."

Winter flashed her a grateful smile, relieved as she followed her outside. She was pleased to find no one else had ventured out into the night air. They rested on the railing to take in the view of the city lights. "This is really pleasant," she said, her pulse settling to normal.

But they were only there for a few moments before the very familiar, well-modulated voice echoed behind them. "Enjoying the exhibition?"

A chill shot through Winter, her heart immediately pounding again. She took her time to collect her thoughts before she turned around.

"Chris," she said quietly. "Fancy seeing you here."

Perfectly sculptured eyebrows shot up. "Tsk, tsk. Really, Winter, you haven't forgotten that I enjoy opening nights as much as you? But then again, you always thought you were more of an authority when it came to art."

Winter's fingers tensed around her glass. Christine managed to haul out the inner bitch without turning an eye. "Come on. Can't we be civil to each other?"

"Have you given more thought to our date?"

"I said no and I meant it. I've moved on with my life."

"I can see that." She gave Veronica a slow, appraising look and tilted her head. "From one woman to the next."

Reluctantly, Winter made the introduction.

"Hello, Veronica," Christine said, giving her one of her most charming smiles.

Winter sizzled out the breath she was holding. Maybe she was going to play the captivating television personality and forget about being bitchy. She could be very appealing when she wanted to be. And she did look quite stunning in a Donatella Versace creation that suited her shape and colouring to perfection.

"I love your dress," Veronica said. "It's beautiful."

At this, the doctor received a more intimate smile. When they began to discuss fashion, Winter didn't contribute to the conversation, instead she quietly studied her ex. The cracks were beginning to show. Her makeup was thicker, her hair had a brassy bottled-blond look and her lips were puffy. Why she had to cling to youth was beyond her. She had poise, class, and beauty, but knowing Christine, she wouldn't be prepared to age gracefully.

"So, Winter," Christine said, turning her attention back to her. "You're over your other little fling, I see."

"Fling?"

"Fling...crush...whatever you choose to call it. Surely you haven't forgotten Pandora already? You know...sexy siren, all legs. You were hanging on her every word at the garden party."

The hairs on Winter's neck stood up. It had been too much to hope that she would get out of the encounter unscathed. "That's none of your business."

Christine gave her a measured stare and distaste fluttered across her face. "I must admit, I never could see how you could keep a woman like that."

Winter's jaw worked. "A woman like what?" she asked. She darted her eyes to Veronica, who flashed her a sympathetic look.

"Come now. She's a singer in a nightclub and would be used to accepting certain...ah...liberties, if you get my meaning."

Winter stared at her. "No, I haven't a clue what you're inferring. Pandora earns a respectable living singing in a reputable club. Don't make her out to be something she's not."

"Rubbish." Christine's voice had turned haughty with a cutting edge. "She's a woman who likes attention. You'd never have been able to satisfy her."

When Veronica protested, Winter grasped her arm. "Let me handle this." She turned back to Christine, her eyes squinted in anger. "This isn't about me at all, is it? Pandora turned you down flat at the club and you've never been able to take rejection. And that she preferred me over you, really rubbed salt into the wound."

A hiss exploded. "How dare you."

"You know what?" Winter said, her anger under control. Her fears bled away. Pandora had liberated her, made her realize what a true relationship meant. Not the farce she had endured with this vitriolic woman—the demoralizing, the abuse, the put-downs. "You're not worth losing sleep over. Whatever you say can't hurt me anymore. You're an egotistical show pony who's got the emotional depth of a cartoon cutout."

Christine's eyes widened in shock. Then her features hardened. She leaned forward and ground out, "You'll never be able to satisfy anyone. You're dull. Boring."

Strangely, the viciousness had no effect on Winter this time. Water off a duck's back. At long last, Christine had lost the capacity to hurt her. She was truly free. "Just go," she said quietly. "You're making a fool of yourself."

"Damn you to hell, Winter," she snapped, then turned abruptly and strode off without another word.

Winter stared into the distance, too mortified to look the woman beside her in the eye. She only turned to look at her when Veronica said vehemently, "That woman is a really, really nasty piece of work."

"Yes, she is. I'm sorry you had to hear all that. It must have been totally embarrassing for you," Winter said, then added with conviction. "But you know what. It was the first time I've had the gumption to really stand up to her."

"And good for you." Veronica touched her arm with her fingertips. "I hope you didn't take what she said to heart. You're anything *but* boring."

Winter smiled, grateful for the support. "I endured those hateful remarks for the most of our relationship. All that time I thought it was my fault."

"You don't think that now?"

"No. Not now. I've been shown what true respect and affection is like."

Veronica's gaze sharpened. Uncertainty played across her face. Winter knew she was struggling to find a way to ask the question that had to be eating into her. She didn't have to wait long.

"What exactly is going on with you and Pandora, Winter? You flew to her defence like she means more to you than just a friend."

She gave her an apologetic shrug. "She does."

Confusion clouded Veronica's features. "You and Pandora are together?"

"Yes. I was going to tell you later on tonight."

"Oh. Aren't I the fool. I thought she was with Jessie." Veronica's flinch was barely noticeable, but it was there.

Heat flooded Winter's cheeks. Christ, she'd made a mess of things. "Sorry. It's complicated. That was an act for Michael's sake. We were trying to stop him annoying Pandora at the club."

"I don't think Jessie was acting."

"No, she wasn't," Winter agreed, shifting uneasily under her scrutiny. "I intend having a word with her during the week."

"I feel stupid. I assumed you were interested in getting to know me…or hoped anyway. I thought we suited each other."

"I didn't mean to hurt you or lead you on. I feel like a shit for doing this to you. We do have a lot in common, but the heart wants what the heart wants. I'd like to be your friend if you'd let me."

"Being new in town, I guess I need a friend just as much as a lover, so I'm okay with that. Disappointed, but I've learnt to be pragmatic about things. Win a few, lose a few as the saying goes." Veronica regarded her kindly. "I hope it works out for you. After meeting that dreadful woman tonight, you deserve someone who makes you happy."

"Thank you for saying that. I haven't earned your generosity. Pandora and I have just started dating, so who knows what will happen." Winter forced back the prick of tears. *Yeah…right.* She knew perfectly well what was going to happen. She was going to have her heart broken and there was nothing she could do about it. Her feelings for Pandora had as much chance to burning out as stopping the sun rising.

Then respite came from an unexpected quarter. Someone at the balcony door caught her eye and she looked around to see Brenda approaching.

"Ah, here you two are. I was wondering where you disappeared to. Come on inside. I'd like you to meet Andre, our other artist in the exhibition. He knows no one, poor boy, and looks overwhelmed with it all."

Winter smiled with relief at the gallery owner. Now they could quit discussing her love life and concentrate on someone else. Her emotional state was frayed. However well Veronica was taking her rejection, she still hated being the cause of someone's pain. God knows she had been the one in that situation often enough.

The rest of the night passed pleasantly enough. They stayed until midnight chatting with Brenda and her friends. On the footpath outside, they shared a rather awkward hug before Veronica climbed into her cab.

In her own taxi, Winter sat in silence to digest the events of the evening. The ghastly scene with Christine and the subsequent "talk" with Veronica, had left her emotionally exhausted. She hated conflict and having to justify herself was always a strain. Now she was alone, all the old misgivings came seeping back. Was she really boring? Would Pandora tire of her soon? Had someone at the club caught her eye tonight. Even though she knew it was a reaction to stress, she couldn't help wallowing in doubt.

By the time she walked up to her front door, she felt like weeping. She fumbled with the key which refused to go in after four tries. She rummaged in her purse for her phone to light up the door. *Crap!* At this time of night, she needed this like a hole in the head.

She felt the air shift beside her. Her heart gave an almighty thump. She swung around to find Pandora standing beside the door, a lopsided smile on her face.

"Holy hell, Pandora," she gasped. "You nearly gave me a heart attack." Then she threw her arms around her and burst into tears.

"Hey, hey. What's wrong, babe?"

"Tough evening and I'm just so glad to see you," Winter snuffled out. "I wasn't expecting you tonight."

"I know. I didn't feel like socialising at the club. All I wanted was to see you."

"You…*sniff*…did?"

Pandora planted a soft kiss on her forehead. "I wanted to wake up beside you. Um…how did your date go?"

Something in Pandora's voice made Winter pull back and look at her closely. "Were you worried I went out with Veronica?"

"A little. She's a hot doctor. That's hard to compete with."

"Not as hot as you. And I've seen you *stark naked.* Wow!"

"Wanna see me *nekid* again?" Pandora said, waggling her eyebrows.

"Yes please."

She plucked the key from Winter's fingers. "Good. As soon as I get this door open, I'm taking you to bed. You can tell me in the morning what upset you. Tonight will only be about your pleasure."

CHAPTER TWENTY-SEVEN

As the days slipped by, Pandora was starting to forget this wasn't permanent. She found herself longing to see Winter, wanting her touch. If they couldn't be together, they talked on the phone. Long conversations, about everything and nothing.

The days became weeks.

The atmosphere at the Fox seemed to be getting tenser, though she didn't know if this was because of her ever-increasing disquiet over the club's heightened security, or it was a genuine vibe. Real or not, it was becoming harder and harder to remain comfortable in her role. She dreaded she would accidently blow her cover at any moment.

On top of that, more people on the Interpol list had visited the club in the last month, and she had to find inventive ways of contacting Adriana. If she was exposed, it was essential no one else was compromised. She rang her with coded instructions where to meet, but never told her anything more over the phone. They didn't linger face-to-face, just discreet, quick drop-offs in dark places. Then she changed her work phone number using the list of numbers in the Hushed app after each call. As for her daily habits, she kept the same routine when she was home. A jog around the park in the morning, a takeaway morning coffee at the café around the corner, a weekly visit to the gym.

She made no attempt to hide she was seeing Winter and stayed over at her house on her nights off. And Winter occasionally slept at her apartment. It was normal for a woman her age to be dating and the mob would know who it was. The organization wouldn't be worth their salt if they didn't have tabs on all their employees. Yuri had never interfered in her life outside the club. As long as she turned up for work and performed to his satisfaction, the rest was her business.

And then it finally happened.

On Wednesday evening, Yuri sent his office girl home until the following Monday and began locking his office door.

As soon as she was home after the show, Pandora sent word to Adriana that Boris and crew would more than likely be at the club on the weekend.

Then she texted Winter. *U still up.*

Yes

Be there 20 min

The outside light was on when she parked her car round the side of the house. Feeling the familiar tightening in her stomach, she pressed the doorbell. Winter opened it almost immediately.

Pandora's face must have said it all.

Winter didn't say a word, instead kissed her with a hunger that surprised them both. She kissed her back with matched ferocity. Then she was pulled through the door and led upstairs.

When Pandora slipped off her clothes and lay beside her, Winter rolled over into her arms. Then she began to cry quietly. Pandora held her tightly, rocking her gently until the tears ceased.

"You're going." It was a statement, not a question.

"I have to," she whispered into her hair. "We have all day and night tomorrow."

Winter pulled away, throwing an arm over her face. "Why am I torturing myself?"

"We knew the day would come."

"But you also said this would burn itself out." Winter gave her an anguished, slightly accusatory stare. "But it hasn't for me. It might be easy for you to move on, but I didn't realize it was going to hurt quite so much."

Pandora took a deep breath. "You think I can just walk away like that?" She clicked her fingers irritably. "That I want to leave you? I don't have a damn *choice*."

Winter didn't reply, instead rolled over to the other side of the bed.

Pandora felt despair engulf her. Was this how it was going to end, their connection crumbling before she'd even gone? She tentatively placed a hand on her shoulder. "Babe." Her voice broke. "I…I—"

Then Winter was in her arms, stroking her hair, peppering little kisses over her face. "I'm sorry…I'm sorry. I promised myself I wasn't going to make it any harder for you. I know you don't want to go. So let's make the best of the time we have left."

Pandora pulled her closer. "Let me make love to you. I want to touch every part to keep in my memories."

* * *

Pandora shrugged on her coat, then tucked the little box into her pocket. On her way out the door, she took a last look round. Everything was in order, her belongings stacked against the wall for the clean-up crew. She had no qualms leaving the small apartment, but she was sorry to have to part with the rented RAV4. It was a great car in traffic.

Now that they had confirmed that Boris and crew were flying in Saturday morning, Captain Milton had organized for a convenient "accident" to happen on her way to the club tomorrow afternoon. At two o'clock, a motorcycle would knock her down as she stepped off the curb. An ambulance would be waiting around the corner to answer the bike rider's call. Yuri would be notified that she had sustained a fractured leg and her "father" was taking her home to Sydney. She would be unable to continue to sing at the club.

All quick and neat. Extraction complete.

In truth, the ambulance would be taking her to the Amberley aerodrome, where she would board an air force plane for some R & R at an overseas destination only Milton knew. Four months later she'd be ready for the next assignment.

Pandora squeezed her eyes shut, feeling sick. She had to sever all ties with anyone associated with this current mission. How was she going to be without Winter? She had already claimed a large piece of her heart.

Today, they had spent leisurely hours in Toowoomba, lunching at a winery, strolling through the botanical gardens, and browsing the antique shops. Doing ordinary things, like normal people. But she wasn't normal people. She was an undercover agent for the bloody government.

Great dating material.

She had dropped Winter off and gone home to dress for dinner. When Pandora told her she had booked a reservation at the exclusive Aria restaurant, Winter had just given a sad little smile. "Our last supper."

Nevertheless, sad though it was, Pandora went all out to make it a memorable evening. She bought a bouquet of flowers and hired a luxury car to take them to the Aria.

By the time she drove into Winter's driveway, she was well in control of her emotions.

Jinx greeted her with an excited meow when she pushed open the door, rubbing himself against her legs. She looked down at him fondly—another thing she was going to miss. He had wormed his way into her affections as effortlessly as his mistress.

Winter's voice floated down from her bedroom. "I'll be there in a moment."

"No hurry," she called back. "We've three quarters of an hour before our ride arrives. Time for a drink before we go."

When Winter appeared in the doorway, Pandora caught her breath. She looked stunning, dressed in a tailored cream dress with a single pearl pendant around her neck. Her hair was piled high on her head, held in place with a mother-of-pearl comb. The heavenly scent of her perfume wafted in the air.

"Wow," Pandora exclaimed. "Don't you look terrific."

Winter gave a twirl. "You think?"

"Uh-huh." She produced the bouquet of flowers. "For you."

"Oh, Pan. That's so sweet. Thank you. Could you pour us a drink while I put these in water? There's a bottle of white wine in the fridge."

Pandora stood for a moment watching her arrange the flowers in a vase—she even did that without any fuss. Pandora handed her a glass. "Come into the lounge. I've got something to give you."

"You've bought me something more than flowers? You're spoiling me."

"I want to give you something special. Something to remember me by." She reached in her pocket for the box.

Winter laid her hand on her forearm and squeezed gently. "I'll never forget you, with or without a present."

"I know. Me too, babe."

Winter slipped off the red bow and unwrapped the box. When she opened the lid to reveal the pearl drop earrings, she gave a cry of delight. "Oh, they're so beautiful."

Seeing the light in her eyes, Pandora felt a flush of pleasure. "I noticed you like pearls."

Winter laughed, waving a hand at the jewellery she was wearing. "How did you guess?" She bounced up from the chair. "Wait there. I've got something for you upstairs. I was going to give it to you tomorrow, but now will be the right time." She picked up the earrings. "I'll put these on while I'm up there."

Pandora stretched out her legs, brushing her fingers over the stem of the glass. Oddly enough, the exchanging of gifts made their relationship feel more intimate, even though it spelled the end of their affair. The look on Winter's face when she'd seen the earrings had made Pandora feel ten feet tall. She wondered what her gift was going to be—knowing Winter it would be practical not frivolous. She was surprised though, when she returned with an envelope.

"I hope you like it," Winter said shyly.

Pandora turned it over in her hand, noting the words on the front. *With all my love, Winter.* Consumed with curiosity, she pulled open the flap. She skimmed her eyes over the letter inside, not realizing at first what she was seeing. It was an invitation from a major record label to audition for an album. If successful, she would be signed up for a two-year contract.

For a moment she was speechless. This was every aspiring singer's dream. What she wouldn't have done for a chance at a plum opportunity like this when she was trying to get her big break. "Wow. Thank you, Winter. This is absolutely fantastic."

"I wanted to give you something you would really value."

"I…I don't know what to say."

"Then don't say anything."

Pandora swallowed back the lump in her throat. "I'm leaving you…I don't deserve it."

"If anyone deserves a break, it's you, sweetheart. You're a wonderful singer."

"How on earth were you able to swing this? This company only handles well-known artists."

"Believe it or not, I know the CEO quite well. I did some of their legal work when they were expanding overseas and we've remained friends." Winter smiled reassuringly at her. "You can take some credit. He'd heard of you and was quite enthusiastic when I asked for the favour. Once you sign the contract, you have a year to take them up on the offer."

"You're an extraordinarily kind person. I just wish…well, that things were different."

"I'm going to miss you dreadfully."

"Me too," Pandora replied feeling guilty. "Now we'd better get out the front. The car is due any minute."

"Right," said Winter, rising from the chair. "Let's go and enjoy ourselves."

CHAPTER TWENTY-EIGHT

Pandora looked over at Winter sleeping peacefully in the faint glow of the approaching dawn. Her eyes took in the soft curves, the sweeping planes and angles, the full lips and arch of her brow. Reluctantly, she forced herself not to linger, and glanced at the clock on the side table. 5:00. Time to go if she wanted to be back by eight thirty. She slipped out from under the sheets, careful not to wake her. It took only a minute to pull on her track suit and tiptoe out of the room with her joggers in hand.

Downstairs, she scribbled out a note saying she'd gone for a run, then hurried through the side door to the garage. As quietly as she could, she eased her car down the driveway into the gloom without turning on the lights. There was no traffic in the quiet suburban street, nor were there any vehicles parked on the side of the road. To be on the safe side, she kept the headlights off until she had turned the corner. Better to be paranoid than sorry.

Twenty minutes later, she parked the car in an alley half a block away from the secondhand bookstore in the side street. She pulled up her hoodie and jogged to the staircase in the recess next to the shop. With a last look around, she ran up the stairs. At her third knock, it was opened by the guard.

He stared at her in surprise. "Colly. What are you doing here? I wasn't told you were coming."

"Hey, Bart. I need to see the captain. He in yet?" she said a little impatiently.

He gestured for her to come in after a quick perusal of the stairway behind her. "Got here half an hour ago. He's in his office."

When she tapped on the door, Milton's deep voice echoed from within, "Enter." He looked up, his eyes widening as she came in. His brows drew together as she took a seat opposite. "What the hell are you doing here, Colly? Has something happened at the club?"

She cleared her throat and shook her head. "No. Everything's fine there."

"If that's the case, you'd better have a good excuse for coming here. You were given specific orders this office was off limits until you go."

Pandora's stomach gave a hitch. From the sour look on his face, this wouldn't be easy. Perhaps it was better just to come straight out with it. She took a deep breath and blurted it out. "I want to stay in Brisbane. I've given ten years of my life to the agency and I've had enough. I want a normal life."

"Take a deep breath and calm down," Milton said sternly. He put down the pen and studied her. "Now, let's get this straight. You don't want to be extracted as planned but want to stay here. You also don't want to do any more undercover work again."

When she nodded, he continued, "I suppose this is about the woman you're seeing? Adriana told me you were dating someone."

She squirmed in the chair. Though she never used alcohol as a crutch, she could do with a brandy right now. A large one.

"Yes, she's the corporate lawyer who helped me get away from Boris Anasenko. We've become close."

"Close? What's that's supposed to mean—an affair, or something more serious?"

Pandora cleared her throat. He looked properly annoyed now. "More serious. It's only been a couple of months, but I really want to continue seeing her."

"Ignoring the fact that you broke one of the cardinal rules of undercover work—no romantic attachments—how do you propose to stay here without any repercussions? Once we fake that accident, you'll have to go. They'll put two and two together and you won't last a week after that. Your body will be found in some dark alley."

"I've been turning that over in my head all night," Pandora replied with more enthusiasm. At least he was prepared to listen. "Up 'til now, they don't suspect I'm anything other than an entertainer. I'm very sure about that. So the only way for me to pull this off, is to continue to go to work and be picked up in the raid. Throw me in the watch house with the rest of them."

"You really want this?"

She nodded, waiting, holding her breath.

Milton thrummed his fingers on the desk, then his expression softened as he made his decision. "The operation is being handled by the police. Detective Rachel Anderson will be going in with their SWAT team who will be armed to the teeth. They haven't any idea we have someone on the inside, and they'll never know. They have a warrant to search the place, and all employees and persons of interest in the club will be taken in for questioning."

"Will you have anything to do with the cross-examinations?"

"I'll be out of sight directing it. Most of the guests will only have to give a statement, but anyone suspected of involvement, will be in for a grilling."

Pandora felt a stab of remorse for the friends she'd made there. Not only would they be hauled in for questioning, Kurt, Frankie and the rest of them would be out of a job when the smoke settled. "What about the staff?"

"They will be held and questioned. The Russians and Yuri will be charged immediately—we have enough proof for that. We're hoping to find something in Yuri's files that will uncover the financial expert behind the laundering."

"So...do you think I can stay?" she asked anxiously.

He looked at her thoughtfully. "It should work. The trick will be to convince the Russians that the leak came from down south, not a whistleblower in the club. The officer interrogating the Melbourne thugs could insinuate that—we know enough people on their payroll to name drop. I'll have a word with Detective Anderson when we have them in the lock-up."

"What will happen after I'm released, Captain?"

"Do you mean do we break all ties with you?"

"I guess I do."

Milton gave a soft chuckle. "You're not the first 'spy who wanted to come in from the cold,' Agent Collins. And you won't be the last. There usually comes a time when undercover gets too stressful, and the agent wants out. You've given us ten years...I guess it's time you had a background role."

"Does that mean I've still have a job?"

"Of course, Colly. We're an organization who look after their own. Give me a ring in four months' time and we'll talk. I suspect Adriana is reaching her cut-off point as well. She'll miss you."

"I know. She'll be pissed off that I'm staying here."

He glanced at her over the top of his reading glasses. "Do you want me to tell her?"

"Would you?" she asked, pleased he had offered. Adriana was going to blow her top.

"I will after the raid. She will be staying for a few more weeks, so you may see her before she goes. But you're to have no more contact with the rest of us for four months once you leave this room. Is that understood?"

"Yes, Captain. Thank you."

"Good. Then off you go. And Colly," he added as she turned to go. "Keep your head down and keep out of trouble. We're going to miss you. You did well. When all this settles down, we'll have a quiet get-together somewhere off the radar."

* * *

The glare of the sun through the window forced Winter awake. After taking a moment to collect her wits, she felt the sheet behind her. It was cool. Pandora had been gone for a while, she guessed for a dip in the pool. Exercise was her way of facing problems.

And it was after all, D-day.

She dragged herself out of bed straight to the shower. The night with Pandora had left her mind fuzzy and clouded with hormones. Once the hot spray had cleared her head, she pulled on a pair of shorts and T-shirt and walked onto the balcony. But in the cold light of day, her predicament returned with relentless pressure.

She felt drained, the emotional highs and lows exhausting. She'd be a jittery mess by this afternoon. Maybe it would be better to get it over with, rip Pandora from her life quickly like plaster off a wound. Say goodbye immediately after breakfast. Then she could go to the office and lose herself in work. At the sound of a car in the driveway, she hurried downstairs. When Pandora walked in, all thoughts of work vanished.

"Hi, babe. I picked up coffee and bagels from the bakery," she said, pecking her on the cheek. Though she wore her usual grin, Winter thought she looked more relaxed than last night. When they'd arrived home from dinner, she had an air of quiet desperation and her lovemaking showed it.

"Thanks. I just got up. Let's sit on the verandah in the sun and eat," Winter said, "I'll put the bagels in the microwave."

Since it was such a barmy morning, they ate in silence, enjoying the peace and quiet. Then Winter asked the question the answer to which she was dreading, "When are you leaving?"

"About twelve. I've some things to organize and have to run over the program with Kurt."

"You're singing tonight?"

"Yes."

"You're going Saturday then? I thought you intended to go today: Friday," she whispered. Then forced out a deep breath. "I'm sorry. I know you couldn't tell me…I just presumed. It doesn't matter. I know you've made it plain I won't see you after today." She threw aside the last of her bagel. "For Christ sake, why am I torturing myself?"

"I've decided not to go," Pandora said softly. "I'm not leaving."

Winter shot upright. "*What! Really?*"

"Yes, really. I want to give *us* a go. You and me…see where it takes us. I've had to walk away from a lot of things in my life, but I'll be damned if I'm going to walk away from you."

Winter eyed her, totally confused. "But you said you *had* to go, and now you make it sound like you have a choice. Not that I don't want you to stay," she added hastily.

Pandora leaned over and took her hand. "It's complicated. Please, babe. I'm not at liberty to discuss it."

"You're not mixed up with anything illegal, are you?" Winter asked, tightening her grip on her hand.

"Trust me, I'm not," Pandora said soothingly. "Singing at the Fox is my second job. I have another one, or should say *had*. I've resigned this morning. The firm is quite respectable, but for security reasons I can't divulge what it is."

Winter rose, feeling jubilant but mostly overwhelmed. "You…you actually gave up your job for me?" And then she was in Pandora's arms, laughing and hugging her. "You're wonderful," she cried, and kissed her full on the mouth.

Pandora slid her hands into her hair, loosening the twist until the stands fell free. "I love playing with your hair…and," she murmured, "other parts of your anatomy."

"Let's go back upstairs."

"You bet."

At the door of the bedroom, Winter twisted her round to face her. "Sweetheart. Promise me you'll be careful if Boris comes back to the club."

"Don't worry, I'll avoid him like the plague."

Winter fondly tucked a strand of hair away from her forehead. “Make sure you do. I couldn’t bear anything to happen to you.”

CHAPTER TWENTY-NINE

Pandora stepped in front of the microphone, fighting her nerves as she gazed around the club. As was usual on a Saturday night, the Silver Fox was full. Though she recognized some of the old regulars, Lawrence Partridge included, the crowd was mostly young professionals. Already rowdy, they were clearly out for a good time. When she shifted her attention to the alcove at the back, a sinking feeling hit the pit of her stomach. Boris was sitting there with the same bastards from Melbourne.

Frankie gave her a wave as she scooted past with a tray of drinks. Her romance was going well with Dana, and Pandora was happy for them. They made a nice couple, two honest hardworking down-to-earth people. Dana often came to pick Frankie up after work but had never frequented the club again as a patron. Nor did Jessie. Winter had never really told her what had transpired when she had her talk with her, but judging by her strained expression, it hadn't gone well. After all this was over, she'd have a conversation with the doctor herself. Their friendship meant too much to Winter, and probably for Jessie as well, for Pandora to come between them.

With a guilty start, she realized her daydreaming had nearly made her miss her cue. She caught the first note and launched into the song. By interval, her nerves were jangling. She went to the bar for a mineral water, though longed for something stronger to calm her down. She nearly ordered a brandy sour but bit her tongue in time. A fatal mistake to get careless at the last moment.

She smelt his cloying aftershave before she heard his voice. "I want to see you after the show, Pandora."

Willing herself not to flinch, she didn't turn but continued to sip her water.

His fingers dug into the tender flesh on her hipbone as he growled out, "You can ignore me all you like, but you *will* join me tonight."

With an effort, she prised off his hand and turned to face him. "Listen to me, Boris. I will *not* be harassed, and I won't be joining you tonight or any time in the future. I hope I've made myself perfectly clear. Now if you don't mind, get out of my way so I can get back to work," she ground out in a low voice.

Boris's eyes went cold. "You'll do what—"

"Shall we go over the next songs, Pandora," Kurt interrupted, sliding in between them. She nearly kissed him in gratitude.

"Let's go." She jostled quickly through the crowd waiting to be served. She didn't glance back at the Russian left at the bar.

When they stepped onto the stage, she squeezed in beside Kurt on the piano stool. "Thanks. Man, that guy is a fucking creep."

"I know," he said, then added in a low voice, "I'll help you skip out as soon as you finish."

"You're a good friend, Kurt."

"No worries. Yuri has tunnel vision when it comes to his brother," he replied with a frown.

With tight shoulders, she left his side to walk to the microphone. She let the applause wash over her, then began to sing. She was halfway through the lyrics, when a commotion erupted at the front door. Aware of what was coming, she continued to croon out the words until the SWAT team appeared in full riot gear. They quickly took up positions along the perimeters of the room, while others fanned out to the hallway leading to the back rooms.

Someone yelled out, "Cops," but the crowd stood fidgeting nervously, watching the assault rifles held at the ready.

A large man with a foghorn-like voice shouted orders. "POLICE! Everyone sit down with your hands on your head. No one is to touch a phone." He sliced a hand signal toward the annex. "Cuff those six men, then search 'em."

Though Boris threw him a murderous look and although the mobsters hissed out a stream of violent oaths in Russian, they didn't resist. Pandora dropped onto the stool on the stage with her hands on her head. She watched the proceedings with interest. The squad was very professional. The raid went like clockwork.

Once everyone was sitting either on a seat or on the floor, a tall striking woman in plain clothes and a tactical vest, swept into the room. There was no doubt she was in charge. She looked around impatiently, and when her eyes rested on the men in the annex, she regarded them with narrowed eyes. "Take them out now. Put them in the special cells."

One of the Russians spat on the floor. "Suka."

She curled her lip. "Use force if you have to."

Immediately, they were bustled protesting out the door.

The policewoman watched them depart before she turned back to address the room. "I'm the officer in charge of this operation. Detective Rachel Anderson. If you cooperate, this will be quick and painless. You will be treated with respect. All customers will be searched and asked to give a statement before you are allowed to leave. It will be an offence to use your phones before you leave this building. Do so and you will be charged." She swept her eyes round the room with a hard glare.

She gestured to five uniformed officers, two men and three women, waiting at the door. "Set up tables over in the right corner. Start with the younger partygoers and get them through as quickly as possible. Regulars need to be questioned. I've organized for one of the bartenders to point them out." She handed over a piece of paper to each officer. "Also those on this list. They will be taken to the station on one of the buses."

She waved to one of the riot squad. "Gather the staff together, Dennis."

"Yes, ma'am."

Pandora glanced around for Kurt. He had disappeared. There was no time to look for him as she joined the line shuffling to the designated area at the left of the bar. Yuri wasn't amongst them. She guessed he was being held somewhere secure while his office was being searched.

Everyone crowded together, eyeing the detective warily.

Anderson looked them over, resting her gaze a moment on Pandora. "All staff members will be taken to the city watch house where you will be questioned," she ordered in a flat decisive voice. "You will be kept overnight. An officer will be collecting your phones before you leave. You will be allowed one phone call at the station to notify your families you won't be coming home until sometime tomorrow. Any questions?"

"I have to get my little girl from the babysitter," called out a teary waitress.

"Ring her now to say you'll be late. You can be questioned first as soon as we get back to the watch house and then you may go home." She tapped the side of her leg irritably. "Anyone else *has* to get home?"

No one else spoke. Pandora didn't blame them. The cop looked like she had a temper. Then two more plainclothes detectives, a bear of a man in a boxy jacket, and an athletic well-built woman with brown hair cut in a bob, appeared from the back.

"Find much, Martin?" asked Rachel.

"A good haul," he replied, a grin splitting his face. "The boys have taken everything back to the station."

"Good, then go with Kerry to the watch house with these people. I'll stay here."

Pandora followed the others in line as they obediently filed through the front door. The pavement fronting the club was in chaos. In the glare of the police spotlights, she could see numerous police cars and two buses parked nearby. In between the vehicles, a pack of reporters were snapping photos and screaming questions.

Detective Anderson, her face like thunder, was trying to maintain order. Down the side of the building, the partygoers that had already been processed had started dribbling out of the club and were being escorted down the street to a taxi rank.

"Some wanker must have texted the press despite my warning," Kerry said testily behind her. "Okay, listen up all of you. All staff are to board that first bus as quickly as possible. No one is to speak to the press."

Easier said than done, thought Pandora. They were hedged in by the press hounds, who were baying for a story. Then out of the blue, a microphone was shoved into her face. Christine Dumont appeared in front of her, dressed in a snazzy two-piece silver cocktail dress as if she'd rushed over from a fancy do. Her cameraman had his lens trained on them.

Crap! She was on live TV.

Christine flashed a practised smile at the camera. "I'm here tonight at the Silver Fox nightclub, where a police raid is in progress. With me is their lounge singer. Pandora, can you tell us what prompted this action by the police?"

"No comment," Pandora replied, attempting to weave her way past.

"I have it on good authority you are very closely associated to one of the family."

Pandora bristled. "Closely associated? What's that supposed to mean?"

"You aren't romantically involved with the owner of the club, Yuri Anasenko?"

Bitch! "I'm employed as an entertainer. I sing. That's it."

Christine's eye sharpened into a calculating stare. "That's not the information I've received."

Aware it was the cardinal sin in her profession to talk to the press, something short-circuited in Pandora's brain. This woman needed to be taken down a peg big-time. "It's a pity you didn't bother to check the so-called information. Any good reporter doing her job would have."

Christine's eyes glinted shards of ice. "Really? What would a person like you know about integrity?"

She thrust the mike a foot from Pandora's nose for her reply. At that moment, someone behind pushed hard against Pandora's back. She cannoned forward into Christine, who teetered precariously on her stiletto heels. In an effort to save herself, she frantically clutched Pandora's arm. With a reflex action as the nails dug in, Pandora slapped the hand away.

Bedlam followed.

Dumont's offsider, a fit young man in his twenties, lunged at Pandora. When he caught her roughly by the shoulders, instinctively she went into combat mode. With a quick movement, she ducked her head and kneed him in the groin. He went down in a heap. But not before his flailing arm caught Christine in the jaw. She screamed and collapsed backward. Pandora made a grab at the front of her skirt to save her fall. The material ripped down to her knees.

The next thing she knew, Pandora was flat on the ground with two burly cops on top of her and cuffed. She groaned as her face bit into the concrete. *So much for keeping a low profile.*

A female voice echoed above her. "Put her in the back of my car. I'll take her in with me later."

They heaved her to her feet. Anderson stood in front of her with hands on hips, livid. Pandora avoided her eye, instead snuck a look around. Christine was leaning against the Seven Network van, glaring at her, looking unusually dishevelled. Her perfectly styled hair hung in clumps, her makeup was streaked, and for modesty an old grey blanket was wound around her waist.

Her offsider was still hunched over, and the cameraman had his camera rolling. As did the rest of the press. Pandora chuckled to herself. One consolation out of all of this: Christine was going to be on primetime news looking very unglamorous.

The witch was going to hate it. She hoped someone got a good shot of the torn dress.

But then she had no more time to think. She was grasped firmly by the arm, pushed into the back of an unmarked car and the door slammed shut. She lay back, trying to get comfortable with her hands cuffed behind her. After wriggling over on one side against the door, she shut her eyes. An hour later the press were gone and the SWAT team were nowhere in sight. The few uniformed police still there, were moving off to their cars.

Yellow tape cordoned off the area.

Then the door opened and Rachel slid into the driver's seat. "Are you all right back there?"

Pandora winced as sharp pain shot through her wrists when she straightened in the seat. "Yeah, everything's dandy."

* * *

Pandora woke with an ache in her back and head. The top bunk had been hard as a rock, and the waitress and the assistant chef who shared the cell, had kept her awake moaning and griping half the night. After a very early, very basic breakfast, two cops appeared at the door.

"Ms. Cameron and Ms. McNally please."

Fabulous! She was left to twiddle her thumbs while they got out of the place. The cell wasn't exactly the Ritz. It had only the bare necessities, no TV, no books and it smelt of sweat, urine, and strong disinfectant. She could even see something on the ceiling that looked suspiciously like crud.

Hours later she was still there. She wished they would hurry up. The place was noisy: the phones, loud voices, angry swearing had begun to grate on her nerves. The fact that this was the first time in her career she had ever been in a lock-up, was a blessing. Her fingerprints wouldn't be on file. Her records were kept secure in a vault at the Home Office, officially classified "secret."

When they'd arrived at the watch house, the detective informed her she was entitled to a phone call. She refused, feeling pathetic. She was handed over to a large female cop, who took her to a room to be searched, fingerprinted, and photographed. The process was not only demoralizing, the surly woman seemed to get enjoyment out of humiliating her. Then after her clothes and personal effects were catalogued into a bag, she was given prison-issue clothes and slip-on shoes, and sent to take a shower.

Pandora made a mental note not to antagonize Detective Anderson in the interrogation room. She didn't want to spend any more time in the place if it could be helped.

Lunch came and went. By midafternoon she was beginning to think they'd forgotten her when the latch of her cell snapped open.

"Follow me, please," ordered a young male constable who eyed her appreciatively.

He led her to a room down the back, where both female detectives were waiting behind a desk. She took the seat opposite gingerly and waited for them to begin.

Anderson flipped open her notes, perused them for a moment and gave her a friendly smile. "Hello Pandora. This is Detective Kerry Donaldson who is assisting with the interviews. May I have your full name please."

Pandora gave them both an amicable nod and answered immediately, "Alice Maria Flinders." She had no qualms about quoting her undercover identity. The bureau was thorough—the name would check out as authentic with a driver's license, Medicare number and passport. "But I just go by Pandora."

"Right then, Pandora. How long have you been working at the Silver Fox?"

The cross-examination went on, routine questions about her work, her impression of the club, the people she worked with. How she was treated. But after twenty minutes, Rachel's tone changed. More forceful, less friendly. "Have you had any financial dealings with the owner of the club?"

"I'm paid to entertain."

"I see it's a good wage."

"It's the going rate. It's a specialist industry."

Rachel studied her and folded her arms. "Singing only?"

"What else would I be paid to do?"

"Some entertainers are expected to keep the customers happy. You don't go home straightaway after your show finishes?"

Pandora held her temper. "I always stay to socialise for a while."

"Ah yes…to talk. And drink of course."

"I like a brandy to wind down. It relaxes me after a show. I never drink to excess at the club," said Pandora, and added with a delicate shrug. "Nor do I go home with any customers, in case you were going to ask that next."

Rachel raised her eyebrows but didn't comment. She tapped her pen on the table. "Christine Dumont accused you of being Yuri Anasenko's lover. Is it true?"

"Definitely not."

"Why so emphatic? He's a handsome man and your boss. You work closely together. It's only natural you feel something for him," said Rachel with a smile.

Pandora held her gaze warily. *Beware the smile on the face of the tiger.* "Not my type."

"Ms. Dumont has a reputation of digging up facts and substantiating them. She'd hardly make that statement on live TV without proof." Rachel's voice had more than a hint of scepticism and censure.

"Well, she was wrong this time."

"You better be able to prove that. I'd like to remind you this is a police investigation and I don't like being lied to," Rachel said sharply.

"Then you'd better ask Christine why she said it. I couldn't possibly be Yuri's lover."

Rachel leaned over the table and shot her a cold look. "And why not?"

"Because I'm a lesbian."

"You're a *what*?" She turned to Kerry Donaldson and snapped. "Why the fuck wasn't *that* in her notes?"

Kerry, who was trying to suppress a chuckle, waved her hands in the air. "Have you seen her dressed up when she sings? She super-hot and super-feminine. No one knew."

"Tell me," Rachel grated out, "why would Christine Dumont say what she did?"

"Because she came on to me one night at the club and I knocked her back. And I'm going out with her ex," Pandora said with satisfaction.

Rachel flopped back in her chair. "That's what this is all about? A Goddamn dyke drama?"

"Well…yes."

"Huh! For Christ sake, I just wasted an hour of my time here." She gestured to Kerry impatiently and stood up. "We're finished. Come on, let's get a cup of coffee and I'll make mine strong." She turned to Pandora. "There's someone else who wants to interview you and then you can go."

On the threshold, she paused and looked back. Her face switched into a genuine smile this time. "And say hello to Winter. I'm guessing that's the ex you're referring to."

Pandora nodded.

"You're a lucky woman. And off the record, it was about time that conceited reporter got what was coming to her. For the record, I never said that." And then she was gone.

Lance Milton entered the room a minute later, carrying two takeaway coffees. When she saw *Coffee Club* stamped on the disposable cups, her taste buds salivated. "Real coffee. The black tar here would take the lining off your stomach," she said gratefully.

Milton handed over a cup and launched into a tirade without any preamble. "What the hell was that about last night, Colly? Are you mad? That was hardly a quiet exit. You're splashed all over the news and social media."

She held his gaze, then dissolved into laughter. "It wasn't intended, but as it turned out, it was the best way to get out. The police have written me off as a jealous girlfriend, the Russians will think I sang at the club because I've a crush on Yuri, and that bitch Christine will look a fool on primetime TV."

He gave a wry smile. "I suppose you're right. You've always been lucky, that's why you're such a good agent. Look how you stuffed up your exit and you come up smelling of roses." His face turned serious. "How did you handle the questioning?"

"No probs. Anderson prodded a bit about my association with Yuri, but I doubt she really thought I was involved in any of the heavy stuff. When she found out the reason Christine disliked me had nothing to do with the Fox, she told me to go. Was the raid successful?"

"Very. We have more than enough evidence for a conviction and to shut down their network up here in the north. Everything's been handed over to the Feds, so we'll be working with them in the following weeks. It's beginning to look like Boris called the shots when it came to the club and Yuri did what he was told."

Pandora absently rubbed a finger down the side of the cup. "How did they launder the money? Boris is a thug, not a businessman. He'll be able to handle clubs and casinos, but I doubt he'd have the know-how for large corporate investments."

"The Feds are tracking the paper trail."

"Did Kurt ever turn up? He disappeared when the squad arrived."

"He was found with Yuri. We think he's the brains behind it. He's more than a piano player. Apparently, he was an accountant for years," Milton said.

Pandora took a sip of coffee, sighing in pleasure when it hit her stomach. "Wow, that's good." She eyed him thoughtfully. "I've had all day in that rotten cell to figure out things. Kurt was always a puzzle. He seemed to have a lot of sway with Yuri. Then it came to me. It was under my nose and I never twigged. He was a great friend, but never once did I get the vibe he was attracted to me sexually. Then I'd see him often in Yuri's office. I think they're lovers. Because the Anasenko family is very traditional to the point of archaism, their relationship would have had to stay buried in the closet."

"A couple. That explains a lot." He adjusted his glasses and stood up. "Come on. Time for you to go." He thrust out his hand. "Take care, Colly. We'll see you in a few months."

She clasped his hand. "Yes sir. And thank you again."

With a farewell smile, he stepped back to let her pass through the door. As she walked down the corridor, she'd never felt so lonely. Even though she was grateful for Milton's offer, she knew she'd never go back to the agency. She had to move on, to chase her dreams, but that would also mean leaving most of her friends in the service behind. Soon she would have nothing in common with them.

And there was a good probability that she had blown it with Winter. The classy woman would hate having a girlfriend who made such a public spectacle of herself, especially after her own experience in the limelight with that bitch Dumont. It was a cert her run-in with Christine would be splashed all over social media.

When she collected her belongings, the duty officer eyed the glittery gown and heels and offered kindly. "You can keep the clothes. Easier than going out in that dress. Someone picking you up, love?"

"No. I'll take a cab home."

Her expression turned to pity. "Ask the officer at the front desk to order you one."

CHAPTER THIRTY

Winter woke early Sunday morning, worry eating at her. There had been no word from Pandora since she'd left on Friday morning. She mooched down to the kitchen, plugged in her phone and made a cup coffee. Figuring the best way to calm her anxiety was to bury herself in work, she went to her office.

When her phone rang, she nearly fell over the cat getting to it. She breathed a sigh of relief—it could be only one person at this time of day. She didn't bother checking the ID before she answered with a breathy, "Where are you, Pan? I've been so worried."

"Hey. It's me…Jessie."

Winter opened her mouth, then shut it again. After their talk, Jessie had stormed off and hadn't contacted her since. "Oh, sorry. What do you want? You said I could go to hell last time I saw you."

"Yeah…well. I was pissed off with you then."

"So," asked Winter, curious now. "Why are you ringing me now?"

"Have you seen the morning news?"

"I never turn the TV on this time of day."

Jessie's voice took on a tone of urgency. "Switch it on. The ABC has a news at seven thirty."

"What's wrong? Has something happened?"

"Just turn on the damn thing."

Panicked, Winter mumbled "Okay," then ran into the lounge and quickly flipped through the channels. "It'll be on in a minute. Aren't you going to tell me what's so important?"

"You'll have to see for yourself. It's not something I can adequately describe over the phone. I've been called over to the hospital, so I'll give you a ring in a couple of hours. Bye."

Winter shook her head in frustration. Typical Jessie, whetted her appetite then hung up. But at least she was talking to her now. She stuffed the phone into her pocket, pausing long enough to rub her eyes before she dropped into a lounge chair.

The announcer began. *"The police conducted a raid on the Silver Fox, a well-known nightclub in inner city Brisbane late last night, causing major disruption to traffic. It is not known at this stage if the police were looking for drugs or if it was terrorism related. Numerous suspects were taken into custody."*

Scenes of patrons exiting the club accompanied by police in riot gear flashed onto the screen. It looked chaotic. The area was cordoned off. Police cars, press vans, and two buses filled the street. Uniformed police were trying to control the press as well as a crowd of onlookers.

"Tension escalated when there was an incident involving well-known television personality, Christine Dumont and the club's singer, Pandora, outside the club."

Winter shot upright, eyes glued to the unfolding drama.

She watched as Christine began interviewing Pandora. Winter couldn't believe she was suggesting Pandora was her Russian boss's lover. They exchanged words, then Pandora stumbled forward. From the angle of the video, it was a little difficult to see all the action. Christine was knocked backwards, and the man next her, a Seven network's employee judging by the logo on his cap, lunged at Pandora. She retaliated with a knee in his groin and he collapsed with a scream. On his way down his arm hit Christine in the face and she disappeared from view. When the crowd parted, Christine was on the ground with her skirt around her knees. The camera lingered on her skimpy lace panties and bare upper thighs.

Winter broke into a belly laugh—Christine was so, so going to hate that footage. Then she quickly sobered when the video clip moved to Pandora. She was facedown on the pavement, being cuffed by two hefty cops. *Oh crap!*

Winter bounded up to her laptop. The footage had gone viral on social media, though most viewers were more interested in Christine's bared body than the arrest. In fact, for some viewers Pandora had reached star status, and labelled the arrest as police brutality.

The phone rang again and this time it was her mother. "Did you see the news, dear?"

"Yes, Mum."

"So…what did you think?"

Winter chuckled. "Christine's going to go ballistic."

"It'll do her good. Have you heard from Pandora?"

Winter's smile faded. "No. I'll ring the police station in a minute. Er…what did you think of it all, Mum?"

"I think that girlfriend of yours is Wonder Woman. Did you see how she handled that lout in the baseball cap? Now, get on that phone and find out what happened to her. She's going to need your support."

"Right. Love you."

But after three attempts to get any information from the police, she gave up for the time being. Stewing, she went back to her computer. Half an hour later her phone rang again. Her excitement faded when she saw who was on the other end of the line.

"Hi, Aunt."

"Winter. No doubt you've seen the news. I told you that woman was no good. Thank god Michael came to his senses," Gussie said smugly.

Winter curled her lips. Gussie sure had a selective memory. "Did you ring to gloat, Aunt?" she snapped. "Or to say something constructive. For your information, Pandora and I are dating. She has become important in my life so don't run her down."

"Just so long as you're not jumping from the frying pan into the fire."

"She's nothing like Christine."

"No, she's nothing like that conceited woman, I grant you that. But not exactly a suitable partner for you either. Not after that display on TV." Gussie lowered her voice. "My friend Edith from bridge, said that the entire staff have been taken into custody and being questioned about illegal activities at the club."

Winter gritted her teeth with exasperation. "What the hell would Edith know about it?"

"There's no need to use that tone. Her husband's a judge. I told you that."

"How could I forget," muttered Winter. "So what else did she say?"

"It's not about drugs or terrorism. It's money laundering."

Winter went silent while she processed this. Somewhere in her brain, pieces of information began to click together. Pandora had quizzed her about money laundering. The real woman was nothing like the vamp she played on stage. She had been set to leave Brisbane on Friday, which meant she knew the raid was going down on Saturday.

But who did she really work for? A rival gang? Unlikely. She wouldn't want to get caught in the raid—she'd have a criminal record. Some sort of law enforcement agency? The most feasible explanation. Not Queensland Police—this was the first time Pandora had been in the state. Interpol perhaps?

"Are you still there?" Gussie's voice echoed in her ear.

"Yes, yes. Just thinking. Did Edith say anything else?" Winter winced. She couldn't believe she had actually asked that question. She was getting information from the Bridge Club gossip circle.

"Just that all the staff are suspects." Gussie lowered her voice. "You will treat this as confidential, won't you Winter? I was told this in the strictest confidence."

Winter nearly laughed. It would be all over town in a day. "Of course I will."

"Good, Then I'll say goodbye."

Winter went to make herself a cup of coffee. She wasn't going to let it shake her. What she needed to do was to work out how she could help Pandora. And floating somewhere was an elusive memory. Something she had discovered long before this ridiculous business with Michael. Then it came to her. She brought up the archived file and settled down to probe.

It took the rest of the morning to trace the discrepancy and the paper trail. When satisfied there was enough concrete proof to launch a proper investigation, she printed out her figures and tucked the papers into a plain yellow envelope. As she tidied up her desk, she tackled the next problem—where to send it. She couldn't very well lob up to the police station and hand it in. If the authorities suspected where it came from, she could lose her practising certificate for breach of client confidentiality.

Then she thought of the perfect go-between. Adriana. Pandora had said, "*We've worked together for years*," which meant they were employed by the same organization, and in all probability, still were. It wouldn't take much to find out. She'd go to the Blue Peacock. She needed to find out if it was open. Thankfully, after an Internet search she found they did lunches. She prayed Adriana would be there.

After another fruitless call to the police station, she headed for the garage with the envelope.

* * *

The Blue Peacock was humming with the Sunday luncheon crowd, a mixture of ethnic and alternate-lifestyle people. Winter circled a group waiting to be seated and made her way to the counter. A young African woman with colourfully braided hair was taking orders, while a Chris Hemsworth lookalike was the barista. The enticing aroma of roasted coffee beans wafted over her. Unable to resist, she ordered a cup.

"A skinny latte, please. Um…would Adriana be here?" she asked, wishing she could at least remember the singer's last name.

It didn't seem to matter. The woman barely gave her a second glance as she answered, "She's busy out the back. Can I give her a message?"

"I don't want to disturb her, but it's really urgent. Could you tell her Winter Carlyle needs to see her at once."

She had the woman's attention now. "Of course. I'll send someone to find her. Please take a seat."

Adriana appeared before her coffee, which was no surprise. She would know about the raid and Pandora's public arrest.

"Winter," she said, her voice bitter. "You're the last person I expected to turn up here. Come with me out the back so we can talk in private."

Winter plucked her mug from the waiter's tray. "Lead on."

They entered a small dressing room filled with a mirror, a row of cosmetics and a rack of clothes. Two chairs and a small table were jammed in the corner.

Adriana waved to a chair and took the other. "What do you want?" From her tone it was clear she was furious.

"Firstly, I'd like to say I've told nobody I've come here. I came entirely off my own bat," Winter said, keeping her voice calm. "I'm presuming you and Pandora work for the same organization. If I'm wrong, then I'll apologise and go immediately. Do you?"

Adriana eyed her with dislike. "What's this all about?"

"I won't say unless you answer my question."

Silence hung heavily in the air between them as doubt and concern flittered over Adriana's face. Eventually, she simply nodded.

"And you work for some sort of government enforcement agency?" Winter watched her closely, trying to read her face.

"Yes. We're the good guys."

Even though she was sure that Pandora wouldn't be mixed up with anything illegal, she let out the breath she was holding. She pulled the envelope from her bag. "This contains information relating to the criminal activities at the Silver Fox. I want you to give it to your superior. Pandora is being held in custody."

"Don't you think I damn well know that? It's splattered all over the news. Why don't you take it to the police yourself?"

Winter made a rueful face. "I shouldn't be sharing this without a court order under the Freedom of Information Act. There isn't time for that if I'm to help Pandora. I can't deliver it myself and I thought you would have a person you could secretly slip it to."

"What's in it?" Adriana asked, her antagonism slipping to curiosity.

"Just facts and figures. A paper trail."

Adriana looked at her incredulously. "To do with this case?"

"Yes. Now that's all I can say."

"Okay, I'll make sure the right person gets it as soon as I can." Then she pushed back in the chair and the antagonism flooded back into her voice. "What's going on with you and Pandora?"

"We've been seeing each other."

"You mean screwing, don't you!"

Even though it was clearly meant as an accusation, Winter had to smile. "Why, yes. That too."

Adriana seem to deflate at that. "Do you realize she's in all this shit because of you? She was supposed to be gone. Holidaying on some tropical island, not locked up in a prison cell."

"I know," said Winter quietly. "But I can't pretend to be sorry she stayed. I love her for it. She's become special." She leaned forward and touched Adriana gently on the arm. "It must hurt to see her find someone else. You love her, don't you?"

Tears sparkled in the singer's eyes. "I did. Desperately for years. I guess I still do a bit, but I've learnt to accept she'll never feel the same way about me. It just hurts, you know, to see her finally find someone she cares enough about to want to stay with."

"I need you to understand I never asked her to give up her job. It was her decision. But I sense, even without me, she was ready to move on. She still wants to see where her music can take her and she's good enough to reach the top."

Adriana nodded, offering a smile for the first time. "You're right. She's been restless for a while now, even if she couldn't see it. You were simply the catalyst." She glanced at her watch. "I was talking to the boss just before you came in. She's due to be cross-examined shortly. If you hurry you can be there when she comes out."

"Really?" Winter leapt to her feet and was already halfway out the door when she called out. "Thanks. Come over for a meal when everything settles down."

* * *

Winter crossed the pavement to where the distinctive blue and white police sign indicated the public entrance of the watch house.

The woman behind the front desk appeared stern. But when she enquired after Pandora, she smiled and her face softened, her blue eyes crinkling at the corners. "She hasn't come out yet. Would you like to take a seat and wait? She shouldn't be too much longer. Most of the people have been processed."

Winter nodded her thanks, plucked a magazine from the rack and settled in a chair in the corner. For an hour, people came and went. Finally the door opened and there she was. Winter stood up quickly. At the sound of the scraping of the chair, Pandora swivelled around and their eyes met. She looked dejected and washed out, but Winter hadn't seen a more beautiful sight in her entire life.

The next thing she was in her arms, laughing and crying at the same time. "I've been waiting for ages. I thought they'd never let you go."

Pandora clutched her tightly. "You came," she murmured into her hair. "I…I badly wanted you to but didn't like to ask."

"Why on earth not?"

"I know how you hate public displays. I made a complete idiot of myself with Christine."

Winter pulled back and cradled her face between her hands. "Are you kidding me? You're my hero. It's the first time I've seen anyone get the better of her. And," she gave a snicker, "it's gone viral. They've dubbed it *Pantygate*. It's hilarious. She must be furious. I bet she takes time off from her show and goes into hiding."

"Huh! I'll have to as well. The press will be all over it."

"Then you can hide out with me. The others can take over my workload…I haven't had a decent break in years. My uncle owns a holiday house up the coast on the beach. It's probably vacant at the moment. Would you like to go with me?"

"Just you and me?"

"Yep."

"I'd love it."

"Come on then. Let's get you home."

When they reached her car in the parking lot, Winter swept her eyes over Pandora. "What *have* you got on?"

With a laugh, Pandora gave a twirl. "New fashion statement, babe."

"Gorgeous," Winter said with a laugh. "Get in and you can tell me what happened on the way home. Do you want to pick anything up from your apartment?"

"No. We can do that tomorrow. I want a hot shower and just chill out with you." As Winter drove home, Pandora related the events of the night. When she finished, Winter reached down and squeezed her thigh lightly. "They think Kurt was the mastermind of the operation?"

"Yes. Boris was the muscle, but Kurt had the financial nous." Pandora let out a long breath. "I was sorry it turned out to be him. He was a really good friend."

Winter pulled up at the red light and shot her a glance. "It wasn't him."

"What do you mean?"

"When I saw the news this morning, I was worried sick about you." She waved a hand. "Not that argument with Chris if that's what you're thinking, but what she said about you and Yuri. I thought maybe they might try to tie you in with whatever the Russians were doing. Guilty by association. Then Gussie rang—mainly to gloat of course—but she did have some gossip. She'd heard from a friend, whose husband's a judge, that the raid wasn't about drugs but money laundering."

"So much for secrecy," said Pandora dryly.

Winter gave a snort. "You have no idea. Anyhow, normally I don't listen, but this time I did. I remembered something you said. Something that had me puzzled at the time. I alluded to it that first night I came to the club. I was negotiating for a client to buy one of Lawrence Partridge's companies. A multimillion-dollar sale. Partridge was unlucky he got me. We're a busy firm, with heavy workloads. We always do checks, but I'm pedantic. I investigated much deeper. I won't go into the finer details, but I discovered there were funds in one of Partridge's company's branches that couldn't be accounted for. It was cleverly done, and surface checks wouldn't have picked it up. Since we still had the files in our system, I went through them with a fine-tooth comb all morning. I found enough to prove he was laundering money through his companies. A lot of money."

"Geez, Winter. The Feds have been working on this for a year. Partridge was investigated, though was never considered a front runner."

"But he was always at the club."

"Yeah. To see me. He made that pretty clear to everyone. The flowers, the attention."

Winter laughed. "He really wasn't pining after you. You were his smokescreen."

Pandora let out a chuckle too. "I've been called worse. Bit of a blow to the ego though." Then her voice lowered with concern. "These are really bad people, babe, the lowest form of humanity. They can't find out it was you who found the evidence."

"I know. The envelope only contains figures and bank accounts. They can't trace it back to me and it's really only a start. The police will subpoena all his finances and they're sure to find a lot more. This was only one company he has a stake in. He has a finger in many pies: real estate, clubs, casinos, charities, you name it."

"What did you do with the information?"

"I gave it to Adriana to take to your people."

Pandora shot up straight in the seat. "You went to *Adriana.* Shit, Winter, how did you even know she was a colleague?"

"You said you've worked with her for years."

"Huh…I guess I did, didn't I. Um…how was she?"

By Pandora's tone, it dawned on Winter that she hadn't told her friend she was not leaving Brisbane. "Angry, bitter. Didn't you tell her you weren't going?"

"No. It's my business what I do with my life. I didn't want any drama about it. Adriana and I, we go back a long way. We've looked after each other in the field for years, and danger brings you really close to someone. Even more than sex. Your life depends on that person. She's become possessive of me to the point it's becomes stifling."

Winter listened, amazed. Pandora was clueless about how Adriana felt about her. "She was fine by the end," she said reassuringly. "When all this settles down, perhaps we can invite her over to dinner if she's still here."

"Thank you. She's a good friend. Oh, and babe," Pandora said with emotion resonating in her voice, "I like the way you said *we* can invite her."

"Pandora, it is *we* now isn't it?"

"It is."

"Then, sweetheart, isn't it about time you told me your real name."

"I guess it is. My name is Hope Collins and I'm very pleased to meet you, Winter Carlyle."

Winter burst into laughter. "That figures. Pandora opens the box and Hope flutters out."

EPILOGUE

Twenty months later

"Here. You carry these in," Winter said, passing over a cheesecake and salad, "and I'll get Matilda."

Pandora took the dishes, smiling to herself as she remembered her first family dinner at the Carlyle's. Winter had been annoyingly blasé about it, but it had been a big deal for her. It was the first time she had ever been taken home to meet the parents—well, technically speaking they had all met, but not as their daughter's partner.

Having gained notoriety from the run-in with Christine, every one of Winter's relations turned up that day to look her over in a new light. When she entered the house she was met with a wall of noise and been examined, quizzed, and dissected. A far scarier experience than any undercover work.

Now here they were, a married couple with a baby. How life had changed, and so much for the better.

Everyone here still called her Pandora, as did Winter who said she couldn't imagine her as anything else. When she registered Pandora as her professional name with the recording studio, it seemed pointless to go back to Hope. She had been known as Colly for the last ten years anyhow. Then with the success of her first album, "Pandora" became permanent.

Joyce Carlyle met them at the door and immediately took Matilda from Winter's arms. "How's my little cherub," she cooed, then beckoned them in.

"She's smiling, Mum."

"Wonderful. When is your mother arriving, Pandora?"

"Next week."

"Bring her over for lunch one day," Joyce said. "Now go on through to the garden and say hello to the birthday girl. Everyone's here."

When they stepped through the back door, Jessie appeared with a tray of champagne flutes. "This'll put you into the mood, my friends."

Pandora plucked one off, but Winter shook her head. "Can't. Breastfeeding."

"Where is the little one?"

"Mum's claimed her. I'll be lucky to get her back."

"Is she smiling yet?"

"Yes, she is," piped in Pandora proudly. "Seven weeks old and cute as a button."

Jessie broke into a laugh. "Oh, you two are so freaking domesticated."

Pandora threw her arm around Winter's shoulders and pulled her close. "Yep," she said with a satisfied smile. "I'm well and truly hooked. Sometimes I wonder how I ever got so lucky."

"Me too," murmured Winter, melting into her embrace.

Jessie looked amused. "Am I the only sane one around here?"

"You should try it, Jess," Winter said, her voice losing a little of its light-heartedness.

"Well, girlfriend, while you have been out of circulation wallowing in home bliss and having babies, I've been taking out someone."

"Really? Who?"

"Her name's Meg. I've been treating her son."

Winter's lips twitched. "Jessie, you're blushing."

"Yeah…well…she's nice. And she doesn't take any shit from me, so there's no need for you to be telling her any stories."

"Oh, I'm sure someone has filled her in," Winter said, chuckling. "Where is she?"

"Coming over now," Jessie muttered.

The woman approaching was attractive in a girl-next-door sort of way. Average height, brown wavy hair, a pleasant face, big blue eyes, and a trim curvy figure. She was dressed in a pretty yellow dress with a high neckline and knee-high skirt. She looked to be in her early thirties.

"Hi," she said shyly. "I'm guessing you're Winter and Pandora. Jessie has told me so much about you."

"Hey there," said Pandora, eyeing her in wonder. So not Jessie's usual type. But then again, she mused, knowing Jessie's history, this was just the sort of woman who could make her happy. And a child would be a bonus. Jessie loved children.

"Jessie said you have a son, Meg," said Winter happily. Pandora smiled to herself—since having Matilda, Winter embraced everything and everyone associated with motherhood.

"I have a girl as well. She's just started preschool."

"Really. How wonderful," Winter said, looping her arm through hers. "Come on and introduce me to them. Then I'll show you Matilda."

Fondly, Pandora watched them wander off, then turned back to Jessie. "Meg's very sweet."

"Yes…she is. She gets me, if you know what I mean. We've only been going out for four months but I'm keen." She gave a little cough. "And she is too."

"You think you can handle two children?"

Jessie gazed at her intently. "I've never known how to have a relationship, never thought I'd be any good at one. But all I've ever wanted was a family. Meg is wonderful and so are her kids. It's like I've been given a second miracle."

Pandora put her hand on her shoulder. "Good for you, Jessie. You'll make a great parent and partner."

"Thanks, and I have to say I've never seen Winter looking so happy."

"Motherhood suits her."

Jessie smiled. "It does. And you too. Now I'll have to continue taking these around or I'll be in trouble. Gussie has her eye on me. I'll see that little tyke of yours shortly. I bet she's ruling the roost already."

"We've had a few sleepless nights," Pandora said with a laugh. "Where is Gussie?"

Jessie rolled her eyes. "Over there. You'll be pleased to know you're finally off the hook. Michael's in love again."

"Thank God. Who with?"

"The skinny babe in the Armani dress." Jessie hooked her index fingers in the air. "Apparently her family is very wealthyyyy."

"Huh! Good. Gussie won't be thinking she's after Michael's money. Who's the attractive young woman with them."

Jessie gave a hearty chuckle. "That's Tracey."

"No kidding," gasped Pandora. "Cripes! Dracula's daughter has morphed into a butterfly. We have been out of circulation for too long." She nodded toward the group in the garden. "I'll catch up with you later. I'd better wish Grandma happy birthday."

The yard was alive with the sound of laughter, buzz of conversations, and children squealing. Winter's grandmother reclined back in one of the outdoor padded chairs, her body frail but mind still alert. She was enjoying the attentions of her family as they took turns to sit with her, and when she caught sight of Pandora, she patted the next chair. "Come and talk to me, dear."

Pandora planted a kiss on the aged cheek. "Happy ninetieth birthday, Grandma."

"So, how are my three girls?"

"We're fine. Better than fine actually. Matilda's smiling now and sleeping through."

The old woman patted her on the leg. "Winter is blooming. And so are you. They tell me your album has been nominated for an ARIA award."

"Yes. And my second is due out next month."

"So, my dear, you've become very successful. And good for you. What happens next?"

Pandora looked over with a smile at Winter who was proudly showing the baby to Meg. "They want me to go on tour, but I've refused. I'll probably never hit the really big time if I don't, but it doesn't matter. I have everything I want here, the love of my life and our gorgeous daughter. Years ago it would have been important, but not now. I have no intention of jeopardising what I have."

"Good for you." Then a twinkle flashed in the faded eyes. "You know, Pandora, you've had a remarkable transformation since that first time we met. You remember…you were clinging to Jessie's arm in that rather bold outfit, which I imagine was for Gussie's benefit. I'll never know why she thought you were leading the boy on. Everyone could see it was ridiculous."

Pandora felt herself blush. "This was always the real me. The woman at the Silver Fox was just an act."

"I like this you so much better—a woman in charge. My granddaughter is very lucky. You're so much more suitable than her other choice."

"Thanks, but I'm the lucky one."

The next minute she felt Winter's fingertips push gently on her shoulders. "Take Matilda, sweetheart, and show her to Grandma," she said and passed over the baby.

Pandora watched silently as the old lady cuddled her closely. When Winter pulled up a chair on the other side, she reached over and took her hand. They sat there, marvelling at the grand old lady cradling the little baby in the crook of her arm and smiled at each other.

Life couldn't get any better.

Bella Books, Inc.

Women. Books. Even Better Together.

P.O. Box 10543
Tallahassee, FL 32302

Phone: 800-729-4992
www.bellabooks.com

CPSIA information can be obtained
at www.ICGtesting.com
Printed in the USA
JSHW032006160320
4775JS00001BA/2